"Have you had protective spells put on your locks and bars?" Lord Darcy asked.

"Oh, yes, your lordship; indeed I have. Wouldn't be without 'em, your lordship. The usual kind, your lordship; cost me a five-sovereign a year to have 'em kept up, but it's worth every bit. . ."

Except for a very slight dampness, there was no trace of the ink that had been spilled across the pages, although the clear, neat curves of Lord Darcy's handwriting remained without change. The handwriting had been put there with intention, while the spilled ink had got there by accident. Removal was simply a matter of differentiation by intention. . .

"A dead man," said Journeyman Henry after a moment. That was obvious. . . the eyelids were sunken and the skin waxy. . . . To make the horror even worse, the nude body — from crown of head to tip of toe — was a deep, almost indigo, blue. . .

Murder and Magic

RANDALL GARRETT

SF

ace books

A Division of Charter Communications Inc.
A GROSSET & DUNLAP COMPANY
51 Madison Avenue
New York, New York 10010

CONTENTS

THE EYES HAVE IT

Sir Pierre Morlaix, Chevalier of the Angevin Empire, Knight of the Golden Leopard, and secretary-in-private to my lord, the Count D'Evreux, pushed back the lace at his cuff for a glance at his wrist watch—three minutes of seven. The Angelus had rung at six, as always, and my lord D'Evreux had been awakened by it, as always. At least, Sir Pierre could not remember any time in the past seventeen years when my lord had not awakened at the Angelus. Once, he recalled, the sacristan had failed to ring the bell, and the Count had been furious for a week. Only the intercession of Father Bright, backed by the Bishop himself, had saved the sacristan from doing a turn in the dungeons of Castle D'Evreux.

Sir Pierre stepped out into the corridor, walked along the carpeted flagstones, and cast a practiced eye around him as he walked. These old castles were difficult to keep clean, and my lord the Count was fussy about nitre collecting in the seams between the stones of the walls. All appeared quite in order, which was a good thing. My lord the Count had been making a night of it last evening, and that always made him the

1

more peevish in the morning. Though he always
woke at the Angelus, he did not always wake up
sober.

Sir Pierre stopped before a heavy, polished,
carved oak door, selected a key from one of the
many at his belt, and turned it in the lock. Then
he went into the elevator and the door locked
automatically behind him. He pressed the switch
and waited in patient silence as he was lifted up
four floors to the Count's personal suite.

By now, my lord the Count would have
bathed, shaved, and dressed. He would also have
poured down an eye-opener consisting of half a
water glass of fine Champagne brandy. He
would not eat breakfast until eight. The Count
had no valet in the strict sense of the term. Sir
Reginald Beauvay held that title, but he was never called upon to exercise the more personal
functions of his office. The Count did not like to
be seen until he was thoroughly presentable.

The elevator stopped. Sir Pierre stepped out
into the corridor and walked along it toward the
door at the far end. At exactly seven o'clock, he
rapped briskly on the great door which bore the
gilt-and-polychrome arms of the House
D'Evreux.

For the first time in seventeen years, there was
no answer.

Sir Pierre waited for the growled command to
enter for a full minute, unable to believe his ears.
Then, almost timidly, he rapped again.

There was still no answer.

Then, bracing himself for the verbal onslaught
that would follow if he had erred, Sir Pierre
turned the handle and opened the door just as if

he had heard the Count's voice telling him to come in.

"Good morning, my lord," he said, as he always had for seventeen years.

But the room was empty, and there was no answer.

He looked around the huge room. The morning sunlight streamed in through the high mullioned windows and spread a diamond-checkered pattern across the tapestry on the far wall, lighting up the brilliant hunting scene in a blaze of color.

"My lord?"

Nothing. Not a sound.

The bedroom door was open. Sir Pierre walked across to it and looked in.

He saw immediately why my lord the Count had not answered, and that, indeed, he would never answer again.

My lord the Count lay flat on his back, his arms spread wide, his eyes staring at the ceiling. He was still clad in his gold and scarlet evening clothes. But the great stain on the front of his coat was not the same shade of scarlet as the rest of the cloth, and the stain had a bullet hole in its center.

Sir Pierre looked at him without moving for a long moment. Then he stepped over, knelt, and touched one of the Count's hands with the back of his own. It was quite cool. He had been dead for hours.

"I knew someone would do you in sooner or later, my lord," said Sir Pierre, almost regretfully.

Then he rose from his kneeling position and

walked out without another look at his dead
lord. He locked the door of the suite, pocketed
the key, and went back downstairs in the
elevator.

Mary, Lady Duncan stared out of the window
at the morning sunlight and wondered what to
do. The Angelus bell had awakened her from a
fitful sleep in her chair, and she knew that, as a
guest of Castle D'Evreux, she would be expected
to appear at Mass again this morning. But how
could she? How could she face the Sacramental
Lord on the altar—to say nothing of taking the
Blessed Sacrament Itself.

Still, it would look all the more conspicuous if
she did not show up this morning after having
made it a point to attend every morning with
Lady Alice during the first four days of this visit.

She turned and glanced at the locked and
barred door of the bedroom. *He* would not be
expected to come. Laird Duncan used his wheelchair as an excuse, but since he had taken up
black magic as a hobby he had, she suspected,
been actually afraid to go anywhere near a
church.

If only she hadn't lied to him! But how could
she have told the truth? That would have been
worse—infinitely worse. And now, because of
that lie, he was locked in his bedroom doing only
God and the Devil knew what.

If only he would come out. If he would only
stop whatever it was he had been doing for all
these long hours—or at least finish it! Then they
could leave Evreux, make some excuse—any excuse—to get away. One of them could feign

sickness. Anything, anything to get them out of France, across the Channel, and back to Scotland, where they would be safe!

She looked back out of the window, across the courtyard, at the towering stone walls of the Great Keep and at the high window that opened into the suite of Edouard, Count D'Evreux.

Last night she had hated him, but no longer. Now there was only room in her heart for fear.

She buried her face in her hands and cursed herself for a fool. There were no tears left for weeping—not after the long night.

Behind her, she heard the sudden noise of the door being unlocked, and she turned.

Laird Duncan of Duncan opened the door and wheeled himself out. He was followed by a malodorous gust of vapor from the room he had just left. Lady Duncan stared at him.

He looked older than he had last night, more haggard and worn, and there was something in his eyes she did not like. For a moment he said nothing. Then he wet his lips with the tip of his tongue. When he spoke, his voice sounded dazed.

"There is nothing to fear any more," he said. "Nothing to fear at all."

The Reverend Father James Valois Bright, Vicar of the Chapel of Saint-Esprit, had as his flock the several hundred inhabitants of the Castle D'Evreux. As such, he was the ranking priest —socially, not hierarchically—in the County. Not counting the Bishop and the Chapter at the Cathedral, of course. But such knowledge did

little good for the Father's peace of mind. The
turnout of his flock was abominably small for its
size—especially for weekday Masses. The Sunday Masses were well attended, of course; Count
D'Evreux was there punctually at nine every
Sunday, and he had a habit of counting the
house. But he never showed up on weekdays,
and his laxity had allowed a certain further laxity to filter down through the ranks.

The great consolation was Lady Alice
D'Evreux. She was a plain, simple girl, nearly
twenty years younger than her brother, the
Count, and quite his opposite in every way. She
was quiet where he was thundering, self-effacing
where he was flamboyant, temperate where he
was drunken, and chaste where he was—

Father Bright brought his thoughts to a full
halt for a moment. He had, he reminded himself,
no right to make judgments of that sort. He was
not, after all, the Count's confessor; the Bishop
was.

Besides, he should have his mind on his
prayers just now.

He paused and was rather surprised to notice
that he had already put on his alb, amice, and
girdle, and he was aware that his lips had formed
the words of the prayer as he had donned each of
them.

Habit, he thought, *can be destructive to the
contemplative faculty.*

He glanced around the sacristy. His server, the
young son of the Count of Saint Brieuc, sent
here to complete his education as a gentleman
who would some day be the King's Governor of

one of the most important counties in Brittany, was pulling his surplice down over his head. The clock said 7:11.

Father Bright forced his mind Heavenward and repeated silently the vesting prayers that his lips had formed meaninglessly, this time putting his full intentions behind them. Then he added a short mental prayer asking God to forgive him for allowing his thoughts to stray in such a manner.

He opened his eyes and reached for his chasuble just as the sacristy door opened and Sir Pierre, the Count's Privy Secretary, stepped in.

"I must speak to you, Father," he said in a low voice. And glancing at the young De Saint-Brieuc, he added: "Alone."

Normally, Father Bright would have reprimanded anyone who presumed to break into the sacristy as he was vesting for Mass, but he knew that Sir Pierre would never interrupt without good reason. He nodded and went outside in the corridor that led to the altar.

"What is it, Pierre?" he asked.

"My lord the Count is dead. Murdered."

After the first momentary shock, Father Bright realized that the news was not, after all, totally unexpected. Somewhere in the back of his mind, it seemed he had always known that the Count would die by violence long before debauchery ruined his health.

"Tell me about it," he said quietly.

Sir Pierre reported exactly what he had done and what he had seen.

"Then I locked the door and came straight

here," he told the priest.

"Who else has the key to the Count's suite?" Father Bright asked.

"No one but my lord himself," Sir Pierre answered, "at least as far as I know."

"Where is his key?"

"Still in the ring at his belt. I noticed that particularly."

"Very good. We'll leave it locked. You're certain the body was cold?"

"Cold and waxy, Father."

"Then he's been dead many hours."

"Lady Alice will have to be told," Sir Pierre said.

Father Bright nodded. "Yes. The Countess D'Evreux must be informed of her succession to the County Seat." He could tell by the sudden momentary blank look that came over Sir Pierre's face that the Privy Secretary had not yet realized fully the implications of the Count's death. "I'll tell her, Pierre. She should be in her pew by now. Just step into the church and tell her quietly that I want to speak to her. Don't tell her anything else."

"I understand, Father," said Sir Pierre.

There were only twenty-five or thirty people in the pews—most of them women—but Alice, Countess D'Evreux was not one of them. Sir Pierre walked quietly and unobtrusively down the side aisle and out into the narthex. She was standing there, just inside the main door, adjusting the black lace mantilla about her head, as though she had just come in from outside. Suddenly, Sir Pierre was very glad he would not have to be the one to break the news.

She looked rather sad, as always, her plain face unsmiling. The jutting nose and square chin which had given her brother the Count a look of aggressive handsomeness only made her look very solemn and rather sexless, although she had a magnificent figure.

"My lady," Sir Pierre said, stepping towards her, "the Reverend Father would like to speak to you before Mass. He's waiting at the sacristy door."

She held her rosary clutched tightly to her breast and gasped. Then she said, "Oh. Sir Pierre. I'm sorry; you quite surprised me. I didn't see you."

"My apologies, my lady."

"It's all right. My thoughts were elsewhere. Will you take me to the good Father?"

Father Bright heard their footsteps coming down the corridor before he saw them. He was a little fidgety because Mass was already a minute overdue. It should have started promptly at 7:15.

The new Countess D'Evreux took the news calmly, as he had known she would. After a pause, she crossed herself and said: "May his soul rest in peace. I will leave everything in your hands, Father, Sir Pierre. What are we to do?"

"Pierre must get on the teleson to Rouen immediately and report the matter to His Highness. I will announce your brother's death and ask for prayers for his soul—but I think I need say nothing about the manner of his death. There is no need to arouse any more speculation and fuss than necessary."

"Very well," said the Countess. "Come, Sir
Pierre; I will speak to the Duke, my cousin, myself."

"Yes, my lady."

Father Bright returned to the sacristy, opened
the missal, and changed the placement of the rib-
bons. Today was an ordinary Feria; a Votive
Mass would not be forbidden by the rubrics. The
clock said 7:17. He turned to young De Saint-
Brieuc, who was waiting respectfully. "Quickly,
my son—go and get the unbleached beeswax
candles and put them on the altar. Be sure you
light them before you put out the white ones.
Hurry, now; I will be ready by the time you
come back. Oh, yes—and change the altar fron-
tal. Put on the black."

"Yes, Father." And the lad was gone.

Father Bright folded the green chasuble and
returned it to the drawer, then took out the
black one. He would say a Requiem for the
Souls of All the Faithful Departed—and hope
that the Count was among them.

His Royal Highness, the Duke of Normandy,
looked over the official letter his secretary had
just typed for him. It was addressed to
*Serenissimo Domino Nostro Iohanni Quarto, Dei
Gratia, Angliae, Franciae, Scotiae, Hiberniae,
Novae Angliae et Novae Franciae, Rex, Im-
perator, Fidei Defensor, . . .* "Our Most Serene
Lord, John IV, by the Grace of God King and
Emperor of England, France, Scotland, Ireland,
New England and New France, Defender of the
Faith, . . ."

It was a routine matter; simple notification to his brother, the King, that His Majesty's most faithful servant, Edouard, Count of Evreux, had departed this life, and asking His Majesty's confirmation of the Count's heir-at-law, Alice, Countess of Evreux as his lawful successor.

His Highness finished reading, nodded, and scrawled his signature at the bottom: *Ricardus Dux Normaniae*.

Then, on a separate piece of paper, he wrote: "Dear John, May I suggest you hold up on this for a while? Edouard was a lecher and a slob, and I have no doubt he got everything he deserved, but we have no notion who killed him. For any evidence I have to the contrary, it might have been Alice who pulled the trigger. I will send you full particulars as soon as I have them. With much love, Your brother and servant, Richard."

He put both papers into a prepared envelope and sealed it. He wished he could have called the King on the teleson, but no one had yet figured out how to get the wires across the channel.

He looked absently at the sealed envelope, his handsome blond features thoughtful. The House of Plantagenet had endured for eight centuries, and the blood of Henry of Anjou ran thin in its veins, but the Norman strain was as strong as ever, having been replenished over the centuries by fresh infusions from Norwegian and Danish princesses. Richard's mother, Queen Helga, wife of His late Majesty, Charles III, spoke very few words of Anglo-French, and those with a heavy Norse accent.

Nevertheless, there was nothing Scandinavian
in the language, manner, or bearing of Richard,
Duke of Normandy. Not only was he a member
of the oldest and most powerful ruling family of
Europe, but he bore a Christian name that was
distinguished even in that family. Seven Kings of
the Empire had borne the name, and most of
them had been good Kings—if not always
"good" men in the nicey-nicey sense of the
word. Even old Richard I, who'd been pretty
wild during the first forty-odd years of his life,
had settled down to do a magnificent job of
kinging for the next twenty years. The long and
painful recovery from the wound he'd received
at the Siege of Chaluz had made a change in him
for the better.

There was a chance that Duke Richard might
be called upon to uphold the honor of that name
as King. By law, Parliament must elect a Plantagenet as King in the event of the death of the
present Sovereign, and while the election of one
of the King's two sons, the Prince of Britain and
the Duke of Lancaster, was more likely than the
election of Richard, he was certainly not
eliminated from the succession.

Meantime, he would uphold the honor of his
name as Duke of Normandy.

Murder had been done; therefore justice must
be done. The Count D'Evreux had been known
for his stern but fair justice almost as well as he
had been known for his profligacy. And, just as
his pleasures had been without temperance, so
his justice had been untempered by mercy. Whoever had killed him would find both justice and

mercy—in so far as Richard had it within his power to give it.

Although he did not formulate it in so many words, even mentally, Richard was of the opinion that some debauched woman or cuckolded man had fired the fatal shot. Thus he found himself inclining toward mercy before he knew anything substantial about the case at all.

Richard dropped the letter he was holding into the special mail pouch that would be placed aboard the evening trans-Channel packet, and then turned in his chair to look at the lean, middle-aged man working at a desk across the room.

"My lord Marquis," he said thoughtfully.

"Yes, Your Highness?" said the Marquis of Rouen, looking up.

"How true are the stories one has heard about the late Count?"

"True, Your Highness?" the Marquis said thoughtfully. "I would hesitate to make any estimate of percentages. Once a man gets a reputation like that, the number of his reputed sins quickly surpasses the number of actual ones. Doubtless many of the stories one hears are of whole cloth; others may have only a slight basis in fact. On the other hand, it is highly likely that there are many of which we have never heard. It is absolutely certain, however, that he has acknowledged seven illegitimate sons, and I dare say he has ignored a few daughters—and these, mind you, with unmarried women. His adulteries would be rather more difficult to establish, but I think your Highness can take it for granted that such escapades were far from uncommon."

He cleared his throat and then added, "If Your Highness is looking for motive, I fear there is a superabundance of persons with motive."

"I see," the Duke said. "Well, we will wait and see what sort of information Lord Darcy comes up with." He looked up at the clock. "They should be there by now."

Then, as if brushing further thoughts on that subject from his mind, he went back to work, picking up a new sheaf of state papers from his desk.

The Marquis watched him for a moment and smiled a little to himself. The young Duke took his work seriously, but was well-balanced about it. A little inclined to be romantic—but aren't we all at nineteen? There was no doubt of his ability, nor of his nobility. The Royal Blood of England always came through.

"My lady," said Sir Pierre gently, "the Duke's Investigators have arrived."

My Lady Alice, Countess D'Evreux, was seated in a gold-brocade upholstered chair in the small receiving room off the Great Hall. Standing near her, looking very grave, was Father Bright. Against the blaze of color on the walls of the room, the two of them stood out like ink blots. Father Bright wore his normal clerical black, unrelieved except for the pure white lace at collar and cuffs. The Countess wore unadorned black velvet, a dress which she had had to have altered hurriedly by her dressmaker; she had always hated black and owned only the mourning she had worn when her mother died eight years before. The somber looks on their faces seemed to make the black blacker.

"Show them in, Sir Pierre," the Countess said calmly.

Sir Pierre opened the door wider, and three men entered. One was dressed as one gently born; the other two wore the livery of the Duke of Normandy.

The gentleman bowed. "I am Lord Darcy, Chief Criminal Investigator for His Highness, the Duke, and your servant, my lady." He was a tall, brown-haired man with a rather handsome, lean face. He spoke Anglo-French with a definite English accent.

"My pleasure, Lord Darcy," said the Countess. "This is our vicar, Father Bright."

"Your servant, Reverend Sir." Then he presented the two men with him. The first was a scholarly-looking, graying man wearing pince-nez glasses with gold rims, Dr. Pateley, Chirurgeon. The second, a tubby, red-faced, smiling man, was Master Sean O Lochlainn, Sorcerer.

As soon as Master Sean was presented he removed a small, leather-bound folder from his belt pouch and proffered it to the priest. "My license, Reverend Father."

Father Bright took it and glanced over it. It was the usual thing, signed and sealed by the Archbishop of Rouen. The law was rather strict on that point; no sorcerer could practice without the permission of the Church, and a license was given only after careful examination for orthodoxy of practice.

"It seems to be quite in order, Master Sean,"

said the priest, handing the folder back. The tubby little sorcerer bowed his thanks and returned
the folder to his belt pouch.

Lord Darcy had a notebook in his hand.
"Now, unpleasant as it may be, we shall have to
check on a few facts." He consulted his notes,
then looked up at Sir Pierre. "You, I believe, discovered the body?"

"That is correct, your lordship."

"How long ago was this?"

Sir Pierre glanced at his wrist watch. It was
9:55. "Not quite three hours ago, your
lordship."

"At what time, precisely?"

"I rapped on the door precisely at seven, and
went in a minute or two later—say 7:01 or 7:02."

"How do you know the time so exactly?"

"My lord the Count," said Sir Pierre with
some stiffness, "insisted upon exact punctuality.
I have formed the habit of referring to my watch
regularly."

"I see. Very good. Now, what did you do then?"

Sir Pierre described his actions briefly.

"The door to his suite was not locked, then?"
Lord Darcy asked.

"No, sir."

"You did not expect it to be locked?"

"No, sir. It has not been for seventeen years."

Lord Darcy raised one eyebrow in a polite
query. "Never?"

"Not at seven o'clock, your lordship. My lord
the Count always rose promptly at six and unlocked the door before seven."

"He did lock it at night, then?"

"Yes, sir."

Lord Darcy looked thoughtful and made a note, but he said nothing more on that subject. "When you left, you locked the door?"

"That is correct, your lordship."

"And it has remained locked ever since?"

Sir Pierre hesitated and glanced at Father Bright. The priest said: "At 8:15, Sir Pierre and I went in. I wished to view the body. We touched nothing. We left at 8:20."

Master Sean O Lochlainn looked agitated. "Er ... excuse me, Reverend Sir. You didn't give him Holy Unction, I hope?"

"No," said Father Bright. "I thought it would be better to delay that until after the authorities had seen the ... er ... scene of the crime. I wouldn't want to make the gathering of evidence any more difficult than necessary."

"Quite right," murmured Lord Darcy.

"No blessings, I trust, Reverend Sir?" Master Sean persisted. "No exorcisms or—"

"Nothing," Father Bright interrupted somewhat testily. "I believe I crossed myself when I saw the body, but nothing more."

"Crossed *yourself*, sir. Nothing else?"

"No."

"Well, that's all right, then. Sorry to be so persistent, Reverend Sir, but any miasma of evil that may be left around is a very important clue, and it shouldn't be dispersed until it's been checked, you see."

"*Evil?*" My lady the Countess looked shocked.

"Sorry, my lady, but—" Master Sean began contritely.

But Father Bright interrupted by speaking to the Countess. "Don't distress yourself, my daughter; these men are only doing their duty."

"Of course. I understand. It's just that it's so—" She shuddered delicately.

Lord Darcy cast Master Sean a warning look, then asked politely, "Has my lady seen the deceased?"

"No," she said. "I will, however, if you wish."

"We'll see," said Lord Darcy. "Perhaps it won't be necessary. May we go up to the suite now?"

"Certainly," the Countess said. "Sir Pierre, if you will?"

"Yes, my lady."

As Sir Pierre unlocked the emblazoned door, Lord Darcy said: "Who else sleeps on this floor?"

"No one else, your lordship," Sir Pierre said. "The entire floor is . . . *was* . . . reserved for my lord the Count."

"Is there any way up besides that elevator?"

Sir Pierre turned and pointed toward the other end of the short hallway. "That leads to the staircase," he said, pointing to a massive oaken door, "but it's kept locked at all times. And, as you can see, there is a heavy bar across it. Except for moving furniture in and out or something like that, it's never used."

"No other way up or down, then?"

Sir Pierre hesitated. "Well, yes, your lordship, there is. I'll show you."

"A secret stairway?"

"Yes, your lordship."

"Very well. We'll look at it after we've seen the body."

Lord Darcy, having spent an hour on the train down from Rouen, was anxious to see the cause of all the trouble at last.

He lay in the bedroom, just as Sir Pierre and Father Bright had left him.

"If you please, Dr. Pateley," said his lordship.

He knelt on one side of the corpse and watched carefully while Pateley knelt on the other side and looked at the face of the dead man. Then he touched one of the hands and tried to move an arm. "Rigor has set in—even to the fingers. Single bullet hole. Rather small caliber—I should say a .28 or .34—hard to tell until I've probed out the bullet. Looks like it went right through the heart, though. Hard to tell about powder burns; the blood has soaked the clothing and dried. Still, these specks . . . hm-m-m. Yes. Hm-m-m."

Lord Darcy's eyes took in everything, but there was little enough to see on the body itself. Then his eye was caught by something that gave off a golden gleam. He stood up and walked over to the great canopied four-poster bed, then he was on his knees again, peering under it. A coin? No.

He picked it up carefully and looked at it. A button. Gold, intricately engraved in an Arabesque pattern, and set in the center with a single diamond. How long had it lain there? Where had it come from? Not from the Count's clothing, for his buttons were smaller, engraved with his arms, and had no gems. Had a man or a woman dropped it? There was no way of knowing at this stage of the game.

Darcy turned to Sir Pierre. "When was this room last cleaned?"

"Last evening, your lordship," the secretary said promptly. "My lord was always particular about that. The suite was always to be swept and cleaned during the dinner hour."

"Then this must have rolled under the bed at some time after dinner. Do you recognize it? The design is distinctive."

The Privy Secretary looked carefully at the button in the palm of Lord Darcy's hand without touching it. "I . . . I hesitate to say," he said at last. "It looks like . . . but I'm not sure—"

"Come, come, Chevalier! Where do you think you *might* have seen it? Or one like it." There was a sharpness in the tone of his voice.

"I'm not trying to conceal anything, your lordship," Sir Pierre said with equal sharpness. "I said I was not sure. I still am not, but it can be checked easily enough. If your lordship will permit me—" He turned and spoke to Dr. Pateley, who was still kneeling by the body. "May I have my lord the Count's keys, doctor?"

Pateley glanced up at Lord Darcy, who nodded silently. The chirurgeon detached the keys from the belt and handed them to Sir Pierre.

The Privy Secretary looked at them for a moment, then selected a small gold key. "This is it," he said, separating it from the others on the ring. "Come with me, your lordship."

* * *

Darcy followed him across the room to a broad wall covered with a great tapestry that must have dated back to the sixteenth century. Sir Pierre reached behind it and pulled a cord. The entire tapestry slid aside like a panel, and Lord Darcy saw that it was supported on a track some ten feet from the floor. Behind it was what looked at first like ordinary oak paneling, but Sir Pierre fitted the small key into an inconspicuous hole and turned. Or, rather, tried to turn.

"That's odd," said Sir Pierre. "It's not locked!"

He took the key out and pressed on the panel, shoving sideways with his hand to move it aside. It slid open to reveal a closet.

The closet was filled with women's clothing of all kinds, and styles.

Lord Darcy whistled soundlessly.

"Try that blue robe, your lordship," the Privy Secretary said. "The one with the—Yes, that's the one."

Lord Darcy took it off its hanger. The same buttons. They matched. And there was one missing from the front! Torn off! "Master Sean!" he called without turning.

Master Sean came with a rolling walk. He was holding an oddly-shaped bronze thing in his hand that Sir Pierre didn't quite recognize. The sorcerer was muttering. "Evil, that there is! Faith, and the vibrations are all over the place. Yes, my lord?"

"Check this dress and the button when you get round to it. I want to know when the two parted company."

"Yes, my lord." He draped the robe over one arm and dropped the button into a pouch at his belt. "I can tell you one thing, my lord. You talk about an evil miasma, this room has got it!" He held up the object in his hand. "There's an underlying background—something that has been here for years, just seeping in. But on top of that, there's a hellish big blast of it superimposed. Fresh it is, and very strong."

"I shouldn't be surprised, considering there was murder done here last night—or very early this morning," said Lord Darcy.

"Hm-m-m, yes. Yes, my lord, the death is there—but there's something else. Something I can't place."

"You can tell that just by holding that bronze cross in your hand?" Sir Pierre asked interestedly.

Master Sean gave him a friendly scowl. " 'Tisn't quite a cross, sir. This is what is known as a *crux ansata*. The ancient Egyptians called it an *ankh*. Notice the loop at the top instead of the straight piece your true cross has. Now, your true cross—if it were properly energized, blessed, d'ye see—your true cross would tend to dissipate the evil. The *ankh* merely vibrates to evil because of the closed loop at the top, which makes a return circuit. And it's not energized by blessing, but by another . . . um . . . spell."

"Master Sean, we have a murder to investigate," said Lord Darcy.

The sorcerer caught the tone of his voice and nodded quickly. "Yes, my lord." And he walked rollingly away.

"Now, where's that secret stairway you mentioned, Sir Pierre?" Lord Darcy asked.

"This way, your lordship."

He led Lord Darcy to a wall at right angles to the outer wall and slid back another tapestry.

"Good Heavens," Darcy muttered, "does he have something concealed behind every arras in the place?" But he didn't say it loud enough for the Privy Secretary to hear.

This time, what greeted them was a solid-seeming stone wall. But Sir Pierre pressed in on one small stone, and a section of the wall swung back, exposing a stairway.

"Oh, yes," Darcy said. "I see what he did. This is the old spiral stairway that goes round the inside of the Keep. There are two doorways at the bottom. One opens into the courtyard, the other is a postern gate through the curtain wall to the outside—but that was closed up in the sixteen century, so the only way out is into the courtyard."

"Your lordship knows Castle D'Evreux, then?" Sir Pierre said. Sir Pierre had no recollection of Darcy's having been in the Castle before.

"Only by the plans in the Royal Archives. But I have made it a point to—" He stopped. "Dear me," he interrupted himself mildly, "what is that?"

"That" was something that had been hidden by the arras until Sir Pierre had slid it aside, and was still showing only a part of itself. It lay on the floor a foot or so from the secret door.

Darcy knelt down and pulled the tapestry

back from the object. "Well, well. A .28 two-
shot pocket gun. Gold-chased, beautifully engraved, mother-of-pearl handle. A regular gem."
He picked it up and examined it closely. "One
shot fired."

He stood up and showed it to Sir Pierre. "Ever
see it before?"

The Privy Secretary looked at the weapon
closely. Then he shook his head. "Not that I recall, your lordship. It certainly isn't one of the
Count's guns."

"You're certain?"

"Quite certain, your lordship. I'll show you
the gun collection if you want. My lord the
Count didn't like tiny guns like that; he preferred a larger caliber. He would never have
owned what he considered a toy."

"Well, we'll have to look into it." He called
over Master Sean again and gave the gun into
his keeping. "And keep your eyes open for anything else of interest, Master Sean. So far, everything of interest besides the late Count himself
has been hiding under beds or behind arrases.
Check everything. Sir Pierre and I are going for
a look down this stairway."

The stairway was gloomy, but enough light
came in through the arrow slits spaced at intervals along the outer wall to illuminate the interior. It spiraled down between the inner and
outer walls of the Great Keep, making four complete circuits before it reached ground level.
Lord Darcy looked carefully at the steps, the
walls, and even the low, arched overhead as he
and Sir Pierre went down.

After the first circuit, on the floor beneath the Count's suite, he stopped. "There was a door here," he said, pointing to a rectangular area in the inner wall.

"Yes, your lordship. There used to be an opening at every floor, but they were all sealed off. It's quite solid, as you can see."

"Where would they lead if they were open?"

"The county offices. My own office, the clerk's offices, the constabulary on the first floor. Below are the dungeons. My lord the Count was the only one who lived in the Keep itself. The rest of the household live above the Great Hall."

"What about guests?"

"They're usually housed in the east wing. We only have two house guests at the moment. Laird and Lady Duncan have been with us for four days."

"I see." They went down perhaps four more steps before Lord Darcy asked quietly, "Tell me, Sir Pierre, were you privy to *all* of Count D'Evreux's business?"

Another four steps down before Sir Pierre answered. "I understand what your lordship means," he said. Another two steps. "No, I was not. I was aware that my lord the Count engaged in certain . . . er . . . shall we say, liaisons with members of the opposite sex. However—"

He paused, and in the gloom, Lord Darcy could see his lips tighten. "However," he continued, "I did not procure for my lord, if that is what you're driving at. I am not and never have been a pimp."

"I didn't intend to suggest that you had, good knight," said Lord Darcy in a tone that strongly implied that the thought had actually never crossed his mind. "Not at all. But certainly there is a difference between 'aiding and abetting' and simple knowledge of what is going on."

"Oh. Yes. Yes, of course. Well, one cannot, of course, be the secretary-in-private of a gentleman such as my lord the Count for seventeen years without knowing something of what is going on, you're right. Yes. Yes. Hm-m-m."

Lord Darcy smiled to himself. Not until this moment had Sir Pierre realized how much he actually *did* know. In loyalty to his lord, he had literally kept his eyes shut for seventeen years.

"I realize," Lord Darcy said smoothly, "that a gentleman would never implicate a lady nor besmirch the reputation of another gentleman without due cause and careful consideration. However,"—like the knight, he paused a moment before going on—"although we are aware that he was not discreet, was he particular?"

"If you mean by that, did he confine his attentions to those of gentle birth, your lordship, then I can say, no he did not. If you mean did he confine his attentions to the gentler sex, then I can only say that, as far as I know, he did."

"I see. That explains the closet full of clothes."

"Beg pardon, your lordship?"

"I mean that if a girl or woman of the lower classes were to come here, he would have proper clothing for them to wear."

"Quite likely, your lordship. He was most particular about clothing. Couldn't stand a woman who was sloppily dressed or poorly dressed."

"In what way?"

"Well. Well, for instance, I recall once that he saw a very pretty peasant girl. She was dressed in the common style, of course, but she was dressed neatly and prettily. My lord took a fancy to her. He said, 'Now there's a lass who knows how to wear clothes. Put her in decent apparel, and she'd pass for a princess.' But a girl, who had a pretty face and a fine figure, made no impression on him unless she wore her clothing well, if you see what I mean, your lordship."

"Did you never know him to fancy a girl who dressed in an offhand manner?" Lord Darcy asked.

"Only among the gently born, your lordship. He'd say, 'Look at Lady So-and-so! Nice wench, if she'd let me teach her how to dress.' You might say, your lordship, that a woman could be dressed commonly or sloppily, but not both."

"Judging by the stuff in that closet," Lord Darcy said, "I should say that the late Count had excellent taste in feminine dress."

Sir Pierre considered. "Hm-m-m. Well, now, I wouldn't exactly say so, your lordship. He knew *how* clothes should be worn, yes. But he couldn't pick out a woman's gown of his accord. He could choose his own clothing with impeccable taste, but he'd not any real notion of how a woman's clothing should go, if you see what I mean. All he knew was how good clothing should be worn. But he knew nothing about design for women's clothing."

"Then how did he get that closet full of clothes?" Lord Darcy asked, puzzled.

Sir Pierre chuckled. "Very simply, your lordship. He knew that the Lady Alice had good taste, so he secretly instructed that each piece that Lady Alice ordered should be made in duplicate. With small variations, of course. I'm certain my lady wouldn't like it if she knew."

"I dare say not," said Lord Darcy thoughtfully.

"Here is the door to the courtyard," said Sir Pierre. "I doubt that it has been opened in broad daylight for many years." He selected a key from the ring of the late Count and inserted it into a keyhole. The door swung back, revealing a large crucifix attached to its outer surface. Lord Darcy crossed himself. "Lord in Heaven," he said softly, "what is this?"

He looked out into a small shrine. It was walled off from the courtyard and had a single small entrance some ten feet from the doorway. There were four prie-dieus—small kneeling benches—ranged in front of the doorway.

"If I may explain, your lordship—" Sir Pierre began.

"No need to," Lord Darcy said in a hard voice. "It's rather obvious. My lord the Count was quite ingenious. This is a relatively newly-built shrine. Four walls and a crucifix against the castle wall. Anyone could come in here, day or night, for prayer. No one who came in would be suspected." He stepped out into the small enclosure and swung around to look at the door. "And when that door is closed, there is no sign that there is a door behind the crucifix. If a woman came in here, it would be assumed that she came for prayer. But if she knew of that door—" His voice trailed off.

"Yes, your lordship," said Sir Pierre. "I did not approve, but I was in no position to disapprove."

"I understand." Lord Darcy stepped out to the doorway of the little shrine and took a quick glance about. "Then anyone within the castle walls could come in here," he said.

"Yes, your lordship."

"Very well. Let's go back up."

In the small office which Lord Darcy and his staff had been assigned while conducting the investigation, three men watched while a fourth conducted a demonstration on a table in the center of the room.

Master Sean O Lochlainn held up an intricately engraved gold button with an Arabesque pattern and a diamond set in the center.

He looked at the other three. "Now, my lord, your Reverence, and colleague Doctor, I call your attention to this button."

Dr. Pateley smiled and Father Bright looked stern. Lord Darcy merely stuffed tobacco—imported from the southern New England counties on the Gulf—into a German-made porcelain pipe. He allowed Master Sean a certain amount of flamboyance; good sorcerers were hard to come by.

"Will you hold the robe, Dr. Pateley? Thank you. Now, stand back. That's it. Thank you. Now, I place the button on the table, a good ten feet from the robe." Then he muttered something under his breath and dusted a bit of powder on the button. He made a few passes over it with his hands, paused, and looked up at Father Bright. "If you will, Reverend Sir?"

Father Bright solemnly raised his right hand, and, as he made the Sign of the Cross, said: "May this demonstration, O God, be in strict accord with the truth, and may the Evil One not in any way deceive us who are witnesses thereto. In the Name of the Father and of the Son and of the Holy Spirit. Amen."

"Amen," the other three chorused.

Master Sean crossed himself, then muttered something under his breath.

The button leaped from the table, slammed itself against the robe which Dr. Pateley held before him, and stuck there as though it had been sewed on by an expert.

"Ha!" said Master Sean. "As I thought!" He gave the other three men a broad, beaming smile. "The two were definitely connected!"

Lord Darcy looked bored. "Time?" he asked.

"In a moment, my lord," Master Sean said apologetically. "In a moment." While the other three watched, the sorcerer went through more spells with the button and the robe, although none were so spectacular as the first demonstration. Finally, Master Sean said: "About eleven thirty last night they were torn apart, my lord. But I shouldn't like to make it any more definite than to say between eleven and midnight. The speed with which it returned to its place shows that it was ripped off very rapidly, however."

"Very good," said Lord Darcy. "Now the bullet, if you please."

"Yes, my lord. This will have to be a bit different." He took more paraphernalia out of his large, symbol-decorated carpet bag. "The Law of Contagion, gently-born sirs, is a tricky thing to work with. If a man doesn't know how to handle it, he can get himself killed. We had an apprentice o' the Guild back in Cork who might have made a good sorcerer in time. He had the Talent—unfortunately, he didn't have the good sense to go with it. According to the Law of Contagion any two objects which have ever been in contact with each other have an affinity for each other which is directly proportional to the product of the degree of relevancy of the contact and the length of time they were in contact and inversely proportional to the length of time since they have ceased to be in contact." He gave a smiling glance to the priest. "That doesn't apply strictly to relics of the saints, Reverend Sir; there's another factor enters in there, as you know."

As he spoke, the sorcerer was carefully clamping the little handgun into a padded vise so that its barrel was parallel to the surface of the table.

"Anyhow," he went on, "this apprentice, all on his own, decided to get rid of the cockroaches in his house—a simple thing, if one knows how to go about it. So he collected dust from various cracks and crannies about the house, dust which contained, of course, the droppings of the pests. The dust, with the appropriate spells and ingredients, he boiled. It worked fine. The roaches all came down with a raging fever and died. Unfortunately, the clumsy lad had poor laboratory technique. He allowed three drops of his own perspiration to fall into the steaming pot over which he was working, and the resulting fever killed him, too."

By this time, he had put the bullet which Dr. Pateley had removed from the Count's body on a small pedestal so that it was exactly in line with the muzzle of the gun. "There, now," he said softly.

Then he repeated the incantation and the powdering that he had used on the button. As the last syllable was formed by his lips, the bullet vanished with a *ping!* In its vise, the little gun vibrated.

"Ah!" said Master Sean. "No question there, eh? That's the death weapon, all right, my lord. Yes. Time's almost exactly the same as that of the removal of the button. Not more than a few seconds later. Forms a picture, don't it, my lord? His lordship the Count jerks a button off the girl's gown, she outs with a gun and plugs him."

Lord Darcy's handsome face scowled. "Let's not jump to any hasty conclusions, my good Sean. There is no evidence whatever that he was killed by a woman."

"Would a man be wearing that gown, my lord?"

"Possibly," said Lord Darcy. "But who says that anyone was wearing it when the button was removed?"

"Oh." Master Sean subsided into silence. Using a small ramrod, he forced the bullet out of the chamber of the little pistol.

"Father Bright," said Lord Darcy, "will the Countess be serving tea this afternoon?"

The priest looked suddenly contrite. "Good heavens! None of you has eaten yet! I'll see that something is sent up right away, Lord Darcy. In the confusion—"

Lord Darcy held up a hand. "I beg your pardon, Father; that wasn't what I meant. I'm sure Master Sean and Dr. Pateley would appreciate a little something, but I can wait until tea time. What I was thinking was that perhaps the Countess would ask her guests to tea. Does she know Laird and Lady Duncan well enough to ask for their sympathetic presence on such an afternoon as this?"

Father Bright's eyes narrowed a trifle. "I dare say it could be arranged, Lord Darcy. You will be there?"

"Yes—but I may be a trifle late. That will hardly matter at an informal tea."

The priest glanced at his watch. "Four o'clock?"

"I should think that would do it," said Lord Darcy.

Father Bright nodded wordlessly and left the room.

Dr. Pateley took off his pince-nez and polished the lenses carefully with a silk handkerchief. "How long will your spell keep the body incorrupt, Master Sean?" he asked.

"As long as it's relevant. As soon as the case is

solved, or we have enough data to solve the case
—as the case may be, heh heh—he'll start to go.
I'm not a saint, you know; it takes powerful
motivation to keep a body incorrupt for years
and years."

Sir Pierre was eying the gown that Pateley had
put on the table. The button was still in place, as
if held there by magnetism. He didn't touch it.
"Master Sean, I don't know much about magic," he said, "but can't you find out who was
wearing this robe just as easily as you found out
that the button matched?"

Master Sean wagged his head in a firm
negative. "No, sir. 'Tisn't relevant, sir. The relevancy of the integrated dress-as-a-whole is
quite strong. So is that of the seamstress or tailor
who made the garment, and that of the weaver
who made the cloth. But, except in certain
cirumstances, the person who wears or wore the
garment has little actual relevancy to the
garment itself."

"I'm afraid I don't understand," said Sir
Pierre, looking puzzled.

"Look at it like this, sir: That gown wouldn't
be what it is if the weaver hadn't made the cloth
in that particular way. It wouldn't be what it is if
the seamstress hadn't cut it in a particular way and
sewed it in a specific manner. You follow, sir?
Yes. Well, then, the connections between
garment-and-weaver and garment-and-
seamstress are strongly relevant. But this dress
would still be pretty much what it is if it had
stayed in the closet instead of being worn. No
relevance—or very little. Now, if it were a well-

worn garment, that would be different—that is, if it had always been worn by the same person. Then, you see, sir, the garment-as-a-whole is what it is because of the wearing, and the wearer becomes relevant."

He pointed at the little handgun he was still holding in his hand. "Now you take your gun, here, sir. The—"

"It isn't *my* gun," Sir Pierre interrupted firmly.

"I was speaking rhetorically, sir," said Master Sean with infinite patience. "This gun or any other gun in general, if you see what I mean, sir. It's even harder to place the ownership of a gun. Most of the wear on a gun is purely mechanical. It don't matter *who* pulls the trigger, you see; the erosion by the gases produced in the chamber, and the wear caused by the bullet passing through the barrel will be the same. You see, sir, 'tisn't relevant *to the gun* who pulled its trigger or what it's fired at. The bullet's a slightly different matter. To the bullet, it *is* relevant which gun it was fired from and what it hit. All these things simply have to be taken into account, Sir Pierre."

"I see," said the knight. "Very interesting, Master Sean." Then he turned to Lord Darcy. "Is there anything else, your lordship? There's a great deal of county business to be attended to."

Lord Darcy waved a hand. "Not at the moment, Sir Pierre. I understand the pressures of government. Go right ahead."

"Thank you, your lordship. If anything further should be required, I shall be in my office."

As soon as Sir Pierre had closed the door, Lord Darcy held out his hand toward the sorcerer. "Master Sean; the gun."

Master Sean handed it to him. "Ever see one like it before?" he asked, turning it over in his hands.

"Not *exactly* like it, my lord."

"Come, come, Sean; don't be so cautious. I am no sorcerer, but I don't need to know the Laws of Similarity to be able to recognize an *obvious* similarity."

"Edinburgh," said Master Sean flatly.

"Exactly. Scottish work. The typical Scot gold work; remarkable beauty. And look at that lock. It has 'Scots' written all over it—and more, 'Edinburgh', as you said."

Dr. Pateley, having replaced his carefully polished glasses, leaned over and peered at the weapon in Lord Darcy's hand. "Couldn't it be Italian, my lord? Or Moorish? In Moorish Spain, they do work like that."

"No Moorish gunsmith would put a hunting scene on the butt," Lord Darcy said flatly, "and the Italians wouldn't have put heather and thistles in the field surrounding the huntsman."

"But the *FdM* engraved on the barrel," said Dr. Pateley, "indicates the—"

"Ferrari of Milano," said Lord Darcy. "Exactly. But the barrel is of much newer work than the rest. So are the chambers. This is a fairly old gun—fifty years old, I'd say. The lock and the butt are still in excellent condition, indicating that it has been well cared for, but frequent usage—or a single accident—could ruin the barrel and require the owner to get a replacement. It was replaced by Ferrari."

"I see," said Dr. Pateley, somewhat humbled.

"If we open the lock . . . Master Sean, hand me your small screwdriver. Thank you. If we open the lock, we will find the name of one of the finest gunsmiths of half a century ago—a man whose name has not yet been forgotten— Hamish Graw of Edinburgh. Ah! There! You see?" They did.

Having satisfied himself on that point, Lord Darcy closed the lock again. "Now, men, we have the gun located. We also know that a guest in this very castle is Laird Duncan of Duncan. The Duncan of Duncan himself. A Scot's laird who was, fifteen years ago, His Majesty's Minister Plenipotentiary to the Grand Duchy of Milano. That suggests to me that it would be indeed odd if there were not some connection between Laird Duncan and this gun. Eh?"

"Come, come, Master Sean," said Lord Darcy rather impatiently, "We haven't all the time in the world."

"Patience, my lord; patience," said the little sorcerer calmly. "Can't hurry these things, you know." He was kneeling in front of a large, heavy traveling chest in the bedroom of the guest apartment occupied temporarily by Laird and Lady Duncan, working with the lock. "One position of a lock is just as relevant as the other so you can't work with the bolt. But the pin-tumblers in the cylinder, now, that's a different matter. A lock's built so that the breaks in the

tumblers are not related to the surface of the
cylinder when the key is out, but there *is* a rela-
tion when the key's *in,* so by taking advantage of
that relevancy—Ah!"

The lock clicked open.

Lord Darcy raised the lid gently.

"Carefully, my lord!" Master Sean said in a
warning voice. "He's got a spell on the thing!
Let me do it." He made Lord Darcy stand back
and then lifted the lid of the heavy trunk himself.
When it was leaning back against the wall, gap-
ing open widely on its hinges, Master Sean took
a long look at the trunk and its lid without
touching either of them. There was a second lid
on the trunk, a thin one obviously operated by a
simple bolt.

Master Sean took his sorcerer's staff, a five-
foot, heavy rod made of the wood of the quicken
tree or mountain ash, and touched the inner lid.
Nothing happened. He touched the bolt. Nothing.

"Hm-m-m," Master Sean murmured thoughtfully. He glanced around the room, and his eyes
fell on a heavy stone doorstop. "That ought to
do it." He walked over, picked it up, and carried
it back to the chest. Then he put it on the rim of
the chest in such a position that if the lid were to
fall it would be stopped by the doorstop.

Then he put his hand in as if to lift the inner
lid.

The heavy outer lid swung forward and down
of its own accord, moving with blurring speed,
and slammed viciously against the doorstop.

Lord Darcy massaged his right wrist gently, as

if he felt where the lid would have hit if he had tried to open the inner lid. "Triggered to slam if a human being sticks a hand in there, eh?"

"Or a head, my lord. Not very effectual if you know what to look for. There are better spells than that for guarding things. Now we'll see what his lordship wants to protect so badly that he practices sorcery without a license." He lifted the lid again, and then opened the inner lid. "It's safe now, my lord. *Look at this!*"

Lord Darcy had already seen. Both men looked in silence at the collection of paraphernalia on the first tray of the chest. Master Sean's busy fingers carefully opened the tissue paper packing of one after another of the objects. "A human skull," he said. "Bottles of graveyard earth. Hm-m-m—this one is labeled 'virgin's blood.' And this! A Hand of Glory!"

It was a mummified human hand, stiff and dry and brown, with the fingers partially curled, as though they were holding an invisible ball three inches or so in diameter. On each of the fingertips was a short candlestub. When the hand was placed on its back, it would act as a candelabra.

"That pretty much settles it, eh, Master Sean?" Lord Darcy said.

"Indeed, my lord. At the very least, we can get him for possession of materials. Black magic is a matter of symbolism and intent."

"Very well. I want a complete list of the contents of that chest. Be sure to replace everything as it was and relock the trunk." He tugged thoughtfully at an earlobe. "So Laird Duncan has the Talent, eh? Interesting."

"Aye. But not surprising, my lord," said Master Sean without looking up from his work. "It's in the blood. Some attribute it to the Dedannans, who passed through Scotland before they conquered Ireland three thousand years ago, but, however that may be, the Talent runs strong in the Sons of Gael. It makes me boil to see it misused."

While Master Sean talked, Lord Darcy was prowling around the room, reminding one of a lean tomcat who was certain that there was a mouse concealed somewhere.

"It'll make Laird Duncan boil if he isn't stopped," Lord Darcy murmured absently.

"Aye, my lord," said Master Sean. "The mental state necessary to use the Talent for black sorcery is such that it invariably destroys the user—but, if he knows what he's doing, a lot of other people are hurt before he finally gets his."

Lord Darcy opened the jewel box on the dresser. The usual traveling jewelry—enough, but not a great choice.

"A man's mind turns in on itself when he's taken up with hatred and thoughts of revenge," Master Sean droned on. "Or, if he's the type who *enjoys* watching others suffer, or the type who doesn't care but is willing to do anything for gain, then his mind is already warped and the misuse of the Talent just makes it worse."

Lord Darcy found what he was looking for in a drawer, just underneath some neatly folded lingerie. A small holster, beautifully made of Florentine leather, gilded and tooled. He didn't need Master Sean's sorcery to tell him that the little pistol fit it like a hand a glove.

* * *

Father Bright felt as though he had been walking a tightrope for hours. Laird and Lady Duncan had been talking in low, controlled voices that betrayed an inner nervousness, but Father Bright realized that he and the Countess had been doing the same thing. The Duncan of Duncan had offered his condolences on the death of the late Count with the proper air of suppressed sorrow, as had Mary, Lady Duncan. The Countess had accepted them solemnly and with gratitude. But Father Bright was well aware that no one in the room—possibly, he thought, no one in the world—regretted the Count's passing.

Laird Duncan sat in his wheelchair, his sharp Scots features set in a sad smile that showed an intent to be affable even though great sorrow weighed heavily upon him. Father Bright noticed it and realized that his own face had the same sort of expression. No one was fooling anyone else, of that the priest was certain—but for anyone to admit it would be the most boorish breach of etiquette. But there was a haggardness, a look of increased age about the Laird's countenance that Father Bright did not like. His priestly intuition told him clearly that there was a turmoil of emotion in the Scotsman's mind that was . . . well, *evil* was the only word for it.

Lady Duncan was, for the most part, silent. In the past fifteen minutes, since she and her husband had come to the informal tea, she had spoken scarcely a dozen words. Her face was masklike, but there was the same look of haggardness about her eyes as there was in her husband's face. But the priest's empathic sense told him that the emotion here was fear, simple and direct. His keen eyes had noticed that she wore a shade too much make-up. She had almost succeeded in covering up the faint bruise on her right cheek, but not completely.

My lady the Countess D'Evreux was all sadness and unhappiness, but there was neither fear nor evil there. She smiled politely and talked quietly. Father Bright would have been willing to bet that not one of the four of them would remember a word that had been spoken.

Father Bright had placed his chair so that he could keep an eye on the open doorway and the long hall that led in from the Great Keep. He hoped Lord Darcy would hurry. Neither of the guests had been told that the Duke's Investigator was here, and Father Bright was just a little apprehensive about the meeting. The Duncans had not even been told that the Count's death had been murder, but he was certain that they knew.

Father Bright saw Lord Darcy come in through the door at the far end of the hall. He murmured a polite excuse and rose. The other three accepted his excuses with the same politeness and went on with their talk. Father Bright met Lord Darcy in the hall.

"Did you find what you were looking for, Lord Darcy?" the priest asked in a low tone.

"Yes," Lord Darcy said. "I'm afraid we shall have to arrest Laird Duncan."

"Murder?"

"Perhaps. I'm not yet certain of that. But the

charge will be black magic. He has all the paraphernalia in a chest in his room. Master Sean
reports that a ritual was enacted in the bedroom
last night. Of course, that's out of my juris-
diction. You, as a representative of the Church,
will have to be the arresting officer." He paused.
"You don't seem surprised, Reverence."

"I'm not," Father Bright admitted. "I felt it.
You and Master Sean will have to make out a
sworn deposition before I can act."

"I understand. Can you do me a favor?"

"If I can."

"Get my lady the Countess out of the room on
some pretext or other. Leave me alone with her
guests. I do not wish to upset my lady any more
than absolutely necessary."

"I think I can do that. Shall we go in together?"

"Why not? But don't mention why I am here.
Let them assume I am just another guest."

"Very well."

All three occupants of the room glanced up as
Father Bright came in with Lord Darcy. The in-
troductions were made: Lord Darcy humbly
begged the pardon of his hostess for his lateness.
Father Bright noticed the same sad smile on
Lord Darcy's handsome face as the others were
wearing.

Lord Darcy helped himself from the buffet
table and allowed the Countess to pour him a
large cup of hot tea. He mentioned nothing
about the recent death. Instead, he turned the
conversation toward the wild beauty of Scotland
and the excellence of the grouse shooting there.

Father Bright had not sat down again. Instead, he left the room once more. When he returned, he went directly to the Countess and said, in a low, but clearly audible voice: "My lady, Sir Pierre Morlaix has informed me that there are a few matters that require your attention immediately. It will require only a few moments."

My lady the Countess did not hesitate, but made her excuses immediately. "Do finish your tea," she added. "I don't think I shall be long."

Lord Darcy knew the priest would not lie, and he wondered what sort of arrangement had been made with Sir Pierre. Not that it mattered except that Lord Darcy had hoped it would be sufficiently involved for it to keep the Countess busy for at least ten minutes.

The conversation, interrupted but momentarily, returned to grouse.

"I haven't done any shooting since my accident," said Laird Duncan, "but I used to enjoy it immensely. I still have friends up every year for the season."

"What sort of weapon do you prefer for grouse?" Lord Darcy asked.

"A one-inch bore with a modified choke," said the Scot. "I have a pair that I favor. Excellent weapons."

"Of Scottish make?"

"No, no. English. Your London gunsmiths can't be beat for shotguns."

"Oh. I thought perhaps your lordship had had all your guns made in Scotland." As he spoke, he took the little pistol out of his coat pocket and put it carefully on the table.

There was a sudden silence, then Laird Duncan said in an angry voice: "What is this? Where did you get that?"

Lord Darcy glanced at Lady Duncan, who had turned suddenly pale. "Perhaps," he said coolly, "Lady Duncan can tell us."

She shook her head and gasped. For a moment, she had trouble in forming words or finding her voice. Finally: "No. No. I know nothing. Nothing."

But Laird Duncan looked at her oddly.

"You do not deny that it is your gun, my lord?" Lord Darcy asked. "Or your wife's, as the case may be."

"Where did you get it?" There was a dangerous quality in the Scotsman's voice. He had once been a powerful man, and Lord Darcy could see his shoulder muscles bunching.

"From the late Count D'Evreux's bedroom."

"What was it doing there?" There was a snarl in the Scot's voice, but Lord Darcy had the feeling that the question was as much directed toward Lady Duncan as it was to himself.

"One of the things it was doing there was shooting Count D'Evreux through the heart."

Lady Duncan slumped forward in a dead faint, overturning her teacup. Laird Duncan made a grab at the gun, ignoring his wife. Lord Darcy's hand snaked out and picked up the weapon before the Scot could touch it. "No, no, my lord," he said mildly. "This is evidence in a murder case. We mustn't tamper with King's Evidence."

He wasn't prepared for what happened next. Laird Duncan roared something obscene in

Scots Gaelic, put his hands on the arms of his
wheelchair, and, with a great thrust of his powerful arms and shoulders, shoved himself up and
forward, toward Lord Darcy, across the table
from him. His arms swung up toward Lord
Darcy's throat as the momentum of his body
carried him toward the investigator.

He might have made it, but the weakness of
his legs betrayed him. His waist struck the edge
of the massive oaken table, and most of his forward momentum was lost. He collapsed forward, his hands still grasping toward the surprised Englishman. His chin came down hard on
the table top. Then he slid back, taking the
tablecloth and the china and silverware with
him. He lay unmoving on the floor. His wife did
not even stir except when the tablecloth tugged
at her head.

Lord Darcy had jumped back, overturning his
chair. He stood on his feet, looking at the two
unconscious forms. He hoped he didn't look too
much like King MacBeth.

"I don't think there's any permanent damage
done to either," said Dr. Pateley an hour later.
"Lady Duncan was suffering from shock, of
course, but Father Bright brought her round in a
hurry. She's a devout woman, I think, even if a
sinful one."

"What about Laird Duncan?" Lord Darcy
asked.

"Well, that's a different matter. I'm afraid
that his back injury was aggravated, and that
crack on the chin didn't do him any good. I
don't know whether Father Bright can help him

or not. Healing takes the co-operation of the patient. I did all I could for him, but I'm just a chirurgeon, not a practitioner of the Healing Art. Father Bright has quite a good reputation in that line, however, and he may be able to do his lordship some good."

Master Sean shook his head dolefully. "His Reverence has the Talent, there's no doubt of that, but now he's pitted against another man who has it—a man whose mind is bent on self-destruction in the long run."

"Well, that's none of my affair," said Dr. Pateley. "I'm just a technician. I'll leave healing up to the Church, where it belongs."

"Master Sean," said Lord Darcy, "there is still a mystery here. We need more evidence. What about the eyes?"

Master Sean blinked. "You mean the picture test, my lord?"

"I do."

"It won't stand up in court, my lord," said the sorcerer.

"I'm aware of that," said Lord Darcy testily.

"Eye test?" Dr. Pateley asked blankly. "I don't believe I understand."

"It's not often used," said Master Sean. "It is a psychic phenomenon that sometimes occurs at the moment of death—especially a violent death. The violent emotional stress causes a sort of backfiring of the mind, if you see what I mean. As a result, the image in the mind of the dying person is returned to the retina. By using the proper sorcery, this image can be developed and the last thing the dead man saw can be brought out.

"But it's a difficult process even under the best

of circumstances, and usually the conditions aren't right. In the first place, it doesn't always occur. It never occurs, for instance, when the person is expecting the attack. A man who is killed in a duel, or who is shot after facing the gun for several seconds, has time to adjust to the situation. Also, death must occur almost instantly. If he lingers, even for a few minutes, the effect is lost. And, naturally if the person's eyes are closed at the instant of death, nothing shows up."

"Count D'Evreux's eyes were open," Dr. Pateley said. "They were still open when we found him. How long after death does the image remain?"

"Until the cells of the retina die and lose their identity. Rarely more than twenty-four hours, usually much less."

"It hasn't been twenty-four hours yet," said Lord Darcy, "and there is a chance that the Count was taken completely by surprise."

"I must admit, my lord," Master Sean said thoughtfully, "that the conditions seem favorable. I shall attempt it. But don't put any hopes on it, my lord."

"I shan't. Just do your best, Master Sean. If there is a sorcerer in practice who can do the job, it is you."

"Thank you, my lord. I'll get busy on it right away," said the sorcerer with a subdued glow of pride.

Two hours later, Lord Darcy was striding down the corridor of the Great Hall, Master

Sean following up as best he could, his *caorthainn*-wood staff in one hand and his big carpet bag in the other. He had asked Father Bright and the Countess D'Evreux to meet him in one of the smaller guest rooms. But the Countess came to meet him.

"My Lord Darcy," she said, her plain face looking worried and unhappy, "is it true that you suspect Laird and Lady Duncan of this murder? Because, if so, I must—"

"No longer, my lady," Lord Darcy cut her off quickly. "I think we can show that neither is guilty of murder—although, of course, the black magic charge must still be held against Laird Duncan."

"I understand," she said, "but—"

"Please, my lady," Lord Darcy interrupted again, "let me explain everything. Come."

Without another word, she turned and led the way to the room where Father Bright was waiting.

The priest stood waiting, his face showing tenseness.

"Please," said Lord Darcy. "Sit down, both of you. This won't take long. My lady, may Master Sean make use of that table over there?"

"Certainly, my lord," the Countess said softly, "certainly."

"Thank you, my lady. Please, please—sit down. This won't take long. Please."

With apparent reluctance, Father Bright and my lady the Countess sat down in two chairs facing Lord Darcy. They paid little attention to what Master Sean O Lochlainn was doing; their eyes were on Lord Darcy.

"Conducting an investigation of this sort is
not an easy thing," he began carefully. "Most
murder cases could be easily solved by your
Chief Man-at-Arms. We find that well-trained
county Armsmen, in by far the majority of cases,
can solve the mystery easily—and in most cases
there is very little mystery. But, by His Imperial
Majesty's law, the Chief Man-at-Arms *must* call
in a Duke's Investigator if the crime is insoluble
or if it involves a member of the aristocracy. For
that reason, you were perfectly correct to call
His Highness the Duke as soon as murder had
been discovered." He leaned back in his chair.
"And it has been clear from the first that my
lord the late Count was murdered."

Father Bright started to say something, but
Lord Darcy cut him off before he could speak.
"By 'murder', Reverend Father, I mean that he
did not die a natural death—by disease or heart
trouble or accident or what-have-you. I should,
perhaps, use the word 'homicide'.

"Now the question we have been called upon
to answer is simply this: Who was responsible
for the homicide?"

The priest and the countess remained silent,
looking at Lord Darcy as though he were some
sort of divinely inspired oracle.

"As you know . . . pardon me, my lady, if I
am blunt . . . the late Count was somewhat of a
playboy. No. I will make that stronger. He was
a satyr, a lecher; he was a man with a sexual obsession.

"For such a man, if he indulges in his passions

—which the late Count most certainly did—
there is usually but one end. Unless he is a man
who has a winsome personality—which he did
not—there will be someone who will hate him
enough to kill him. Such a man inevitably leaves
behind him a trail of wronged women and
wronged men.

"One such person may kill him.

"One such person did.

"But we must find the person who did and determine the extent of his or her guilt. That is my
purpose.

"Now, as to the facts. We know that Edouard
had a secret stairway which led directly to his
suite. Actually, the secret was poorly kept. There
were many women—common and noble—who
knew of the existence of that stairway and knew
how to enter it. If Edouard left the lower door
unlocked, anyone could come up that stairway.
He had another lock in the door of his bedroom,
so only someone who was invited could come in,
even if she . . . or he . . . could get into the stairway. He was protected.

"Now here is what actually happened last
night. I have evidence, by the way, and I have
the confessions of both Laird and Lady Duncan.
I will explain how I got those confessions in a
moment.

"*Primus:* Lady Duncan had an assignation
with Count D'Evreux last night. She went up the
stairway to his room. She was carrying with her
a small pistol. She had had an affair with
Edouard, and she had been rebuffed. She was
furious. But she went to his room.

"He was drunk when she arrived—in one of the nasty moods with which both of you are familiar. She pleaded with him to accept her again as his mistress. He refused. According to Lady Duncan, he said: 'I don't want you! You're not fit to be in the same room with *her*!'

"The emphasis is Lady Duncan's, not my own.

"Furious, she drew a gun—the little pistol which killed him."

The Countess gasped. "But Mary *couldn't* have—"

"*Please!*" Lord Darcy slammed the palm of his hand on the arm of his chair with an explosive sound. "My lady, you *will* listen to what I have to say!"

He was taking a devil of a chance, he knew. The Countess was his hostess and had every right to exercise her prerogatives. But Lord Darcy was counting on the fact that she had been under Count D'Evreux's influence so long that it would take her a little time to realize that she no longer had to knuckle under to the will of a man who shouted at her. He was right. She became silent.

Father Bright turned to her quickly and said: "Please, my daughter. Wait."

"Your pardon, my lady," Lord Darcy continued smoothly. "I was about to explain to you why I know Lady Duncan could not have killed your brother. There is the matter of the dress. We are certain that the gown that was found in Edouard's closet was worn by the killer. *And that gown could not possibly have fit Lady Dun-*

can! She's much too . . . er . . . hefty.

"She had told me her story, and, for reasons I will give you later, I believe it. When she pointed the gun at your brother, she really had no intention of killing him. She had no intention of pulling the trigger. Your brother knew this. He lashed out and slapped the side of her head. She dropped the pistol and fell, sobbing, to the floor. He took her roughly by the arm and 'escorted' her down the stairway. He threw her out.

"Lady Duncan, hysterical, ran to her husband.

"And then, when he had succeeded in calming her down a bit, she realized the position she was in. She knew that Laird Duncan was a violent, a warped man—very similar to Edouard, Count D'Evreux. She dared not tell him the truth, but she had to tell him something. So she lied.

"She told him that Edouard had asked her up in order to tell her something of importance; that that 'something of importance' concerned Laird Duncan's safety; that the Count told her that he knew of Laird Duncan's dabbling in black magic; that he threatened to inform Church authorities on Laird Duncan unless she submitted to his desires; that she had struggled with him and ran away."

Lord Darcy spread his hands. "This was, of course, a tissue of lies. But Laird Duncan believed everything. So great was his ego that he could not believe in her infidelity, although he has been paralyzed for five years."

"How can you be certain that Lady Duncan told the truth?" Father Bright asked warily.

"Aside from the matter of the gown—which Count D'Evreux kept only for women of the common class, *not* the aristocracy—we have the testimony of the actions of Laird Duncan himself. We come then to—

"*Secundus:* Laird Duncan could not have committed the murder physically. *How could a man who was confined to a wheelchair go up that flight of stairs?* I submit to you that it would have been physically impossible.

"The possibility that he has been pretending all these years, and that he is actually capable of walking, was disproved three hours ago, when he actually injured himself by trying to throttle me. His legs are incapable of carrying him even one step—much less carrying him to the top of that stairway."

Lord Darcy folded his hands complacently.

"There remains," said Father Bright, "the possibility that Laird Duncan killed Count D'Evreux by psychical, by magical means."

Lord Darcy nodded. "That is indeed possible, Reverend Sir, as we both know. But not in this instance. Master Sean assures me, and I am certain that you will concur, that a man killed by sorcery, by black magic, dies of internal malfunction, not of a bullet through the heart.

"In effect, the Black Sorcerer induces his enemy to kill himself by psychosomatic means. He dies by what is technically known as psychic induction. Master Sean informs me that the commonest—and crudest—method of doing this is by the so-called 'simulacrum induction' method. That is, by the making of an image—usually, but not necessarily, of wax—and, using the Law of Similarity, inducing death. The Law of Contagion is also used, since the fingernails, hair, spittle, and so on, of the victim are usually incorporated into the image. Am I correct, Father?"

The priest nodded. "Yes. And, contrary to the heresies of certain materialists, it is not at all necessary that the victim be informed of the operation—although, admittedly, it can, in certain circumstances, aid the process."

"Exactly," said Lord Darcy. "But it is well known that material objects can be moved by a competent sorcerer—'black' or 'white'. Would you explain to my lady the Countess why her brother could not have been killed in that manner?"

Father Bright touched his lips with the tip of his tongue and then turned to the girl sitting next to him. "There is a lack of relevancy. In this case, the bullet must have been relevant either to the heart or to the gun. To have traveled with a velocity great enough to penetrate, the relevancy to the heart must have been much greater than the relevancy to the gun. Yet the test, witnessed by myself, that was performed by Master Sean indicates that this was not so. The bullet returned to the gun, not to your brother's heart. The evidence, my dear, is conclusive that the bullet was propelled by purely physical means, and was propelled from the gun."

"Then what was it Laird Duncan did?" the Countess asked.

"*Tertius:*" said Lord Darcy. "Believing what his wife had told him. Laird Duncan flew into a rage. He determined to kill your brother. He used an induction spell. But the spell backfired and almost killed him.

"There are analogies on a material plane. If one adds mineral spirits and air to a fire, the fire will be increased. But if one adds ash, the fire will be put out.

"In a similar manner, if one attacks a living being psychically it will die—but if one attacks a dead thing in such a manner, the psychic energy will be absorbed, to the detriment of the person who has used it.

"In theory, we could charge Laird Duncan with attempted murder, for there is no doubt that he did attempt to kill your brother, my lady. *But your brother was already dead at the time!*

"The resultant dissipation of psychic energy rendered Laird Duncan unconscious for several hours, during which Lady Duncan waited in suspenseful fear.

"Finally, when Laird Duncan regained consciousness, he realized what had happened. He knew that your brother was already dead when he attempted the spell. He thought, therefore, that Lady Duncan had killed the Count.

"On the other hand, Lady Duncan was perfectly well aware that she had left Edouard alive and well. So she thought the black magic of her husband had killed her erstwhile lover."

"Each was trying to protect the other," Father Bright said. "Neither is completely evil, then. There may be something we can do for Laird Duncan."

"I wouldn't know about that, Father," Lord Darcy said. "The Healing Art is the Church's business, not mine." He realized with some amusement that he was paraphrasing Dr. Pateley. "What Laird Duncan had not known," he went on quickly, "was that his wife had taken a gun up to the Count's bedroom. That put a rather different light on her visit, you see. That's why he flew into such a towering rage at me—not because I was accusing him or his wife of murder, but because I had cast doubt on his wife's behavior."

He turned his head to look at the table where the Irish sorcerer was working. "Ready, Master Sean?"

"Aye, my lord. All I have to do is set up the screen and light the lantern in the projector."

"Go ahead, then." He looked back at Father Bright and the Countess. "Master Sean has a rather interesting lantern slide I want you to look at."

"The most successful development I've ever made, if I may say so, my lord," the sorcerer said.

"Proceed."

Master Sean opened the shutter on the projector, and a picture sprang into being on the screen.

There were gasps from Father Bright and the Countess.

It was a woman. She was wearing the gown that had hung in the Count's closet. A button had been torn off, and the gown gaped open. Her right hand was almost completely obscured by a dense cloud of smoke. Obviously she had just fired a pistol directly at the onlooker.

But that was not what had caused the gasps.

The girl was beautiful. Gloriously, ravishingly beautiful. It was not a delicate beauty. There was nothing flowerlike or peaceful in it. It was a beauty that could have but one effect on a normal human male. She was the most physically desirable woman one could imagine.

Retro me, Sathanas, Father Bright thought wryly. *She's almost obscenely beautiful.*

Only the Countess was unaffected by the desirability of the image. She saw only the startling beauty.

"Has neither of you seen that woman before? I thought not," said Lord Darcy. "Nor had Laird or Lady Duncan. Nor Sir Pierre.

"Who is she? We don't know. But we can make a a few deductions. She must have come to the Count's room by appointment. This is quite obviously the woman Edouard mentioned to Lady Duncan—the woman, the 'she' that the Scots noblewoman could not compare with. It is almost certain she is a commoner; otherwise she would not be wearing a robe from the Count's collection. She must have changed right there in the bedroom. Then she and the Count quarreled —about what, we do not know. The Count had previously taken Lady Duncan's pistol away from her and had evidently carelessly let it lay on that table you see behind the girl. She grabbed it and shot him. Then she changed clothes again, hung up the robe, and ran away. No one saw her come or go. The Count had designed his stairway for just that purpose.

"Oh, we'll find her, never fear—now that we know what she looks like.

"At any rate," Lord Darcy concluded, "the mystery is now solved to my complete satisfaction, and I shall so report to His Highness."

Richard, Duke of Normandy, poured two liberal portions of excellent brandy into a pair of crystal goblets. There was a smile of satisfaction on his youthful face as he handed one of the goblets to Lord Darcy. "Very well done, my lord," he said, "Very well done."

"I am gratified to hear Your Highness say so," said Lord Darcy, accepting the brandy.

"But how were you so certain that it was *not* someone from outside the castle? Anyone could have come in through the main gate. That's always open."

"True, Your Highness. But the door at the foot of the stairway was *locked*. Count D'Evreux locked it after he threw Lady Duncan out. There is no way of locking or unlocking it from the outside; the door had not been forced. No one could have come in that way, nor left that way, after Lady Duncan was so forcibly ejected. The only other way into the Count's suite was by the other door, and that door was unlocked."

"I see," said Duke Richard. "I wonder why she went up there in the first place?"

"Probably because he asked her to. Any other woman would have known what she was getting into if she accepted an invitation to Count D'Evreux's suite."

The Duke's handsome face darkened. "No.

One would hardly expect that sort of thing from one's own brother. She was perfectly justified in shooting him."

"Perfectly, Your Highness. And had she been anyone but the heiress, she would undoubtedly have confessed immediately. Indeed, it was all I could do to keep her from confessing to me when she thought I was going to charge the Duncans with the killing. But she knew that it was necessary to preserve the reputations of her brother and herself. Not as private persons, but as Count and Countess, as officers of the Government of His Imperial Majesty the King. For a man to be known as a rake is one thing. Most people don't care about that sort of thing in a public official so long as he does his duty and does it well—which, as Your Highness knows, the Count did.

"But to be shot to death while attempting to assault his own sister—that is quite another thing. She was perfectly justified in attempting to cover it up. And she will remain silent unless someone else is accused of the crime."

"Which, of course, will not happen," said Duke Richard. He sipped at the brandy, then said: "She will make a good Countess. She has judgment and she can keep cool under duress. After she had shot her own brother, she might have panicked, but she didn't. How many women would have thought of simply taking off the damaged gown and putting on its duplicate from the closet?"

"Very few," Lord Darcy agreed. "That's why I never mentioned that I knew the Count's wardrobe contained dresses identical to her own. By the way, Your Highness, if any good Healer, like Father Bright, had known of those duplicate dresses, he would have realized that the Count had a sexual obsession about his sister. He would have known that all the other women the Count went after were sister substitutes."

"Yes; of course. And none of them could measure up." He put his goblet on the table. "I shall inform the King my brother that I recommended the new Countess wholeheartedly. No word of this must be put down in writing, of course. You know and I know and the King must know. No one else must know."

"One other knows," said Lord Darcy.

"Who?" The Duke looked startled.

"Father Bright."

Duke Richard looked relieved. "Naturally. He won't tell her that *we* know, will he?"

"I think Father Bright's discretion can be relied upon."

In the dimness of the confessional, Alice, Countess D'Evreux knelt and listened to the voice of Father Bright.

"I shall not give you any penance, my child, for you have committed no sin—that is, in so far as the death of your brother is concerned. For the rest of your sins, you must read and memorize the third chapter of 'The Soul and The World,' by St. James Huntington."

He started to pronounce the absolution, but the Countess said:

"I don't understand one thing. That picture.

That wasn't me. I never saw such a gorgeously beautiful girl in my life. And I'm so plain. I don't understand."

"Had you looked more closely, my child, you would have seen that the face did look like yours —only it was idealized. When a subjective reality is made objective, distortions invariably show up; that is why such things cannot be accepted as evidence of objective reality in court." He paused. "To put it another way, my child: Beauty is in the eye of the beholder."

A CASE OF IDENTITY

The pair of Men-at-Arms strolled along the Rue King John II, near the waterfront of Cherbourg, and a hundred yards south of the sea. In this district, the Keepers of the King's Peace always traveled in pairs, each keeping one hand near the truncheon at his belt and the other near the hilt of his smallsword. The average commoner was not a swordsman, but sailors are not common commoners. A man armed only with a truncheon would be at a disadvantage with a man armed with a cutlass.

The frigid wind from the North Sea whipped the edges of the Men-at-Arms' cloaks, and the light from the mantled gas lamps glowed yellowly, casting multiple shadows that shifted queerly as the Armsmen walked.

There were not many people on the streets. Most of them were in the bistros, where there were coal fires to warm the outer man and fiery bottled goods to warm the inner. There had been crowds in the street on the Vigil of the Feast of the Circumcision, nine days before, but now the Twelfth Day of Christmas had passed and the Year of Our Lord 1964 was in its second week. Money had run short and few could still afford to drink.

The taller of the two officers stopped and pointed ahead. "Ey, Robert. Old Jean hasn't got his light on."

"Hm-m-m. Third time since Christmas. Hate to give the old man a summons."

"Aye. Let's just go in and scare the Hell out of him."

"Aye," said the shorter man. "But we'll promise him a summons next time and keep our promise, Jack."

The sign above the door was a weatherbeaten dolphin-shaped piece of wood, painted blue. The Blue Dolphin.

Armsman Robert pushed open the door and went in, his eyes alert for trouble. There was none. Four men were sitting around one end of the long table at the left, and Old Jean was talking to a fifth man at the bar. They all looked up as the Armsmen came in. Then the men at the table went on with their conversation. The fifth customer's eyes went to his drink. The barkeep smiled ingratiatingly and came toward the two Armsmen.

"Evening, Armsmen," he said with a snaggle-toothed smile. "A little something to warm the blood?" But he knew it was no social call.

Robert already had out his summons book, pencil poised. "Jean, we have warned you twice before," he said frigidly. "The law plainly states that every place of business must maintain a standard gas lamp and keep it lit from sunset to sunrise. You know this."

"Perhaps the wind—" the barkeep said defensively.

"The wind? I will go up with you and we will

see if perhaps the wind has turned the gas cock, ey?"

Old Jean swallowed. "Perhaps I did forget. My memory—."

"Perhaps explaining your memory to my lord the Marquis next court day will help you to improve it, ey?"

"No, no! Please, Armsman! The fine would ruin me!"

Armsman Robert made motions with his pencil as though he were about to write. "I will say it is a first offense and the fine will be only half as much."

Old Jean closed his eyes helplessly. "Please, Armsman. It will not happen again. It is just that I have been so used to Paul—he did everything, all the hard work. I have no one to help me now."

"Paul Sarto has been gone for two weeks now," Robert said. "This is the third time you have given me that same excuse."

"Armsman," said the old man earnestly, "I will not forget again. I promise you."

Robert closed his summons book. "Very well. I have your word? Then you have my word that there will be no excuses next time. I will hand you the summons instantly. Understood?"

"Understood, Armsman! Yes, of course. Many thanks! I will not forget again!"

"See that you don't. Go and light it."

Old Jean scurried up the stairway and was back within minutes. "It's lit now, Armsman."

"Excellent. I expect it to be lit from now on. At sunset. Good night, Jean."

"Perhaps a little—?"

"No, Jean. Another time. Come, Jack."

The Armsmen left without taking the offered drink. It would be ungentlemanly to take it after threatening the man with the law. The Armsman's Manual said that, because of the sword he is privileged to wear, an Armsman must be a gentleman at all times.

"Wonder why Paul left?" Jack asked when they were on the street again. "He was well paid, and he was too simple to work elsewhere."

Robert shrugged. "You know how it is. Wharf rats come and go. No need to worry about him. A man with a strong back and a weak mind can always find a bistro that will take care of him. He'll get along."

Nothing further was said for the moment. The two Armsmen walked on to the corner, where the Quai Sainte Marie turned off to the south.

Robert glanced southwards and said: "Here's a happy one."

"Too happy, if you ask me," said Jack.

Down the Quai Sainte Marie came a man. He was hugging the side of the building, stumbling towards them, propping himself up by putting the flat of his palms on the brick wall one after the other as he moved his feet. He wore no hat, and, as the wind caught his cloak, the two Men-at-Arms saw something they had not expected. He was naked.

"Blind drunk and freezing," Jack said. "Better take him in."

They never got the chance. As they came toward him, the stumbling man stumbled for the last time. He dropped to his knees, looked up at

them with blind eyes that stared past them into
the darkness of the sky, then toppled to one side,
his eyes still open, unblinking.

Robert knelt down. "Sound your whistle! I
think he's dead!"

Jack took out his whistle and keened a note
into the frigid air.

"Speak of the Devil," Robert said softly. "It's
Paul! He doesn't smell drunk. I think . . . *God!*"
He had tried to lift the head of the fallen man
and found his palm covered with blood. "It's
soft," he said wonderingly. "The whole side of
his skull is crushed."

In the distance, they heard the clatter of hoofs
as a mounted Sergeant-at-Arms came at a gallop
toward the sound of the whistle.

Lord Darcy, tall, lean-faced, and handsome,
strode down the hall to the door bearing the
arms of Normandy and opened it.

"Your Highness sent for me?" He spoke
Anglo-French with a definite English accent.

There were three men in the room. The
youngest, tall, blond Richard, Duke of Nor-
mandy and brother to His Imperial Majesty,
John IV, turned as the door opened. "Ah. Lord
Darcy. Come in." He gestured toward the portly
man wearing episcopal purple. "My Lord
Bishop, may I present my Chief Investigator,
Lord Darcy. Lord Darcy, this is his lordship, the
Bishop of Guernsey and Sark."

"A pleasure, Lord Darcy," said the Bishop,
extending his right hand.

Lord Darcy took the hand, bowed, kissed the

ring. "My Lord Bishop." Then he turned and
bowed to the third man, the lean, graying Marquis of Rouen. "My Lord Marquis."

Then Lord Darcy faced the Royal Duke again
and waited expectantly.

The Duke of Normandy frowned slightly.
"There appears to be some trouble with my lord
the Marquis of Cherbourg. As you know, My
Lord Bishop is the elder brother of the Marquis."

Lord Darcy knew the family history. The previous Marquis of Cherbourg had had three sons.
At his death, the eldest had inherited the title
and government. The second had taken Holy
Orders, and the third had taken a commission in
the Royal Navy. When the eldest had died
without heirs, the Bishop could not succeed to
the title, so the Marquisate went to the youngest
son, Hugh, the present Marquis.

"Perhaps you had better explain, My Lord
Bishop," said the Duke. "I would rather Lord
Darcy had the information firsthand."

"Certainly, Your Highness," said the Bishop.
He looked worried, and his right hand kept fid-
dling with the pectoral cross at his breast.

The Duke gestured toward the chairs. "Please,
my lords—sit down."

The four men settled themselves, and the
Bishop began his story.

"My brother the Marquis," he said after a
deep breath, "is missing."

Lord Darcy raised an eyebrow. Normally, if
one of His Majesty's Governors turned up miss-

ing, there would be a hue and cry from one end of the Empire to the other—from Duncansby Head in Scotland to the southernmost tip of Gascony—from the German border on the east to New England and New France, across the Atlantic. If my lord the Bishop of Guernsey and Sark wanted it kept quiet, then there was—there had *better* be!—a good reason.

"Have you met my brother, Lord Darcy?" the Bishop asked.

"Only briefly, my lord. Once, about a year ago. I hardly know him."

"I see."

The Bishop fiddled a bit more with his pectoral cross, then plunged into his story. Three days before, on the tenth of January, the Bishop's sister-in-law, Elaine, Marquise de Cherbourg, had sent a servant by boat to St. Peter Port, Guernsey, the site of the Cathedral Church of the Diocese of Guernsey and Sark. The sealed message which he was handed informed My Lord Bishop that his brother the Marquis had been missing since the evening of the eighth. Contrary to his custom, My Lord Marquis had not notified My Lady Marquise of any intention to leave the castle. Indeed, he implied that he had intended to retire when he had finished with certain Government papers. No one had seen him since he entered his study. My lady of Cherbourg had not missed him until next morning, when she found that his bed had not been slept in.

"This was on the morning of Thursday the ninth, my lord?" Lord Darcy asked.

"That is correct, my lord," said the Bishop.

"May I ask why we were not notified until now?" Lord Darcy asked gently.

My Lord Bishop fidgeted. "Well, my lord . . . you see . . . well, My Lady Elaine believes that . . . er . . . that his lordship, my brother, is not . . . er . . . *may* not be . . . er . . . quite right in his mind."

There! thought Lord Darcy. *He got it out! My Lord of Cherbourg is off his chump! Or, at least, his lady thinks so.*

"What behavior did he display?" Lord Darcy asked quietly.

The Bishop spoke rapidly and concisely. My Lord of Cherbourg had had his first attack on the eve of St. Stephen's Day, the 26th of December, 1963. His face had suddenly taken on a look of utter idiocy; it had gone slack, and the intelligence seemed to fade from his eyes. He had babbled meaninglessly and seemed not to know where he was—and, indeed, to be somewhat terrified of his surroundings.

"Was he violent in any way?" asked Lord Darcy.

"No. Quite the contrary. He was quite docile and easily led to bed. Lady Elaine called in a Healer immediately, suspecting that my brother may have had an apoplectic stroke. As you know, the Marquisate supports a chapter of the Benedictines within the walls of Castle Cherbourg, and Father Patrique saw my brother within minutes.

"But by that time the attack had passed. Father Patrique could detect nothing wrong, and my brother simply said it was a slight dizzy spell, nothing more. However, since then there have been three more attacks—on the evenings of the second, the fifth, and the seventh of this month. And now he is gone."

"You feel, then, My Lord Bishop, that his lordship has had another of these attacks and may be wandering around somewhere . . . ah . . . *non compos mentis,* as it were?"

"That's exactly what I'm afraid of," the Bishop said firmly.

Lord Darcy looked thoughtful for a moment, then glanced silently at His Royal Highness, the Duke.

"I want you to make a thorough investigation, Lord Darcy," said the Duke. "Be as discreet as possible. We want no scandal. If there is anything wrong with my lord of Cherbourg's mind, we will have the best care taken, of course. But we must find him first." He glanced at the clock on the wall. "There is a train for Cherbourg in forty-one minutes. You will accompany My Lord Bishop."

Lord Darcy rose smoothly from his chair. "I'll just have time to pack, Your Highness." He bowed to the Bishop. "Your servant, my lord." He turned and walked out the door, closing it behind him.

But instead of heading immediately for his own apartments, he waited quietly outside the door, just to one side. He had caught Duke Richard's look.

Within, he heard voices.

"My Lord Marquis," said the Duke, "would you see that My Lord Bishop gets some refreshment? If your lordship will excuse me, I have some urgent work to attend to. A report on this matter must be dispatched immediately to the King my brother."

"Of course, Your Highness; of course."

"I will have a carriage waiting for you and Lord Darcy. I will see you again before you leave, my lord. And now, excuse me."

He came out of the room, saw Lord Darcy waiting, and motioned toward another room nearby. Lord Darcy followed him in. The Duke closed the door firmly and then said, in a low voice:

"This may be worse than it appears at first glance, Darcy. De Cherbourg was working with one of His Majesty's personal agents trying to trace down the ring of Polish *agents provocateurs* operating in Cherbourg. If he's actually had a mental breakdown and they've got hold of him, there will be the Devil to pay."

Lord Darcy knew the seriousness of the affair. The Kings of Poland had been ambitious for the past half century. Having annexed all of the Russian territory they could—as far as Minsk to the north and Kiev to the south—the Poles now sought to work their way westwards, toward the borders of the Empire. For several centuries, the Germanic states had acted as buffers between the powerful Kingdom of Poland and the even more powerful Empire. In theory, the Germanic states, as part of the old Holy Roman Empire, owed fealty to the Emperor—but no Anglo-

French King had tried to enforce that fealty for centuries. The Germanic states were, in fact, holding their independence because of the tug-of-war between Poland and the Empire. If the troops of King Casimir IX tried to march into Bavaria, for instance, Bavaria would scream for Imperial help and would get it. On the other hand, if King John IV tried to tax so much as a single sovereign out of Bavaria, and sent troops in to collect it, Bavaria would scream just as loudly for Polish aid. As long as the balance of power remained, the Germanies were safe.

Actually, King John had no desire to bring the Germanies into the Empire forcibly. That kind of aggression hadn't been Imperial policy for a good long time. With hardly any trouble at all, an Imperial army could take over Lombardy or northern Spain. But with the whole New World as Imperial domain, there was no need to add more of Europe. Aggression against her peaceful neighbors was unthinkable in this day and age.

As long as Poland had been moving eastward, Imperial policy had been to allow her to go her way while the Empire expanded into the New World. But that eastward expansion had ground to a halt. King Casimir was now having trouble with those Russians he had already conquered. To hold his quasi-empire together, he had to keep the threat of external enemies always before the eyes of his subjects, but he dared not push any farther into Russia. The Russian states had formed a loose coalition during the last generation, and the King of Poland, Sigismund III, had backed down. If the Russians ever really united, they would be a formidable enemy.

That left the Germanic states to the west and Roumeleia to the south. Casimir had no desire to tangle with Roumeleia, but he had plans for the Germanic states.

The wealth of the Empire, the basis of its smoothly expanding economy, was the New World. The importation of cotton, tobacco, and sugar—to say nothing of the gold that had been found in the southern continent—was the backbone of Imperial economy. The King's subjects were well-fed, well-clothed, well-housed, and happy. But if the shipping were to be blocked for any considerable length of time, there would be trouble.

The Polish Navy didn't stand a chance against the Imperial Navy. No Polish fleet could get through the North Sea without running into trouble with either the Imperial Navy or that of the Empire's Scandinavian allies. The North Sea was Imperial-Scandinavian property, jointly patrolled, and no armed ship was allowed to pass. Polish merchantmen were allowed to come and go freely—after they had been boarded to make sure that they carried no guns. Bottled up in the Baltic, the Polish Navy was helpless, and it wasn't big enough or good enough to fight its way out. They'd tried it once, back in '39, and had been blasted out of the water. King Casimir wouldn't try that again.

He had managed to buy a few Spanish and Sicilian ships and have them outfitted as privateers, but they were merely annoying, not menacing. If caught, they were treated as pirates

—either sunk or captured and their crews hanged—and the Imperial Government didn't even bother to protest to the King of Poland.

But King Casimir evidently had something else up his royal sleeve. Something was happening that had both the Lords of the Admiralty and the Maritime Lords on edge. Ships leaving Imperial ports—Le Havre, Cherbourg, Liverpool, London, and so on—occasionally disappeared. They were simply never heard from again. They never got to New England at all. And the number was more than could be accounted for either by weather or piracy.

That was bad enough, but to make things worse, rumors had been spreading around the waterfronts of the Empire. Primarily the rumors exaggerated the dangers of sailing the Atlantic. The word was beginning to spread that the mid-Atlantic was a dangerous area—far more dangerous than the waters around Europe. A sailor worth his salt cared very little for the threats of weather; give a British or a French sailor a seaworthy ship and a skipper he trusted, and he'd head into the teeth of any storm. But the threat of evil spirits and black magic was something else again.

Do what they would, scientific researchers simply could not educate the common man to understand the intricacies and limitations of modern scientific sorcery. The superstitions of a hundred thousand years still clung to the minds of ninety-nine per cent of the human race, even in a modern, advanced civilization like the Empire. How does one explain that only a small percentage of the population is capable of performing magic? How to explain that all the incantations in the official grimoires won't help a person who doesn't have the Talent? How to explain that, even with the Talent, years of training are normally required before it can be used efficiently, predictably, and with power? People had been told again and again, but deep in their hearts they believed otherwise.

Not one person in ten who was suspected of having the Evil Eye really had it, but sorcerers and priests were continually being asked for counteragents. And only God knew how many people wore utterly useless medallions, charms, and anti-hex shields prepared by quacks who hadn't the Talent to make the spells effective. There is an odd quirk in the human mind that makes a fearful man prefer to go quietly to a wicked-looking, gnarled "witch" for a countercharm than to a respectable licensed sorcerer or an accredited priest of the Church. Deep inside, the majority of people had the sneaking suspicion that evil was more powerful than good and that evil could be counteracted only by more evil. Almost none of them would believe what scientific magical research had shown—that the practice of black magic was, in the long run, more destructive to the mind of the practitioner than to his victims.

So it wasn't difficult to spread the rumor that there was Something Evil in the Atlantic—and, as a result, more and more sailors were becoming leery of shipping aboard a vessel that was bound for the New World.

And the Imperial Government was absolutely certain that the story was being deliberately spread by agents of King Casimir IX.

Two things had to be done: The disappearances must cease, and the rumors must be stopped. And my lord the Marquis of Cherbourg had been working towards those ends when he had disappeared. The question of how deeply Polish agents were involved in that disappearance was an important one.

"You will contact His Majesty's agent as soon as possible," said Duke Richard. "Since there may be black magic involved, take Master Sean along—incognito. If a sorcerer suddenly shows up, they—whoever they may be—might take cover. They might even do something drastic to de Cherbourg."

"I will exercise the utmost care, Your Highness," said Lord Darcy.

The train pulled into Cherbourg Station with a hiss and a blast of steam that made a great cloud of fog in the chill air. Then the wind picked up the cloud and blew it to wisps before anyone had stepped from the carriages. The passengers hugged their coats and cloaks closely about them as they came out. There was a light dusting of snow on the ground and on the platform, but the air was clear and the low winter sun shone brightly, if coldly, in the sky.

The Bishop had made a call on the teleson to Cherbourg Castle before leaving Rouen, and there was a carriage waiting for the three men— one of the newer models with pneumatic tires and spring suspension, bearing the Cherbourg arms on the doors, and drawn by two pairs of fine greys. The footmen opened the near door and the Bishop climbed in, followed by Lord Darcy and a short, chubby man who wore the clothing of a gentleman's gentleman. Lord Darcy's luggage was put on the rack atop the carriage, but a small bag carried by the "gentleman's gentleman" remained firmly in the grasp of his broad fist.

Master Sean O Lochlainn, Sorcerer, had no intention of letting go of his professional equipment. He had grumbled enough about not being permitted to carry his symbol-decorated carpet bag, and had spent nearly twenty minutes casting protective spells around the black leather suitcase that Lord Darcy had insisted he carry.

The footman closed the door of the carriage and swung himself aboard. The four greys started off at a brisk trot through the streets of Cherbourg toward the Castle, which lay across the city, near the sea.

Partly to keep My Lord Bishop's mind off his brother's troubles and partly to keep from being overheard while they were on the train, Lord Darcy and the Bishop had tacitly agreed to keep their conversation on subjects other than the investigation at hand. Master Sean had merely sat quietly by, trying to look like a valet—at which he succeeded very well.

Once inside the carriage, however, the conversation seemed to die away. My lord the Bishop settled himself into the cushions and gazed silently out of the window. Master Sean leaned back, folded his hands over his paunch and closed his eyes. Lord Darcy, like my lord the Bishop, looked out the window. He had only been in Cherbourg twice before, and was not as familiar with the city as he would like to be. It would be worth his time to study the route the carriage was taking.

It was not until they came to the waterfront itself, turned, and moved down the Rue de Mer toward the towers of Castle Cherbourg in the distance, that Lord Darcy saw anything that particularly interested him.

There were, he thought, entirely too many ships tied up at the docks, and there seemed to be a great deal of goods waiting on the wharves to be loaded. On the other hand, there did not seem to be as many men working as the apparent volume of shipping would warrant.

Crews scared off by the "Atlantic Curse," Lord Darcy thought. He looked at the men loafing around in clumps, talking softly but, he thought, rather angrily. *Obviously sailors; out of work by their own choice and resenting their own fears. Probably trying to get jobs as longshoremen and being shut out by the Longshoremen's Guild.*

Normally, he knew, sailors were considered as an auxiliary of the Longshoremen's Guild, just as longshoremen were considered as an auxiliary of the Seamen's Guild. If a sailor decided to spend a little time on land, he could usually get work as a longshoreman; if a longshoreman decided to go to sea, he could usually find a berth somewhere. But with ships unable to find crews, there were fewer longshoremen finding work loading vessels. With regular members of the

Longshoremen's Guild unable to find work, it was hardly odd that the Guild would be unable to find work for the frightened seamen who had caused that very shortage.

The unemployment, in turn, threw an added burden on the Privy Purse of the Marquis of Cherbourg, since, by ancient law, it was obligatory upon the lord to take care of his men and their families in times of trouble. Thus far, the drain was not too great, since it was spread out evenly over the Empire; my lord of Cherbourg could apply to the Duke of Normandy for aid under the same law, and His Royal Highness could, in turn, apply to His Imperial Majesty, John IV, King and Emperor of England, France, Scotland, Ireland, New England and New France, Defender of the Faith, et cetera.

And the funds of the Imperial Privy Purse came from all over the Empire.

Still, if the thing became widespread, the economy of the Empire stood in danger of complete collapse.

There had not been a complete cessation of activity on the waterfront, Lord Darcy was relieved to notice. Aside from those ships that were making the Mediterranean and African runs, there were still ships that had apparently found crews for the Atlantic run to the northern continent of New England and the southern continent of New France.

One great ship, the *Pride of Calais,* showed quite a bit of activity; bales of goods were being loaded over the side amid much shouting of orders. Close by, Lord Darcy could see a sling full of wine casks being lifted aboard, each cask bearing the words: *Ordwin Vayne, Vintner,* and a sorcerer's symbol burnt into the wood, showing that the wine was protected against souring for the duration of the trip. Most of the wine, Lord Darcy knew, was for the crew; by law each sailor was allowed the equivalent of a bottle a day, and, besides, the excellence of the New World wines was such that it did not pay to import the beverage from Europe.

Further on, Lord Darcy saw other ships that he knew were making the Atlantic run loading goods aboard. Evidently the "Atlantic Curse" had not yet frightened the guts out of all of the Empire's seamen.

We'll come through, Lord Darcy thought. *In spite of everything the King of Poland can do, we'll come through. We always have.*

He did not think: *We always will.* Empires and societies, he knew, died and were replaced by others. The Roman Empire had died to be replaced by hordes of barbarians who had gradually evolved the feudal society, which had, in turn, evolved the modern system. It was, certainly, possible that the eight-hundred-year old Empire that had been established by Henry II in the Twelfth Century might some day collapse as the Roman Empire had—but it had already existed nearly twice as long, and there were no threatening hordes of barbarians to overrun it nor were there any signs of internal dissent strong enough to disrupt it. The Empire was still stable and still evolving.

Most of that stability and evolution was due

to the House of Plantagenet, the House which had been founded by Henry II after the death of King Stephen. Old Henry had brought the greater part of France under the sway of the King of England. His son, Richard the Lion-Hearted, had neglected England during the first ten years of his reign, but, after his narrow escape from death from the bolt of a crossbowman at the Siege of Chaluz, he had settled down to controlling the Empire with a firm hand and a wise brain. He had no children, but his nephew, Arthur, the son of King Richard's dead brother, Geoffrey, had become like a son to him. Arthur had fought with the King against the treacheries of Prince John, Richard's younger brother and the only other claimant to the throne. Prince John's death in 1216 left Arthur as the only heir, and, upon old Richard's death in 1219, Arthur, at thirty-two, had succeeded to the Throne of England. In popular legend, King Arthur was often confused with the earlier King Arthur of Camelot—and for good reason. The monarch who was known even today as Good King Arthur had resolved to rule his realm in the same chivalric manner—partly inspired by the legends of the ancient Brittanic leader, and partly because of his own inherent abilities.

Since then, the Plantagenet line had gone through nearly eight centuries of trial and tribulation; of blood, sweat, toil, and tears; of resisting the enemies of the Empire by sword, fire, and consummate diplomacy to hold the realm together and to expand it.

The Empire had endured. And the Empire would continue to endure only so long as every subject realized that it could *not* endure if the entire burden were left to the King alone. *The Empire expects every man to do his duty.*

And Lord Darcy's duty, at this moment, was greater than the simple duty of finding out what had happened to my lord the Marquis of Cherbourg. The problem ran much deeper than that.

His thoughts were interrupted by the voice of the Bishop.

"There's the tower of the Great Keep ahead, Lord Darcy. We'll be there soon."

It was actually several more minutes before the carriage-and-four drew up before the main entrance of Castle Cherbourg. The door was opened by a footman, and three men climbed out, Master Sean still clutching his suitcase.

My Lady Elaine, Marquise de Cherbourg, stood in her salon above the Great Hall, staring out the window at the Channel. She could see the icy waves splashing and dancing and rolling with almost hypnotic effect, but she saw them without thinking about them.

Where are you, Hugh? she thought. *Come back to me, Hugh. I need you. I never knew how much I'd need you.* Then there seemed to be a blank as her mind rested. Nothing came through but the roll of the waves.

Then there was the noise of an opening door behind her. She turned quickly, her long velvet

skirts swirling around her like thick syrup.
"Yes?" Her voice seemed oddly far away in her
ears.

"You rang, my lady." It was Sir Gwiliam, the
seneschal.

My Lady Elaine tried to focus her thoughts.
"Oh," she said after a moment. "Oh, yes." She
waved toward the refreshment table, upon which
stood a decanter of Oporto, a decanter of Xerez,
and an empty decanter. "Brandy. The brandy
hasn't been refilled. Bring some of the Saint
Coeurlandt Michele '46."

"The Saint Coeurlandt Michele '46, my
lady?" Sir Gwiliam blinked slightly "But my
lord de Cherbourg would not—"

She turned to face him directly. "My lord of
Cherbourg would most certainly not deny his
lady his best Champagne brandy at a time like
this, *Sieur* Gwiliam!" she snapped, using the local pronunciation instead of standard Anglo-
French, thus employing a mild and un-
answerable epithet. "Must I fetch it myself?"

Sir Gwiliam's face paled a little, but his expression did not change. "No, my lady. Your
wish is my command."

"Very well. I thank you, Sir Gwiliam." She
turned back to the window. Behind her, she
heard the door open and close.

Then she turned, walked over to the refreshment table, and looked at the glass she had
emptied only a few minutes before.

Empty, she thought. *Like my life. Can I refill
it?*

She lifted the decanter of Xerez, took out the

stopple, and, with exaggerated care, refilled her glass. Brandy was better, but until Sir Gwiliam brought the brandy there was nothing to drink but the sweet wines. She wondered vaguely why she had insisted on the best and finest brandy in Hugh's cellar. There was no need for it. Any brandy would have done, even the *Aqua Sancta '60*, a foul distillate. She knew that by now her palate was so anesthetized that she could not tell the difference.

But where *was* the brandy? Somewhere. Yes. Sir Gwiliam.

Angrily, almost without thinking, she began to jerk at the bell-pull. Once. Pause. Once. Pause. Once . . .

She was still ringing when the door opened.

"Yes, my lady?"

She turned angrily—then froze.

Lord Seiger frightened her. He always had.

"I rang for Sir Gwiliam, my lord," she said, with as much dignity as she could summon.

Lord Seiger was a big man who had about him the icy coldness of the Norse home from which his ancestors had come. His hair was so blond as to be almost silver, and his eyes were a pale iceberg blue. The Marquise could not recall ever having seen him smile. His handsome face was always placid and expressionless. She realized with a small chill that she would be more afraid of Lord Seiger's smile than of his normal calm expression.

"I rang for Sir Gwiliam." my lady repeated.

"Indeed, my lady," said Lord Seiger, "but since Sir Gwiliam seemed not to answer, I felt it my duty to respond. You rang for him a few minutes ago. Now you are ringing again. May I help?"

"No . . . No . . ." What could she say?

He came into the room, closing the door behind him. Even twenty-five feet away, My Lady Elaine fancied she could feel the chill from him. She could do nothing as he approached. She couldn't find her voice. He was tall and cold and blondly handsome—and had no more sexuality than a toad. Less—for a toad must at least have attraction for another toad—and a toad was at least a living thing. My lady was not attracted to the man, and he hardly seemed living.

He came toward her like a battleship—twenty feet—fifteen . . .

She gasped and gestured toward the refreshment table. "Would you pour some wine, my lord? I'd like a glass of the . . . the Xerez."

It was as though the battleship had been turned in its course, she thought. His course toward her veered by thirty degrees as he angled toward the table.

"Xerez, my lady? Indeed. I shall be most happy."

With precise, strong hands, he emptied the last of the decanter into a goblet. "There is less than a glassful, my lady," he said, looking at her with expressionless blue eyes. "Would my lady care for the Oporto instead?"

"No . . . No, just the Xerez, my lord, just the Xerez." She swallowed. "Would you care for anything yourself?"

"I never drink, my lady." He handed her the partially filled glass.

It was all she could do to take the glass from his hand, and it struck her as odd that his fingers, when she touched them, seemed as warm as anyone else's.

"Does my lady really feel that it is necessary to drink so much?" Lord Seiger asked. "For the last four days. . ."

My lady's hand shook, but all she could say was: "My nerves, my lord. My nerves." She handed back the glass, empty.

Since she had not asked for more, Lord Seiger merely held the glass and looked at her. "I am here to protect you, my lady. It is my duty. Only your enemies have anything to fear from me."

Somehow, she knew that what he said was true, but—

"Please. A glass of Oporto, my lord."

"Yes, my lady."

He was refilling her glass when the door opened.

It was Sir Gwiliam, bearing a bottle of brandy. "My lady, my lord, the carriage has arrived."

Lord Seiger looked at him expressionlessly, then turned the same face on My Lady Elaine. "The Duke's Investigators. Shall we meet them here, my lady?"

"Yes. Yes, my lord, of course. Yes." Her eyes were on the brandy.

The meeting between Lord Darcy and My Lady Elaine was brief and meaningless. Lord Darcy had no objection to the aroma of fine brandy, but he preferred it fresh rather than secondhand. Her recital of what had happened dur-

ing the days immediately preceding the disappearance of the Marquis was not significantly
different from that of the Bishop.

The coldly handsome Lord Seiger, who had
been introduced as secretary to the Marquis,
knew nothing. He had not been present during
any of the alleged attacks.

My lady the Marquise finally excused herself,
pleading a headache. Lord Darcy noted that the
brandy bottle went with her.

"My Lord Seiger," he said, "her ladyship
seems indisposed. Whom does that leave in
charge of the castle for the moment?"

"The servants and household are in charge of
Sir Gwiliam de Bracy, the seneschal. The guard
is in the charge of Captain Sir Androu Duglasse.
I am not My Lord Marquis' Privy Secretary; I
am merely aiding him in cataloguing some
books."

"I see. Very well. I should like to speak to Sir
Gwiliam and Sir Androu."

Lord Seiger stood up, walked over to the bell-
pull and signaled. "Sir Gwiliam will be here
shortly," he said. "I shall fetch Sir Androu myself." He bowed. "If you will excuse me, my
lords."

When he had gone, Lord Darcy said: "An impressive looking man. Dangerous, too, I should
say—in the right circumstances."

"Seems a decent sort," said My Lord Bishop.
"A bit restrained ... er ... stuffy, one might
say. Not much sense of humor, but sense of humor isn't everything." He cleared his throat and
then went on. "I must apologize for my sister-in-

law's behavior. She's overwrought. You won't be needing me for these interrogations, and I really ought to see after her."

"Of course, my lord; I quite understand," Lord Darcy said smoothly.

My Lord Bishop had hardly gone when the door opened again and Sir Gwiliam came in. "Your lordship rang?"

"Will you be seated, Sir Gwiliam?" Lord Darcy gestured toward a chair. "We are here, as you know, to investigate the disappearance of My Lord of Cherbourg. This is my man, Sean, who assists me. All you say here will be treated as confidential."

"I shall be happy to co-operate, your lordship," said Sir Gwiliam, seating himself.

"I am well aware, Sir Gwiliam," Lord Darcy began, "that you have told what you know to My Lord Bishop, but, tiresome as it may be, I shall have to hear the whole thing again. If you will be so good as to begin at the beginning, Sir Gwiliam . . ."

The seneschal dutifully began his story. Lord Darcy and Master Sean listened to it for the third time and found that it differed only in viewpoint, not in essentials. But the difference in viewpoint was important. Like My Lord Bishop, Sir Gwiliam told his story as though he were not directly involved.

"Did you actually ever see one of these attacks?" Lord Darcy asked.

Sir Gwiliam blinked. "Why . . . no. No, your lordship, I did not. But they were reported to me in detail by several of the servants."

"I see. What about the night of the disappearance? When did you last see My Lord Marquis?"

"Fairly early in the evening, your lordship. With my lord's permission, I went into the city about five o'clock for an evening of cards with friends. We played until rather late—two or two-thirty in the morning. My host, Master Ordwin Vayne, a well-to-do wine merchant in the city, of course insisted that I spend the night. That is not unusual, since the castle gates are locked at ten and it is rather troublesome to have a guard unlock them. I returned to the castle, then, at about ten in the morning, at which time my lady informed me of the disappearance of My Lord Marquis."

Lord Darcy nodded. That checked with what Lady Elaine had said. Shortly after Sir Gwiliam had left, she had retired early, pleading a slight cold. She had been the last to see the Marquis of Cherbourg.

"Thank you, sir seneschal," Lord Darcy said. "I should like to speak to the servants later. There is—"

He was interrupted by the opening of the door. It was Lord Seiger, followed by a large, heavy-set, mustached man with dark hair and a scowling look.

As Sir Gwiliam rose, Lord Darcy said: "Thank you for your help, Sir Gwiliam. That will be all for now."

"Thank you, your lordship; I am most anxious to help."

As the seneschal left, Lord Seiger brought the

mustached man into the room. "My lord, this is Sir Androu Duglasse, Captain of the Marquis' Own Guard. Captain, Lord Darcy, Chief Investigator for His Highness the Duke."

The fierce-looking soldier bowed. "I am at your service, m' lord."

"Thank you. Sit down, captain."

Lord Seiger retreated through the door, leaving the captain with Lord Darcy and Master Sean.

"I hope I can be of some help, y' lordship," the captain said.

"I think you can, captain," Lord Darcy said. "No one saw my lord the Marquis leave the castle, I understand. I presume you have questioned your guards."

"I have, y' lordship. We didn't know m' lord was missing until next morning, when m' lady spoke to me. I checked with the men who were on duty that night. The only one to leave after five was Sir Gwiliam, at five oh two, according to the book."

"And the secret passage?" Lord Darcy asked. He had made it a point to study the plans of every castle in the Empire by going over the drawings in the Royal Archives.

The captain nodded. "There is one. Used during times of siege in the old days. It's kept locked and barred nowadays."

"And guarded?" Lord Darcy asked.

Captain Sir Androu chuckled. "Yes, y' lordship. Most hated post in the Guard. Tunnel ends up in a sewer, d'ye see. We send a man out there for mild infractions of the rules. Straightens him out to spend a few nights with the smell and the rats, guarding an iron door that hasn't been opened for years and couldn't be opened from the outside without a bomb—or from the inside, either, since it's rusted shut. We inspect at irregular intervals to make sure the man's on his toes."

"I see. You made a thorough search of the castle?"

"Yes. I was afraid he might have come down with another of those fainting spells he's had lately. We looked everywhere he could have been. He was nowhere to be found, y' lordship. Nowhere. He must have got out somewhere."

"Well, we shall have to—" Lord Darcy was interrupted by a rap on the door.

Master Sean, dutifully playing his part, opened it. "Yes, your lordship?"

It was Lord Seiger at the door. "Would you tell Lord Darcy that Henri Vert, Chief Master-at-Arms of the City of Cherbourg, would like to speak to him?"

For a fraction of a second, Lord Darcy was both surprised and irritated. How had the Chief Master-at-Arms known he was here? Then he saw what the answer must be.

"Tell him to come in, Sean," said Lord Darcy.

Chief Henri was a heavy-set, tough-looking man in his early fifties who had the air and bearing of a stolid fighter. He bowed. "Lord Darcy. May I speak to your lordship alone?" He spoke Anglo-French with a punctilious precision that showed it was not his natural way of speaking.

He had done his best to remove the accent of the local *patois,* but his effort to speak properly was noticeable. "Certainly, Chief Henri. Will you excuse us, captain? I will discuss this problem with you later."

"Of course, your lordship."

Lord Darcy and Master Sean were left alone with Chief Henri.

"I *am* sorry to have interrupted, your lordship," said the Chief, "but His Royal Highness gave strict instructions."

"I had assumed as much, Chief Henri. Be so good as to sit down. Now—what has happened?"

"Well, your lordship," he said, glancing at Master Sean, "His Highness instructed me over the teleson to speak to no one but you." Then the Chief took a good look and did a double take. "By the Blue! Master Sean O Lochlainn! I didn't recognize you in that livery!"

The sorcerer grinned. "I make a very good valet, eh, Henri?"

"Indeed you do! Well, then, I may speak freely?"

"Certainly," said Lord Darcy. "Proceed."

"Well, then." The Chief leaned forward and spoke in a low voice. "When this thing came up, I thought of you first off. I must admit that it's beyond me. On the night of the eighth, two of my men were patrolling the waterfront district. At the corner of Rue King John II and Quai Sainte Marie, they saw a man fall. Except for a cloak, he was naked—and if your lordship remembers, that was a very cold night. By the time they got to him, he was dead."

Lord Darcy narrowed his eyes. "How had he died?"

"Skull fracture, your lordship. Somebody'd smashed in the right side of his skull. It's a wonder he could walk at all."

"I see. Proceed."

"Well, he was brought to the morgue. My men both identified him as one Paul Sarto, a man who worked around the bistros for small wages. He was also identified by the owner of the bistro where he had last worked. He seems to have been feeble-minded, willing to do manual labor for bed, board, and spending money. Needed taking care of a bit."

"Hm-m-m. We must trace him and find out why his baron had not provided for him," said Lord Darcy. "Proceed."

"Well, your lordship . . . er . . . there's more to it than that. I didn't look into the case immediately. After all, another killing on the waterfront—" He shrugged and spread his hands, palms up. "My sorcerer and my chirurgeon looked him over, made the usual tests. He was killed by a blow from a piece of oak with a square corner—perhaps a two-by-two or something like that. He was struck about ten minutes before the Armsmen found him. My chirurgeon says that only a man of tremendous vitality could have survived that long—to say nothing of the fact that he was able to walk."

"Excuse me, Henri," Master Sean interrupted. "Did your sorcerer make the FitzGibbon test for post-mortem activation?"

"Of course. First test he made, considering the wound. No, the body had not been activated after death and made to walk away from the scene of the crime. He actually died as the Armsmen watched."

"Just checking," said Master Sean.

"Well, anyway, the affair might have been dismissed as another waterfront brawl, but there were some odd things about the corpse. The cloak he was wearing was of aristocratic cut—not that of a commoner. Expensive cloth, expensive tailoring. Also, he had bathed recently—and, apparently, frequently. His toe- and finger-nails were decently manicured and cut."

Lord Darcy's eyes narrowed with interest. "Hardly the condition one would expect of a common laborer, eh?"

"Exactly, my lord. So when I read the reports this morning, I went to take a look. This time of year, the weather permits keeping a body without putting a preservation spell on it."

He leaned forward, and his voice became lower and hoarser. "I only had to take one look, my lord. Then I had to take action and call Rouen. My lord, it is the Marquis of Cherbourg himself!"

Lord Darcy rode through the chilling wintry night on a borrowed horse, his dark cloak whipping around the palfrey's rump in the icy breeze. The chill was more apparent than real. A relatively warm wind had come in from the sea, bringing with it a slushy rain; the temperature of the air was above the freezing point—but not

much above it. Lord Darcy had endured worse
cold than this, but the damp chill seemed to
creep inside his clothing, through his skin, and
into his bones. He would have preferred a dry
cold, even if it was much colder; at least, a dry
cold didn't try to crawl into a man's cloak with
him.

He had borrowed the horse from Chief Henri.
It was a serviceable hack, well-trained to police
work and used to the cobbled streets of
Cherbourg.

The scene at the morgue, Lord Darcy thought,
had been an odd one. He and Sean and Henri
had stood by while the morgue attendant had
rolled out the corpse. At first glance, Lord
Darcy had been able to understand the con-
sternation of the Chief Master-at-Arms.

He had only met Hugh of Cherbourg once
and could hardly be called upon to make a
positive identification, but if the corpse was not
the Marquis to the life, the face was his in death.

The two Armsmen who had seen the man die
had been asked separately, and without being
told of the new identification, still said that the
body was that of Paul Sarto, although they admitted he looked cleaner and better cared for
than Paul ever had.

It was easy to see how the conflict of opinion
came about. The Armsmen had seen the Marquis only rarely—probably only on state occasions, when he had been magnificently dressed.
They could hardly be expected to identify a wandering, nearly nude man on the waterfront as
their liege lord. If, in addition, that man was im-

mediately identified in their minds with the man they had known as Paul Sarto, the identification of him as my lord the Marquis would be positively forced from their minds. On the other hand, Henri Vert, Chief Master-at-Arms of the City of Cherbourg, knew My Lord Marquis well and had never seen nor heard of Paul Sarto until after the death.

Master Sean had decided that further thaumaturgical tests could be performed upon the deceased. The local sorcerer—a mere journeyman of the Sorcerer's Guild—had explained all the tests he had performed, valiantly trying to impress a Master of the Art with his proficiency and ability.

"The weapon used was a fairly long piece of oak, Master. According to the Kaplan-Sheinwold test, a short club could not have been used. On the other hand, oddly enough, I could find no trace of evil or malicious intent, and—"

"Precisely why I intend to perform further tests, me boy," Master Sean had said. "We haven't enough information."

"Yes, Master," the journeyman sorcerer had said, properly humbled.

Lord Darcy made the observation—which he kept to himself—that if the blow had been dealt from the front, which it appeared to have been, then the killer was either left-handed or had a vicious right-hand backswing. Which, he had to admit to himself, told him very little. The cold chill of the unheated morgue had begun to depress him unduly in the presence of the dead, so he had left that part of the investigation to Mas-

ter Sean and set out on his own, borrowing a
palfrey from Chief Henri for the purpose.

The winters he had spent in London had convinced him thoroughly that no man of intelligence would stay anywhere near a cold
seacoast. Inland cold was fine; seacoast warmth
was all right. But this—!

Although he did not know Cherbourg well,
Lord Darcy had the kind of mind that could
carry a map in its memory and translate that
map easily into the real world that surrounded
him. Even a slight inaccuracy of the map didn't
bother him.

He turned his mount round a corner and saw
before him a gas lamp shielded with blue glass—
the sign of an outstation of the Armsmen of
Cherbourg. An Armsman stood at attention
outside.

As soon as he saw that he was confronted by
a mounted nobleman, the Man-at-Arms came to
attention. "Yes, my lord! Can I aid you, my
lord?"

"Yes, Armsman, you can," Lord Darcy said
as he vaulted from the saddle. He handed the
reins of the horse to the Armsman. "This mount
belongs to Chief Henri at headquarters." He
showed his card with the ducal arms upon it. "I
am Lord Darcy, Chief Investigator for His
Royal Highness the Duke. Take care of the
horse. I have business in this neighborhood and
will return for the animal. I should like to speak
to your Sergeant-at-Arms."

"Very good, my lord. The Sergeant is within,
my lord."

After speaking to the sergeant, Lord Darcy

went out again into the chill night.

It was still several blocks to his destination, but it would have been unwise to ride a horse all the way. He walked two blocks through the dingy streets of the neighborhood. Then, glancing about to make fairly certain he had not been followed or observed, he turned into a dark alley. Once inside, he took off his cloak and reversed it. The lining, instead of being the silk that a nobleman ordinarily wore, or the fur that would be worn in really cold weather, was a drab, worn, brown, carefully patched in one place. From a pocket, he drew a battered slouch hat of the kind normally worn by commoners in this area and adjusted it to his head after carefully mussing his hair. His boots were plain and already covered with mud. Excellent!

He relaxed his spine—normally his carriage was one of military erectness—and slowly strolled out of the other end of the alley.

He paused to light a cheap cigar and then moved on toward his destination.

"Aaiiy?" The blowsy-looking woman in her mid-fifties looked through the opening in the heavy door. "What might you be wanting at this hour?"

Lord Darcy gave the face his friendliest smile and answered in the *patois* she had used. "Excuse me, Lady-of-the-House, but I'm looking for my brother, Vincent Coudé. Hate to call on him so late, but—"

As he had expected, he was interrupted.

"We don't allow no one in after dark unless

they's identified by one of our people."

"As you shouldn't, Lady-of-the-House,"
Lord Darcy agreed politely. "But I'm sure my
brother Vincent will identify me. Just tell him his
brother Richard is here. Ey?"

She shook her head. "He ain't here. Ain't
been here since last Wednesday. My girl checks
the rooms every day, and he ain't been here since
last Wednesday."

Wednesday! thought Lord Darcy. *Wednesday
the eighth! The night the Marquis disappeared!
The night the body was found only a few blocks
from here!*

Lord Darcy took a silver coin from his belt
pouch and held it out between the fingers of his
right hand. "Would you mind going up and taking a look? He might've come in during the day.
Might be asleep up there."

She took the coin and smiled. "Glad to; glad
to. You might be right; he might've come in. Be
right back."

But she left the door locked and closed the
panel.

Lord Darcy didn't care about that. He listened carefully to her footsteps. Up the stairs.
Down the hall. A knock. Another knock.

Quickly, Lord Darcy ran to the right side of
the house and looked up. Sure enough, he saw
the flicker of a lantern in one window. The
Lady-of-the-House had unlocked the door and
looked in to make sure that her roomer was not
in. He ran back to the door and was waiting for
her when she came down.

She opened the door panel and said sadly:
"He still ain't here, Richard."

Lord Darcy handed her another sixth-sovereign piece. "That's all right, Lady-of-the-House. Just tell him I was here. I suppose he's out on business." He paused. "When is his rent next due?"

She looked at him through suddenly narrowed eyes, wondering whether it would be possible to cheat her roomer's brother out of an extra week's rent. She saw his cold eyes and decided it wouldn't.

"He's paid up to the twenty-fourth," she admitted reluctantly. "But if he ain't back by then, I'll be turning his stuff out and getting another roomer."

"Naturally," Lord Darcy agreed. "But he'll be back. Tell him I was here. Nothing urgent. I'll be back in a day or so."

She smiled. "All right. Come in the daytime, if y' can, Friend Richard. Thank y' much."

"Thank y' yourself, Lady-of-the-House," said Lord Darcy. "A good and safe night to y'." He turned and walked away.

He walked half a block and then dodged into a dark doorway.

So! Sir James le Lein, agent of His Majesty's Secret Service, had not been seen since the night of the eighth. That evening was beginning to take on a more and more sinister complexion.

He knew full well that he could have bribed the woman to let him into Sir James' room, but the amount he would have had to offer would have aroused suspicion. There was a better way.

It took him better than twenty minutes to find that way, but eventually he found himself on the

roof of the two-story rooming house where Sir
James had lived under the alias of Vincent
Coudé.

The house was an old one, but the construction had been strong. Lord Darcy eased himself
down the slope of the shingled roof to the rain
gutters at the edge. He had to lie flat, his feet
uphill toward the point of the roof, his hands
braced against the rain gutter to look down over
the edge toward the wall below. The room in
which he had seen the glimmer of light from the
woman's lantern was just below him. The window was blank and dark, but the shutters were
not drawn, which was a mercy.

The question was: Was the window locked?
Holding tight to the rain gutter, he eased himself
down to the very edge of the roof. His body was
at a thirty-degree angle, and he could feel the
increased pressure of blood in his head.
Cautiously, he reached down to see if he could
touch the window. He could!

Just barely, but he could!

Gently, carefully, working with the tips of the
fingers of one hand, he teased the window open.
As was usual with these old houses, the glass
panes were in two hinged panels that swung in-
ward. He got both of them open.

So far, the rain gutter had held him. It seemed
strong enough to hold plenty of weight. He slowly moved himself around until his body was parallel with the edge of the roof. Then he took a
good grasp of the edge of the rain gutter and
swung himself out into empty air. As he swung

round, he shot his feet out toward the lower sill of the window.

Then he let go and tumbled into the room.

He crouched motionlessly for a moment. Had he been heard? The sound had seemed tremendous when his feet had struck the floor. But it was still early, and there were others moving about in the rooming house. Still, he remained unmoving for a good two minutes to make sure there would be no alarm. He was quite certain that if the Lady-of-the-House had heard anything that disturbed her, she would have rushed up the stairs. No sound. Nothing.

Then he rose to his feet and took a special device from the pocket of his cloak.

It was a fantastic device, a secret of His Majesty's Government. Powered by the little zinc-copper couples that were the only known source of such magical power, they heated a steel wire to tremendously high temperature. The thin wire glowed white-hot, shedding a yellow-white light that was almost as bright as a gas-mantle lamp. The secret lay in the magical treatment of the steel filament. Under ordinary circumstances, the wire would burn up in a blue-white flash of fire. But, properly treated by a special spell, the wire was passivated and merely glowed with heat and light instead of burning. The hot wire was centered at the focus of a parabolic reflector, and merely by shoving forward a button with his thumb, Lord Darcy had at hand a light source equal to—and indeed far superior to—an ordinary dark lantern. It was a personal instrument, since the passivation was tuned to Lord Darcy and no one else.

He thumbed the button and a beam of light sprang into existence.

The search of Sir James le Lein's room was quick and thorough. There was absolutely nothing of any interest to Lord Darcy anywhere in the room.

Naturally Sir James would have taken pains to assure that there would not be. The mere fact that the housekeeper had a key would have made Sir James wary of leaving anything about that would have looked out of place. There was nothing here that would have identified the inhabitant of the room as anyone but a common laborer.

Lord Darcy switched off his lamp and brooded for a moment in the darkness. Sir James was on a secret and dangerous mission for His Imperial Majesty, John IV. Surely there were reports, papers, and so on. Where had Sir James kept the data he collected? In his head? That was possible, but Lord Darcy didn't think it was true.

Sir James had been working with Lord Cherbourg. Both of them had vanished on the night of the eighth. That the mutual vanishing was coincidental was possible—but highly improbable. There were too many things unexplained as yet. Lord Darcy had three tentative hypotheses, all of which explained the facts as he knew them thus far, and none of which satisfied him.

It was then that his eyes fell on the flowerpot

silhouetted against the dim light that filtered in from outside the darkened room. If it had been in the middle of the window sill, he undoubtedly would have smashed it when he came in; his feet had just barely cleared the sill. But it was over to one side, in a corner of the window. He walked over and looked at it carefully in the dimness. Why, he asked himself, would an agent of the King be growing an African violet?

He picked up the little flowerpot, brought it away from the window, and shone his light on it. It looked utterly usual.

With a grim smile, Lord Darcy put the pot, flower and all, into one of the capacious pockets of his cloak. Then he opened the window, eased himself over the sill, lowered himself until he was hanging only by his fingertips, and dropped the remaining ten feet to the ground, taking up the jar of landing with his knees.

Five minutes later, he had recovered his horse from the Armsmen and was on his way to Castle Cherbourg.

The monastery of the Order of Saint Benedict in Cherbourg was a gloomy-looking pile of masonry occupying one corner of the great courtyard that surrounded the castle. Lord Darcy and Master Sean rang the bell at the entrance gate early on the morning of Tuesday, January 14th. They identified themselves to the doorkeeper and were invited into the Guests' Common Room to wait while Father Patrique was summoned. The monk would have to get the permission of the Lord Abbot to speak to outsiders, but that was a mere formality.

It was a relief to find that the interior of the monastery did not share the feeling of gloom with its exterior. The Common Room was quite cheerful and the winter sun shone brightly through the high windows.

After a minute or so, the inner door opened and a tall, rather pale man in Benedictine habit entered the room. He smiled pleasantly as he strode briskly across the room to take Lord Darcy's hand. "Lord Darcy, I am Father Patrique. Your servant, my lord."

"And I yours, your reverence. This is my man, Sean."

The priest turned to accept the introduction, then he paused and a gleam of humor came into his eyes. "Master Sean, the clothing you wear is not your own. A sorcerer cannot hide his calling by donning a valet's outfit."

Master Sean smiled back. "I hadn't hoped to conceal myself from a perceptive of your Order, Reverend Sir."

Lord Darcy, too, smiled. He had rather hoped that Father Patrique would be a perceptive. The Benedictines were quite good in bringing out that particular phase of Talent if a member of their Order had it, and they prided themselves on the fact that Holy Father Benedict, their Founder in the early part of the Sixth Century, had showed that ability to a remarkable degree long before the Laws of Magic had been formulated or investigated scientifically. To such a perceptive, identity cannot be concealed without a radical change in the personality itself. Such a man is capable of perceiving, *in toto,* the personality of another; such men are invaluable as Healers, especially in cases of demonic possession and other mental diseases.

"And now, how may I help you, my lord?" the Benedictine asked pleasantly.

Lord Darcy produced his credentials and identified himself as Duke Richard's Chief Investigator.

"Quite so," said the priest. "Concerning the fact that my lord the Marquis is missing, I have no doubt."

"The walls of a monastery are not totally impenetrable, are they, Father?" Lord Darcy asked with a wry smile.

Father Patrique chuckled. "We are wide open to the sight of God and the rumors of man. Please be seated; we will not be disturbed here."

"Thank you, Father," Lord Darcy said, taking a chair. "I understand you were called to attend my lord of Cherbourg several times since last Christmas. My lady of Cherbourg and my lord the Bishop of Guernsey and Sark have told me of the nature of these attacks—that, incidentally, is why this whole affair is being kept as quiet as possible—but I would like your opinion as a Healer."

The priest shrugged his shoulders and spread his hands a little. "I should be glad to tell you what I can, my lord, but I am afraid I know almost nothing. The attacks lasted only a few minutes each time and they had vanished by the time I was able to see My Lord Marquis. By then, he was normal—if a little puzzled. He told me he had no memory of such behavior as my lady reported. He simply blanked out and then came out of it, feeling slightly disoriented and a little dizzy."

"Have you formed no diagnosis, Father?" Lord Darcy asked.

The Benedictine frowned. "There are several possible diagnoses, my lord. From my own observation, and from the symptoms reported by My Lord Marquis, I would have put it down as a mild form of epilepsy—what we call the *petit mal* type, the 'little sickness'. Contrary to popular opinion, epilepsy is not caused by demonic possession, but by some kind of organic malfunction that we know very little about.

"In *grand mal*, or 'great sickness' epilepsy, we find the seizures one normally thinks of as being connected with the disease—the convulsive 'fits' that cause the victim to completely lose control of his muscles and collapse with jerking limbs and so on. But the 'little sickness' merely causes brief loss of consciousness—sometimes so short that the victim does not even realize it. There is no collapse or convulsion; merely a blank daze lasting a few seconds or minutes."

"But you are not certain of that?" Lord Darcy asked.

The priest frowned. "No. If my lady the Marquise is telling the truth—and I see no reason why she should not, his behavior during the . . . well, call them seizures . . . his behavior during the seizures was atypical. During a typical seizure of the *petit mal* type, the victim is totally blank—staring at nothing, unable to speak or move, unable to be roused. But my lord was not that way, according to my lady. He seemed confused, bewildered, and very stupid, but he was *not* unconscious." He paused and frowned.

"Therefore you have other diagnoses, Father?" Lord Darcy prompted.

Father Patrique nodded thoughtfully. "Yes. Always assuming that my lady the Marquise has reported accurately, there are other possible diagnoses. But none of them quite fits, any more than the first one does."

"Such as?"

"Such as attack by psychic induction."

Master Sean nodded slowly, but there was a frown in his eyes.

"The wax-and-doll sort of thing," said Lord Darcy.

Father Patrique nodded an affirmative. "Exactly, my lord—although, as you undoubtedly know, there are far better methods than that—in practice."

"Of course," Lord Darcy said brusquely. In theory, he knew, the simulacrum method *was* the best method. Nothing could be more powerful than an exact duplicate, according to the Laws of Similarity. The size of the simulacrum made little difference, but the accuracy of detail did—including internal organs.

But the construction of a wax simulacrum—aside from the artistry required—entailed complications which bordered on the shadowy area of the unknown. Beeswax was more effective than mineral wax for the purpose because it was an animal product instead of a mineral one, thus increasing the similarity. But why did the addition of sal ammoniac increase the potency? Magicians simply said that sal ammoniac, saltpeter, and a few other minerals increased the similarity in some unknown way and let it go at that; sorcerers had better things to do than grub around in mineralogy.

"The trouble is," said Father Patrique, "that the psychic induction method nearly always involves physical pain or physical illness—intestinal disorders, heart trouble, or other glandular disturbances. There are no traces of such things here unless one considers the malfunction of the brain as a glandular disorder—and even so, it should be accompanied by pain."

"Then you discount that diagnosis, too?" asked Lord Darcy.

Father Patrique shook his head firmly. "I discount none of the diagnoses I have made thus far. My data are far from complete."

"You have other theories, then."

"I do, my lord. Actual demonic possession."

Lord Darcy narrowed his eyes and looked straight into the eyes of the priest. "You don't really believe that, Reverend Sir."

"No," Father Patrique admitted candidly, "I do not. As a perceptive, I have a certain amount of faith in my own ability. If more than one personality were inhabiting my lord's body, I am certain I would have perceived the ... er ... other personality."

Lord Darcy did not move his eyes from those of the Benedictine. "I had assumed as much, your reverence," he said. "If it were a case of multiple personality, you would have detected it, eh?"

"I am certain I would have, my lord," Father Patrique stated positively. "If my lord of Cherbourg had been inhabited by another personality, I would have detected it, even if that other personality had been under cover." He paused, then waved a hand slightly. "You understand, Lord Darcy? Alternate personalities in a single human body, a single human brain, can hide themselves. The personality dominant at any given time conceals to the casual observer the fact that other—different—personalities are present. But the . . . the *alter egos* cannot conceal themselves from a true perceptive."

"I understand," Lord Darcy said.

"There was only one personality in the . . . the *person*, the *brain*, of the Marquis of Cherbourg at the time I examined him. And that personality was the personality of the Marquis himself."

"I see," Lord Darcy said thoughtfully. He did not doubt the priest's statement. He knew the reputation Father Patrique had among Healers. "How about drugs, Father?" he asked after a moment. "I understand that there are drugs which can alter a man's personality."

The Benedictine Healer smiled. "Certainly. Alcohol—the essence of wines and beers—will do it. There are others. Some have a temporary effect; others have no effect in single dosages— or, at least, no detectable effect—but have an accumulative effect if the drug is taken regularly. Oil of wormwood, for instance, is found in sev-

eral of the more expensive liqueurs—in small
quantity, of course. If you get drunk on such a
liqueur, the effect is temporary and hardly dis-
tinguishable from that of alcohol alone. But if
taken steadily, over a period of time, a definite
personality change occurs."

Lord Darcy nodded thoughtfully, then looked
at his sorcerer. "Master Sean, the phial, if you
please."

The tubby little Irish sorcerer fished in a
pocket with thumb and forefinger and brought
forth a small stoppered glass phial a little over
an inch long and half an inch in diameter. He
handed it to the priest, who looked at it with
curiosity. It was nearly filled with a dark amber
fluid. In the fluid were little pieces of dark matter, rather like coarse-cut tobacco, which had
settled to the bottom of the phial and filled perhaps a third of it.

"What is it?" Father Patrique asked.

Master Sean frowned. "That's what I'm not
rightly sure of, Reverend Sir. I checked it to
make certain there were no spells on it before I
opened it. There weren't. So I unstoppered it
and took a little whiff. Smells like brandy, with
just faint overtones of something else. Naturally,
I couldn't analyze it without having some notion
of what it was. Without a specimen standard, I
couldn't use Similarity analysis. Oh, I checked
the brandy part, and that came out all right. The
liquid is brandy. But I can't identify the little
crumbs of stuff. His lordship had an idea that it
might be a drug of some kind, and, since a

Healer has all kinds of *materia medica* around, I thought perhaps we might be able to identify it."

"Certainly," the priest agreed. "I have a couple of ideas we might check right away. The fact that the material is steeped in brandy indicates either that the material decays easily or that the essence desired is soluble in brandy. That suggests several possibilities to my mind." He looked at Lord Darcy. "May I ask where you got it, my lord?"

Lord Darcy smiled. "I found it buried in a flowerpot."

Father Patrique, realizing that he had been burdened with all the information he was going to get, accepted Lord Darcy's statement with a slight shrug. "Very well, my lord; Master Sean and I will see if we can discover what this mysterious substance may be."

"Thank you, Father." Lord Darcy rose from his seat. "Oh—one more thing. What do you know about Lord Seiger?"

"Very little. His lordship comes from Yorkshire ... North Riding, if I'm not mistaken. He's been working with my lord of Cherbourg for the past several months—something to do with books, I believe. I know nothing of his family or anything like that, if that is what you mean."

"Not exactly," said Lord Darcy. "Are you his Confessor, Father? Or have you treated him as a Healer?"

The Benedictine raised his eyebrows. "No. Neither. Why?"

"Then I can ask you a question about his soul.

What kind of man is he? What is the oddness I
detect in him? What is it about him that
frightens my lady the Marquise in spite of his
impeccable behavior?" He noticed the hesitation
in the priest's manner and went on before Father
Patrique could answer. "This is not idle curiosity, Your Reverence. I am investigating a
homicide."

The priest's eyes widened. "Not . . .?" He
stopped himself. "I see. Well, then. Granted, as
a perceptive, I know certain things about Lord
Seiger. He suffers from a grave illness of the
soul. How these things come about, we do not
know, but occasionally a person utterly lacks
that part of the soul we call 'conscience', at
least insofar as it applies to certain acts. We cannot think that God would fail to provide such a
thing; therefore theologists ascribe the lack to an
act of the Devil at some time in the early life of
the child—probably prenatally and, therefore,
before baptism can protect the child. Lord
Seiger is such a person. A psychopathic personality. Lord Seiger was born without an ability to
distinguish between 'right' and 'wrong' as we
know the terms. Such a person performs a given
act or refrains from performing it only according
to the expediency of the moment. Certain acts
which you or I would look upon with abhor-
rence he may even look upon as pleasurable.
Lord Seiger is—basically—a homicidal psycho-
path."

Lord Darcy said, "I thought as much." Then
he added dryly, "He is, I presume, under
restraint?"

"Oh, of course; of course!" The priest looked aghast that anyone should suggest otherwise. "Naturally such a person cannot be condemned because of a congenital deficiency, but neither can he be allowed to become a danger to society." He looked at Master Sean. "You know something of Geas Theory, Master Sean?"

"Something," Master Sean agreed. "Not my field, of course, but I've studied a little of the theory. The symbol manipulation's a little involved for me, I'm afraid. Psychic Algebra's as far as I ever got."

"Of course. Well, Lord Darcy, to put it in layman's terms, a powerful spell is placed upon the affected person—a *geas,* it's called—which forces him to limit his activities to those which are not dangerous to his fellow man. We cannot limit him too much, of course, for it would be sinful to deprive him entirely of his free will. His sexual morals, for instance, are his own—but he cannot use force. The extent of the *geas* depends upon the condition of the individual and the treatment given by the Healer who performed the work."

"It takes an extensive and powerful knowledge of sorcery, I take it?" Lord Darcy asked.

"Oh, yes. No Healer would even attempt it until he had taken his Th.D. and then specialized under an expert for a time. And there are not many Doctors of Thaumaturgy. Since Lord Seiger is a Yorkshireman, I would venture to guess that the work was done by His Grace the Archbishop of York—a most pious and powerful Healer. I, myself, would not think of attempting such an operation."

"You can, however, tell that such an operation has been performed?"

Father Patrique smiled. "As easily as a chirurgeon can tell if an abdominal operation has been performed."

"Can a *geas* be removed? Or partially removed?"

"Of course—by one equally as skilled and powerful. But I could detect that, too. It has not been done in Lord Seiger's case."

"Can you tell what channels of freedom he has been allowed?"

"No," said the priest. "That sort of thing depends upon the fine structure of the *geas,* which is difficult to observe without extensive analysis."

"Then," said Lord Darcy, "you cannot tell me whether or not there are circumstances in which his *geas* would permit him to kill? Such as, for instance . . . er . . . self-defense?"

"No," the priest admitted. "But I will say that it is rare indeed for even such a channel as self-defense to be left open for a psychopathic killer. The *geas* in such a case would necessarily leave the decision as to what constituted 'self-defense' up to the patient. A normal person knows when 'self-defense' requires killing one's enemy, rendering him unconscious, fleeing from him, giving him a sharp retort, or merely keeping quiet. But to a psychopathic killer, a simple insult may be construed as an attack which requires 'self-defense'—which would give him permisson to kill. No Healer would leave such a decision in the hands of the patient." His face grew somber. "Certainly no sane man would leave that decision to the mind of a man like Lord Seiger."

"Then you consider him safe, Father?"

The Benedictine hesitated only a moment. "Yes. Yes, I do. I do not believe him capable of committing an antisocial act such as that. The Healer took pains to make sure that Lord Seiger would be protected from most of his fellow men, too. He is almost incapable of committing any offense against propriety; his behavior is impeccable at all times; he cannot insult anyone; he is almost incapable of defending himself physically except under the greatest provocation.

"I once watched him in a fencing bout with my lord the Marquis. Lord Seiger is an expert swordsman—much better than my lord the Marquis. The Marquis was utterly unable to score a touch upon Lord Seiger's person; Lord Seiger's defense was far too good. *But*—neither could Lord Seiger score a touch upon my lord. He couldn't even try. His brilliant swordsmanship is purely and completely defensive." He paused. "You are a swordsman yourself, my lord?" It was only half a question; the priest was fairly certain that a Duke's Investigator would be able to handle any and all weapons with confidence.

He was perfectly correct. Lord Darcy nodded without answering. To be able to wield a totally defensive sword required not only excellent—superlative—swordsmanship, but the kind of iron self-control that few men possessed. In Lord Seiger's case, of course, it could hardly be called *self*-control. The control had been imposed by another.

"Then you can understand," the priest continued, "why I say that I believe he can be trusted. If his Healer found it necessary to impose so many restrictions and protections, he would most certainly not have left any channel open for Lord Seiger to make any decision for himself as to when it would be proper to kill another."

"I understand, Father. Thank you for your information. I assure you it will remain confidential."

"Thank you, my lord. If there is nothing else . . . ?"

"Nothing for the moment, Reverend Father. Thank you again."

"A pleasure, Lord Darcy. And now, Master Sean, shall we go to my laboratory?"

An hour later, Lord Darcy was sitting in the guest room which Sir Gwiliam had shown him to the day before. He was puffing at his Bavarian pipe, filled with a blend of tobacco grown in the Southern Duchies of New England, his mind working at high speed, when Master Sean entered.

"My lord," said the tubby little sorcerer with a smile, "the good Father and I have identified the substance."

"Good!" Lord Darcy gestured toward a chair. "What was it?"

Master Sean sat down. "We were lucky, my lord. His Reverence *did* have a sample of the drug. As soon as we were able to establish a similarity between our sample and his, we identified it as a mushroom known as the Devil's Throne. The fungus is dried, minced, and steeped in brandy or other spirit. The liquid is then decanted off and the minced bits are thrown away —or, sometimes, steeped a second time. In large doses, the drugged spirit results in insanity, convulsions, and rapid death. In small doses, the preliminary stages are simply mild euphoria and light intoxication. But if taken regularly, the effect is cumulative—first, a manic, hallucinatory state, then delusions of persecution and violence."

Lord Darcy's eyes narrowed. "That fits. Thank you. Now there is one more problem. I want positive identification of that corpse. My Lord Bishop is not certain that it is his brother; that may just be wishful thinking. My Lady Marquise refuses to view the body, saying that it could not possibly be her husband—and that is *definitely* wishful thinking. But *I* must know for certain. Can you make a test?"

"I can take blood from the heart of the dead man and compare it with blood from My Lord Bishop's veins, my lord."

"Ah, yes. The Jacoby transfer method," said Lord Darcy.

"Not quite, my lord. The Jacoby transfer requires at least two hearts. It is dangerous to take blood from a living heart. But the test I have in mind is equally as valid."

"I thought blood tests were unreliable between siblings."

"Well, now, as to that, my lord," Master Sean

said, "in theory there is a certain very low probability that brother and sister, children of the same parents, would show completely negative results. In other words, they would have zero similarity in that test.

"Blood similarity runs in a series of steps from zero to forty-six. In a parent-child relationship, the similarity is always exactly twenty-three—in other words, the child is always related half to one parent and half to the other.

"With siblings, though, we find variations. Identical twins, for instance, register a full forty-six point similarity. Most siblings run much less, averaging twenty-three. There *is* a possibility of two brothers or two sisters having only one-point similarity, and, as I said, my lord, of a brother and sister having zero similarity. But the odds are on the order of one point seven nine million million to one against it. Considering the facial similarity of My Lord Bishop and My Lord Marquis, I would be willing to stake my reputation that the similarity would be substantially greater than zero—perhaps greater than twenty-three."

"Very well, Master Sean. You have not failed me yet; I do not anticipate that you ever will. Get me that data."

"Yes, my lord. I shall endeavor to give satisfaction." Master Sean left suffused with a glow of mixed determination and pride.

Lord Darcy finished his pipe and headed for the offices of Captain Sir Androu Duglasse.

The captain looked faintly indignant at Lord Darcy's question. "I searched the castle quite thoroughly, y' lordship. We looked everywhere that M' Lord Marquis could possibly have gone."

"Come, captain," Lord Darcy said mildly, "I don't mean to impugn your ability, but I dare say there are places you didn't search simply because there was no reason to think my lord of Cherbourg would have gone there."

Captain Sir Androu frowned. "Such as, my lord?"

"Such as the secret tunnel."

The captain looked suddenly blank. "Oh," he said after a moment. Then his expression changed. "But surely, y'lordship, you don't think . . ."

"I don't *know*, that's the point. My lord *did* have keys to every lock in the castle, didn't he?"

"All except to the monastery, yes. My Lord Abbot has those."

"Naturally. I think we can dismiss the monastery. Where else did you not look?"

"Well . . ." The captain hesitated thoughtfully. "I didn't bother with the strongroom, the wine cellar, or the icehouse. I don't have the keys. Sir Gwiliam would have told me if anything was amiss."

"Sir Gwiliam has the keys, you say? Then we must find Sir Gwiliam."

Sir Gwiliam, as it turned out, was in the wine cellar. Lord Seiger informed them that, at Lady Elaine's request, he had sent the seneschal down for another bottle of brandy. Lord Darcy followed Captain Sir Androu down the winding stone steps to the cellars.

"Most of this is used as storage space," the

captain said, waving a hand to indicate the vast, dim rooms around them. "All searched very carefully. The wine cellar's this way, y' lordship."

The wine-cellar door, of heavy, reinforced oak, stood slightly ajar. Sir Gwiliam, who had evidently heard their footsteps, opened it a little more and put his head out. "Who is it? Oh. Good afternoon, my lord. Good afternoon, captain. May I be of service?"

He stepped back, opening the door to let them in.

"I thank you, Sir Gwiliam," said Lord Darcy. "We come partly on business and partly on pleasure. I have noticed that my lord the Marquis keeps an excellent cellar; the wines are of the finest and the brandy is extraordinary. Saint Coeurlandt Michele '46 is difficult to come by these days."

Sir Gwiliam looked rather sad. "Yes, your lordship, it is. I fear the last two cases in existence are right here. I now have the painful duty of opening one of them." He sighed and gestured toward the table, where stood a wooden case that had been partially pried open. A glance told Lord Darcy that there was nothing in the bottles but brandy and that the leaden seals were intact.

"Don't let us disturb you, Sir Gwiliam," Lord Darcy said. "May we look around?"

"Certainly, your lordship. A pleasure." He went back to work on opening the brandy case with a pry bar.

Lord Darcy ran a practiced eye over the racks,

noting labels and seals. He had not really expected that anyone would attempt to put drugs or poison into bottles; My Lady Elaine was not the only one who drank, and wholesale poisoning would be too unselective.

The wine cellar was not large, but it was well stocked with excellent vintages. There were a couple of empty shelves in one corner, but the rest of the shelves were filled with bottles of all shapes and sizes. Over them lay patinas of dust of various thicknesses. Sir Gwiliam was careful not to bruise his wines.

"His lordship's choices, or yours, Sir Gwiliam?" Lord Darcy asked, indicating the rows of bottles.

"I am proud to say that My Lord Marquis has always entrusted the selection of wines and spirits to me, your lordship."

"I compliment both of you," Lord Darcy said. "You for your excellent taste, and his lordship for recognizing that ability in you." He paused. "However, there is more pressing business."

"How may I help you, my lord?" Having finished opening the case, he dusted off his hands and looked with a mixture of pride and sadness at the Saint Coeurlandt Michele '46. Distilled in 1846 and aged in the wood for thirty years before it was bottled, it was considered possibly the finest brandy ever made.

Quietly, Lord Darcy explained that there had been several places where Captain Sir Androu had been unable to search. "There is the possibility, you see, that he might have had a heart attack—or some sort of attack—and collapsed to the floor."

Sir Gwiliam's eyes opened wide. "And he might be there yet? God in Heaven! Come, your lordship! This way! I have been in the icehouse, and so has the chef, but no one has opened the strongroom!"

He took the lead, running, with Lord Darcy right behind him and Sir Androu in the rear. It was not far, but the cellar corridors twisted oddly and branched frequently.

The strongroom was more modern than the wine cellar; the door was of heavy steel, swung on gimbaled hinges. The walls were of stone and concrete, many feet thick.

"It's a good thing the captain is here, your lordship," the seneschal said breathlessly as the three men stopped in front of the great vault door. "It takes two keys to open it. I have one, the captain has the other. My Lord Marquis, of course, has both. Captain?"

"Yes, yes, Gwiliam; I have mine here."

There were four keyholes on each side of the wide door. Lord Darcy recognized the type of construction. Only one of the four keyholes on each side worked. A key put into the wrong hole would ring alarms. The captain would know which hole to put his own key in, and so would Sir Gwiliam—but neither knew the other's proper keyhole. The shields around the locks prevented either man from seeing which keyhole the other used. Lord Darcy could not tell, even though he watched. The shields covered the hands too well.

"Ready, captain?" Sir Gwiliam asked.

"Ready."

"Turn."

Both men turned their keys at once. The six-foot wide door clicked inside itself and swung open when Sir Gwiliam turned a handle on his side of the door.

There was a great deal worthy of notice inside —gold and silver utensils; the jeweled coronets of the Marquis and Marquise; the great Robes of State, embroidered with gold and glittering with gems—in short, all the paraphernalia for great occasions of state. In theory, all this belonged to the Marquis; actually, it was no more his than the Imperial Crown Jewels belonged to King John IV. Like the castle, it was a part of the office; it could be neither pawned nor sold.

But nowhere in the vault was there any body, dead or alive, nor any sign that there had ever been one.

"Well!" said Sir Gwiliam with a sharp exhalation. "I'm certainly glad of that! You had me worried, your lordship." There was a touch of reproach in his voice.

"I am as happy to find nothing as you are. Now let's check the icehouse."

The icehouse was in another part of the cellars and was unlocked. One of the cooks was selecting a roast. Sir Gwiliam explained that he unlocked the icehouse each morning and left the care of it with the Chief of the Kitchen, locking it again each night. A careful search of the insulated, ice-chilled room assured Lord Darcy that there was no one there who shouldn't be.

"Now we'll take a look in the tunnel," Lord Darcy said. "Have you the key, Sir Gwiliam?"

"Why . . . why, yes. But it hasn't been opened for years! Decades! Never since I've been here, at any rate."

"I have a key, myself, y' lordship," said the captain. "I just never thought of looking. Why would he go there?"

"Why, indeed? But we must look, nevertheless."

A bell rang insistently in the distance, echoing through the cellars.

"Dear me!" said Sir Gwiliam. "My lady's brandy! I quite forgot about it! Sir Androu has a key to the tunnel, my lord; would you excuse me?"

"Certainly, Sir Gwiliam. Thank you for your help."

"A pleasure, my lord." He hurried off to answer the bell.

"Did you actually expect to find My Lord Marquis in any of those places your lordship?" asked Sir Androu. "Even if my lord had gone into one of them, would he have locked the door behind him?"

"I did not expect to find him in the wine cellar or the icehouse," Lord Darcy said, "but the strong room presented a strong possibility. I merely wanted to see if there were any indications that he had been there. I must confess that I found none."

"To the tunnel, then," said the captain.

The entrance was concealed behind a shabby, unused cabinet. But the cabinet swung away from the steel door behind it with oiled smoothness. And when the captain took out a dull, patinaed key and opened the door, the lock turned smoothly and effortlessly.

The captain looked at his key, now brightened by abrasion where it had forced the wards, as though it were imbued with magic. "Well, I'll be cursed!" he said softly.

The door swung silently open to reveal a tunnel six feet wide and eight high. Its depths receded into utter blackness.

"A moment, m' lord," said the captain. "I'll get a lamp." He walked back down the corridor and took an oil lamp from a wall bracket.

The two of them walked down the tunnel together. On either side, the niter-stained walls gleamed whitely. The captain pointed down at the floor. "Somebody's been using this lately," he said softly.

"I had already noticed the disturbed dust and crushed crystals of niter," Lord Darcy said. "I agree with you."

"Who's been using the tunnel, then, y'lordship?"

"I am confident that my lord the Marquis of Cherbourg was one of them. His . . . er . . . confederates were here, too."

"But why? And how? No one could have got

out without my guard seeing them."

"I am afraid you are right, my good captain."
He smiled. "But that doesn't mean that the
guard would have reported to you if his liege
lord told him not to . . . eh?"

Sir Androu stopped suddenly and looked at
Lord Darcy. "Great God in Heaven! And I
thought—!" He brought himself up short.

"You thought *what?* Quickly, man!"

"Y' lordship, a new man enlisted in the Guard
two months ago. Came in on m'lord's recom-
mendation. Then m' lord reported that he mis-
behaved and had me put him on the sewer detail
at night. The man's been on that detail ever
since."

"Of course!" Lord Darcy said with a smile of
triumph. "He would put one of his own men on.
Come, captain; I must speak to this man."

"I . . . I'm afraid that's impossible, y'
lordship. He's down as a deserter. Disappeared
from post last night. Hasn't been seen since."

Lord Darcy said nothing. He took the lantern
from the captain and knelt down to peer closely
at the footprints on the tunnel floor.

"I should have looked more closely," he muttered, as if to himself. "I've taken too much for
granted. Ha! Two men—carrying something
heavy. And followed by a third." He stood up.
"This puts an entirely different complexion on
the matter. We must act at once. Come!" He
turned and strode back toward the castle cellar.

"But— What of the rest of the tunnel?"

"There is no need to search it," Lord Darcy
said firmly. "I can assure you that there is no

one in it but ourselves. Come along."

In the shadows of a dingy dockside warehouse
a block from the pier where the Danzig-bound
vessel, *Esprit de Mer,* was tied up, Lord Darcy
stood, muffled in a long cloak. Beside him,
equally muffled in a black naval cloak, his blond
hair covered by a pulled-up cowl, stood Lord
Seiger, his quite handsome face expressionless in
the dimness.

"There she is," Lord Darcy said softly. "She's
the only vessel bound for a North Sea port from
Cherbourg. The Rouen office confirms that she
was sold last October to a Captain Olsen. He
claims to be a Northman, but I will be willing to
wager against odds that he's Polish. If not, then
he is certainly in the pay of the King of Poland.
The ship is still sailing under Imperial registry
and flying the Imperial flag. She carries no
armament, of course, but she's a fast little craft
for a merchant vessel."

"And you think we will find the evidence we
need aboard her?" Lord Seiger asked.

"I am almost certain of it. It will be either here
or at the warehouse, and the man would be a
fool to leave the stuff there now—especially
when it can be shipped out aboard the *Esprit de
Mer.*"

It had taken time to convince Lord Seiger that
it was necessary to make this raid. But once
Lord Darcy had convinced him of how much
was already known and verified everything by a
teleson call to Rouen, Lord Seiger was both willing and eager. There was a suppressed excite-

ment in the man that showed only slightly in the
pale blue eyes, leaving the rest of his face as
placid as ever.

. Other orders had had to be given. Captain Sir
Androu Duglasse had sealed Castle Cherbourg;
no one—*no one*—was to be allowed out for any
reason whatever. The guard had been doubled
during the emergency. Not even My Lord
Bishop, My Lord Abbot, or My Lady Marquise
could leave the castle. Those orders came, not
from Lord Darcy, but from His Royal Highness
the Duke of Normandy himself.

Lord Darcy looked at his wrist watch. "It's
time, my lord," he said to Lord Seiger. "Let's
move in."

"Very well, my lord," Lord Seiger agreed.

The two of them walked openly toward the
pier.

At the gate that led to the pier itself, two
burly-looking seamen stood lounging against the
closed gate. When they saw the two cloaked men
approaching, they became more alert, stepping
away from the gate, toward the oncoming figures. Their hands went to the hilts of the scab-
barded cutlasses at their belts.

Lord Seiger and Lord Darcy walked along the
pier until they were within fifteen feet of the ad-
vancing guards, then stopped.

"What business have ye here?" asked one of
the seamen.

It was Lord Darcy who spoke. His voice was
low and cold. "Don't address me in that manner
if you want to keep your tongue," he said in excellent Polish. "I wish to speak to your captain."

The first seaman looked blank at being addressed in a language he did not understand, but the second blanched visibly. "Let me handle this," he whispered in Anglo-French to the other. Then, in Polish: "Your pardon, lord. My messmate here don't understand Polish. What was it you wanted, lord?"

Lord Darcy sighed in annoyance. "I thought I made myself perfectly clear. We desire to see Captain Olsen."

"Well, now, lord, he's given orders that he don't want to see no one. Strict orders, lord."

Neither of the two sailors noticed that, having moved away from the gate, they had left their rear unguarded. From the skiff that had managed to slip in under the pier under cover of darkness, four of the Marquis' Own silently lifted themselves to the deck of the pier. Neither Lord Darcy nor Lord Seiger looked at them.

"Strict orders?" Lord Darcy's voice was heavy with scorn. "I dare say your orders do not apply to Crown Prince Sigismund himself, do they?"

On cue, Lord Seiger swept the hood back from his handsome blond head.

It was extremely unlikely that either of the two sailors had ever seen Sigismund, Crown Prince of Poland—nor, if they had, that they would have recognized him when he was not dressed for a state occasion. But certainly they had heard that Prince Sigismund was blond and handsome, and that was all Lord Darcy needed. In actuality, Lord Seiger bore no other resemblance, being a good head taller than the Polish prince.

While they stood momentarily dumbfounded

by this shattering revelation, arms silently encircled them, and they ceased to wonder about Crown Princes of any kind for several hours. They were rolled quietly into the shadows behind a pile of heavy bags of ballast.

"Everyone else all set?" Lord Darcy whispered to one of the Guardsmen.

"Yes, my lord."

"All right. Hold this gate. Lord Seiger, let's go on."

"I'm right with you, my lord," said Lord Seiger.

Some little distance away, at the rear door of a warehouse just off the waterfront, a heavily armed company of the Men-at-Arms of Cherbourg listened to the instructions of Chief Master-at-Arms Henri Vert.

"All right. Take your places. Seal every door. Arrest and detain anyone who tries to leave. Move out." With a rather self-important feeling, he touched the Duke's Warrant, signed by Lord Darcy as Agent for His Highness, that lay folded in his jacket pocket.

The Men-at-Arms faded into the dimness, moving silently to their assigned posts. With Chief Henri remained six Sergeants-at-Arms and Master Sean O Lochlainn, Sorcerer.

"All right, Sean," said Chief Henri, "go ahead."

"Give us a little light from your dark lantern, Henri," said Master Sean, kneeling to peer at the lock of the door. He set his black suitcase on the stone pavement and quietly set his corthainn-

wood magician's staff against the wall beside the
door. The Sergeants-at-Arms watched the tubby
little sorcerer with respect.

"Hoho," Master Sean said, peering at the lock.
"A simple lock. But there's a heavy bar across it
on the inside. Take a little work, but not much
time." He opened his suitcase to take out two
small phials of powder and a thin laurel-wood
wand.

The Armsmen watched in silence as the
sorcerer muttered his spells and blew tiny puffs
of powder into the lock. Then Master Sean
pointed his wand at the lock and twirled it coun-
terclockwise slowly. There was a faint sliding
noise and a *snick!* of metal as the lock unlocked
itself.

Then he drew the wand across the door a foot
above the lock. This time, something heavy slid
quietly on the other side of the door.

With an almost inaudible sigh, the door
swung open an inch or so.

Master Sean stepped aside and allowed the
sergeants and their chief to enter the door.
Meanwhile, he took a small device from his
pocket and checked it again. It was a cylinder of
glass two inches in diameter and half an inch
high, half full of liquid. On the surface of the
liquid floated a tiny sliver of oak that would
have been difficult to see if the top of the glass
box had not been a powerful magnifying lens.
The whole thing looked a little like a pocket
compass—which, in a sense, it was.

The tiny sliver of oak had been recovered
from the scalp of the slain man in the morgue,

and now, thanks to Master Sean's thaumaturgical art, the little sliver pointed unerr-
ingly toward the piece of wood whence it had
come.

Master Sean nodded in satisfaction. As Lord
Darcy had surmised, the weapon was still in the
warehouse. He glanced up at the lights in the
windows of the top floor of the warehouse. Not
only the weapon, but some of the plotters were
still here.

He smiled grimly and followed the Armsmen
in, his corthainn-wood staff grasped firmly in
one hand and his suitcase in the other.

Lord Darcy stood with Lord Seiger on one of
the lower decks of the *Esprit de Mer* and looked
around. "So far, so good," he said in a low
voice. "Piracy has its advantages, my lord."

"Indeed it does, my lord," Lord Seiger replied
in the same tone.

Down a nearby ladder, his feet clad in soft-
soled boots, came Captain Sir Androu, com-
mander of the Marquis' Own. "So far, so good,
m' lords," he whispered, not realizing that he
was repeating Lord Darcy's sentiments. "We
have the crew. All sleeping like children."

"*All* the crew?" Lord Darcy asked.

"Well, m' lord, all we could find so far. Some
of 'em are still on shore leave. Not due back 'til
dawn. Otherwise, I fancy this ship would have
pulled out long before this. No way to get word
to the men, though, eh?"

"I have been hoping so," Lord Darcy agreed.
"But the fact remains that we really don't know

how many are left aboard. How about the bridge?"

"The Second Officer was on duty, m' lord. We have him."

"Captain's cabin?"

"Empty, m' lord."

"First Officer's?"

"Also empty, m' lord. Might be both ashore."

"Possibly." There was a distinct possibility, Lord Darcy knew, that both the captain and the first officer were still at the warehouse—in which case, they would be picked up by Chief Henri and his men. "Very well. Let's keep moving down. We still haven't found what we're looking for." *And there will be one Hell of an international incident if we don't find it,* Lord Darcy told himself. *His Slavonic Majesty's Government will demand all sorts of indemnities, and Lady Darcy's little boy will find himself fighting the aborigines in the jungles of New France.*

But he wasn't really terribly worried; his intuition backed up his logic in telling him that he was right.

Nevertheless, he mentally breathed a deep sigh of relief when he and Lord Seiger found what they were looking for some five or six minutes later.

There were four iron-barred cells on the deck just above the lowest cargo hold. They faced each other, two and two, across a narrow passageway. Two bosuns blocked the passageway.

Lord Darcy looked down the tweendecks hatch and saw them. He had gone down the ladders silently, peeking carefully below before at-

tempting to descend, and his caution had paid
off. Neither of the bosuns saw him. They were
leaning casually against the opposite bulkheads
of the passageway, talking in very low voices.

There was no way to come upon them by
stealth, but neither had a weapon in hand, and
there was nothing to retreat behind for either of
them.

Should he, Lord Darcy wondered, wait for re-
inforcements? Sir Androu already had his hands
full for the moment, and Lord Seiger would not,
of course, be of any use. The man was utterly
incapable of physical violence.

He lifted himself from the prone position from
which he had been peeking over the hatch edge
to look below, and whispered to Lord Seiger.
"They have cutlasses. Can you hold your own
against one of them if trouble comes?"

For answer, Lord Seiger smoothly and silently
drew his rapier. "Against both of them if necessary, my lord," he whispered back.

"I don't think it will be necessary, but there's
no need taking chances at this stage of the
game." He paused. Then he drew a five-shot .42
caliber handgun from his belt holster. "I'll cover
them with this."

Lord Seiger nodded and said nothing.

"Stay here," he whispered to Lord Seiger.
"Don't come down the stairs . . . sorry, the *ladder* . . . until I call."

"Very well, my lord."

Lord Darcy walked silently up the ladder that
led to the deck above. Then he came down
again, letting his footfalls be heard.

He even whistled softly but audibly as he did so—an old Polish air he happened to know.

Then, without breaking his stride, he went on down the second ladder. He held his handgun in his right hand, concealed beneath his cloak.

His tactics paid off beautifully. The bosuns heard him coming and assumed that he must be someone who was authorized to be aboard the ship. They stopped their conversation and assumed an attitude of attention. They put their hands on the hilts of their cutlasses, but only as a matter of form. They saw the boots, then the legs, then the lower torso of the man coming down the ladder. And still they suspected nothing. An enemy would have tried to take them by surprise, wouldn't he?

Yes.

And he did.

Halfway down the steps, Lord Darcy dropped to a crouch and his pistol was suddenly staring both of them in the face.

"If either of you moves," said Lord Darcy calmly, "I will shoot him through the brain. Get your hands off those blade hilts and don't move otherwise. Fine. Now turn around. *V-e-r-r-ry slowly.*"

The men obeyed wordlessly. Lord Darcy's powerful hand came down twice in a deft neck-chop, and both men dropped to the floor unconscious.

"Come on down, my lord," said Lord Darcy. "There will be no need for swordplay."

Lord Seiger descended the ladder in silence, his sword sheathed.

There were two cell doors on either side of the

passageway; the cells themselves had been built to discipline crewmen or to imprison sailors or passengers who were accused of crime on the high seas while the ship was in passage. The first cell on the right had a dim light glowing within it. The yellowish light gleamed through the small barred window in the door.

Both Lord Darcy and Lord Seiger walked over to the door and looked inside.

"That's what I was looking for," Lord Darcy breathed.

Within, strapped to a bunk, was a still, white-faced figure. The face was exactly similar to that of the corpse Lord Darcy had seen in the morgue.

"Are you sure it's the Marquis of Cherbourg?" Lord Seiger asked.

"I refuse to admit that there are *three* men who look that much alike," Lord Darcy whispered dryly. "Two are quite enough. Since Master Sean established that the body in the morgue was definitely *not* related to my lord of Guernsey and Sark, *this* must be the Marquis. Now, the problem will be getting the cell door open."

"I vill open idt for you."

At the sound of the voice behind them, both Lord Darcy and Lord Seiger froze.

"To qvote you, Lord Darcy, 'If either of you moves, I vill shoodt him through the brain,'" said the voice. "Drop de gun, Lord Darcy."

As Lord Darcy let his pistol drop from his hand, his mind raced.

The shock of having been trapped, such as it had been, had passed even before the voice be-

hind him had ceased. Shock of that kind could
not hold him frozen long. Nor was his the kind
of mind that grew angry with itself for making a
mistake. There was no time for that.

He had been trapped. Someone had been hidden in the cell across the passageway, waiting for
him. A neat trap. Very well; the problem was,
how to get out of that trap.

"Bot' of you step to de left," said the voice.
"Move avay from de cell port. Dat's it. Fine.
Open de door, Ladislas."

There were two men, both holding guns. The
shorter, darker of the two stepped forward and
opened the door to the cell next to that in which
the still figure of the Marquis of Cherbourg lay.

"Bot' of you step inside," said the taller of the
two men who had trapped the Imperial agents.

There was nothing Lord Seiger and Lord
Darcy could do but obey.

"Keep you de hands high in de air. Dat's fine.
Now listen to me, and listen carefully. You t'ink
you have taken dis ship. In a vay, you have. But
not finally. I have you. I have de Marquis. You
vill order your men off. Odervise, I vill kill all of
you—vun adt a time. Understand? If I hang, I
do not die alone."

Lord Darcy understood. "You want your
crew back, eh, Captain Olsen? And how will you
get by the Royal Navy?"

"De same way I will get out of Cherbourg har-
bor, Lord Darcy," the captain said complacently. "I vill promise release. You vill be able to go
back home from Danzig. Vot goodt is any of
you to us now?"

None, except as hostages, Lord Darcy
thought. What had happened was quite clear.
Somehow, someone had managed to signal to
Captain Olsen that his ship was being taken. A
signal from the bridge, perhaps. It didn't matter.
Captain Olsen had not been expecting invaders,
but when they had come, he had devised a neat
trap. He had known where the invaders would
be heading.

Up to that point, Lord Darcy knew, the Polish
agents had planned to take the unconscious
Marquis to Danzig. There, he would be operated
on by a sorcerer and sent back to Cherbourg—
apparently in good condition, but actually under
the control of Polish agents. His absence would
be explained by his "spells," which would no
longer be in evidence. But now that Captain
Olsen knew that the plot had been discovered, he
had no further use for the Marquis. Nor had he
any use for either Lord Darcy or Lord Seiger.
Except that he could use them as hostages to get
his ship to Danzig.

"What do you want, Captain Olsen?" Lord
Darcy asked quietly.

"Very simply, dis: You vill order de soldiers to
come below. Ve vill lock them up. Ven my men
vake up, and de rest of de crew come aboard, ve
vill sail at dawn. Ven ve are ready to sail, all may
go ashore except you and Lord Seiger and de
Marquis. Your men vill tell de officials in
Cherbourg vhat has happened and vill tell dem
dat ve vill sail to Danzig unmolested. Dere, you

vill be set free and sent back to Imperial territory
I give you my vord."

Oddly, Lord Darcy realized that the man
meant it. Lord Darcy knew that the man's word
was good. But was he responsible for the reactions of the Polish officials at Danzig? Was he
responsible for the reactions of Casimir IX? No.
Certainly not.

But, trapped as they were—

And then a hoarse voice came from across the
passageway, from the fourth cell.

"Seiger? Seiger?"

Lord Seiger's eyes widened. "Yes?"

Captain Olsen and First Officer Ladislas remained unmoved. The captain smiled
sardonically. "Ah, yes. I forgot to mention your
so-brave Sir James le Lein. He vill make an excellent hostage, too."

The hoarse voice said: "They are traitors to
the King, Seiger. Do you hear me?"

"I hear you, Sir James," said Lord Seiger.

"Destroy them," said the hoarse voice.

Captain Olsen laughed. "Shut up, le Lein.
You—"

But he never had time to finish.

Lord Darcy watched with unbelieving eyes as
Lord Seiger's right hand darted out with blurring speed and slapped aside the captain's gun.
At the same time, his left hand drew his rapier
and slashed out toward the first officer.

The first officer had been covering Lord
Darcy. When he saw Lord Seiger move, he
swung his gun toward Lord Seiger and fired. The

slug tore into the Yorkshire nobleman's side as
Captain Olsen spun away and tried to bring his
own weapon to bear.

By that time, Lord Darcy himself was in action. His powerful legs catapulted him toward
First Officer Ladislas just as the point of Lord
Seiger's rapier slashed across Ladislas' chest,
making a deep cut over the ribs. Then Ladislas
was slammed out into the passageway by Lord
Darcy's assault.

After that, Lord Darcy had too much to do to
pay any attention to what went on between Lord
Seiger and Captain Olsen. Apparently oblivious
to the blood gushing from the gash on his chest,
Ladislas fought with steel muscles. Darcy knew
his own strength, but he also knew that this op-
ponent was of nearly equal strength. Darcy held
the man's right wrist in a vise grip to keep him
from bringing the pistol around. Then he
smashed his head into Ladislas' jaw. The gun
dropped and spun away as both men fell to the
deck.

Lord Darcy brought his right fist up in a
smashing blow to the first officer's throat; gag-
ging, the first officer collapsed.

Lord Darcy pushed himself to his knees and
grabbed the unconscious man by the collar, pulling him half upright.

At that second, a tongue of steel flashed by
Lord Darcy's shoulder, plunged itself into
Ladislas' throat, and tore sideways. The first of-
ficer died as his blood spurted fountainlike over
Lord Darcy's arm.

After a moment, Lord Darcy realized that the fight was over. He turned his head.

Lord Seiger stood nearby, his sword red. Captain Olsen lay on the deck, his life's blood flowing from three wounds—two in the chest, and the third, like his first officer's, a slash across the throat.

"I had him," Lord Darcy said unevenly. "There was no need to cut his throat."

For the first time, he saw a slight smile on Lord Seiger's face.

"I had my orders, my lord," said Seiger, as his side dripped crimson.

With twelve sonorous, resounding strokes, the great Bell of the Benedictine Church of Saint Denys, in the courtyard of Castle Cherbourg, sounded the hour of midnight. Lord Darcy, freshly bathed and shaved and clad in his evening wear, stood before the fireplace in the reception room above the Great Hall and waited patiently for the bell to finish its tally. Then he turned and smiled at the young man standing beside him. "As you were saying, Your Highness?"

Richard, Duke of Normandy, smiled back. "Even royalty can't drown out a church bell, eh, my lord?" Then his face became serious again. "I was saying that we have made a clean sweep. Dunkerque, Calais, Boulogne ... all the way down to Hendaye. By now, the English Armsmen will be picking them up in London, Liverpool, and so on. By dawn, Ireland will be clear. You've done a magnificent job, my lord, and you may rest assured that my brother the King will hear of it."

"Thank you, Your Highness, but I really—"

Lord Darcy was interrupted by the opening of the door. Lord Seiger came in, then stopped as he saw Duke Richard.

The Duke reacted instantly. "Don't bother to bow, my lord. I have been told of your wound."

Lord Seiger nevertheless managed a slight bow. "Your Highness is most gracious. But the wound is a slight one, and Father Patrique has laid his hands on it. The pain is negligible, Highness."

"I am happy to hear so." The Duke looked at Lord Darcy. "By the way ... I am curious to know what made you suspect that Lord Seiger was a King's Agent. I didn't know, myself, until the King, my brother, sent me the information I requested."

"I must confess that I was not certain until Your Highness verified my suspicions on the teleson. But it seemed odd to me that de Cherbourg would have wanted a man of Lord Seiger's ... ah ... peculiar talents merely as a librarian. Then, too, Lady Elaine's attitude ... er, your pardon, my lord—"

"Perfectly all right, my lord," said Lord Seiger expressionlessly. "I am aware that many women find my presence distasteful—although I confess I do not know why."

"Who can account for the behavior of women?" Lord Darcy said. "Your manners and behavior are impeccable. Nonetheless, My Lady

Marquise found, as you say, your presence distasteful. She must have made this fact known to her husband the Marquis, eh?"

"I believe she did, my lord," said Lord Seiger.

"Very well," said Lord Darcy. "Would My Lord Marquis, who is notoriously in love with his wife, have kept a *librarian* who frightened her? No. Therefore, either Lord Seiger's purpose here was much more important—or he was blackmailing the Marquis. I chose to believe the former." He did not add that Father Patrique's information showed that it was impossible for Lord Seiger to blackmail anyone.

"My trouble lay in not knowing who was working for whom. We knew only that Sir James was masquerading as a common working man, and that he was working with My Lord Marquis. But until Your Highness got in touch with His Majesty, we knew nothing more. I was working blind until I realized that Lord Seiger—"

He stopped as he heard the door open. From outside came Master Sean's voice: "After you, my lady, my lord, Sir Gwiliam."

The Marquise de Cherbourg swept into the room, her fair face an expressionless mask. Behind her came My Lord Bishop and Sir Gwiliam, followed by Master Sean O Lochlainn.

Lady Elaine walked straight to Duke Richard. She made a small curtsy. "Your presence is an honor, Your Highness." She was quite sober.

"The honor is mine, my lady," replied the Duke.

"I have seen my lord husband. He is alive, as I knew he was. But his mind is gone. Father Patrique says he will never recover. I must know what has happened, Your Highness."

"You will have to ask Lord Darcy that, my lady," the Duke said gently. "I should like to hear the complete story myself."

My lady turned her steady gaze on the lean Englishman. "Begin at the beginning and tell me everything, my lord. I must know."

The door opened again, and Sir Androu Duglasse came in. "Good morning, Y' Highness," he said with a low bow. "Good morning, m'lady, y' lordships, Sir Gwiliam, Master Sean." His eyes went back to Lady Elaine. "I've heard the news from Father Patrique, m'lady. I'm a soldier, m'lady, not a man who can speak well. I cannot tell you of the sorrow I feel."

"I thank you, Sir Captain," said my lady, "I think you have expressed it very well." Her eyes went back to Lord Darcy. "If you please, my lord . . ."

"As you command, my lady," said Lord Darcy. "Er . . . captain, I don't think that what I have to say need be known by any others than those of us here. Would you watch the door? Explain to anyone else that this is a private conference. Thank you. Then I can begin." He leaned negligently against the fireplace, where he could see everyone in the room.

"To begin with, we had a hellish plot afoot— not against just one person, but against the Empire. The 'Atlantic Curse'. Ships sailing from Imperial ports to the New World were never heard from again. Shipping was dropping off badly, not only from ship losses, but because fear kept seamen off trans-Atlantic ships. They feared magic, although, as I shall show, pure magic had nothing to do with it.

"My lord the Marquis was working with Sir James le Lein, one of a large group of King's Agents with direct commissions to discover the cause of the 'Atlantic Curse'. His Majesty had correctly deduced that the whole thing was a Polish plot to disrupt Imperial economy.

"The plot was devilish in its simplicity. A drug, made by steeping a kind of mushroom in brandy, was being used to destroy the minds of the crews of trans-Atlantic ships. Taken in small dosages, over a period of time, the drug causes violent insanity. A ship with an insane crew cannot last long in the Atlantic.

"Sir James, working with My Lord Marquis and other agents, tried to get a lead on what was going on. My Lord Marquis, not wanting anyone in the castle to know of his activities, used the old secret tunnel that leads to the city sewers in order to meet Sir James.

"Sir James obtained a sample of the drug after he had identified the ringleader of the Polish agents. He reported to My Lord Marquis. Then, on the evening of Wednesday, the eighth of January, Sir James set out to obtain more evidence. He went to the warehouse where the ringleader had his headquarters."

Lord Darcy paused and smiled slightly. "By the by, I must say that the details of what happened in the warehouse were supplied to me by

Sir James. My own deductions only gave me a pat of the story.

"At any rate, Sir James obtained entry to the second floor of the warehouse. He heard voices. Silently, he went to the door of the room from which the voices came and looked in through the . . . er . . . the keyhole. It was dark in the corridor, but well-lit in the room.

"What he saw was a shock to him. Two men —a sorcerer and the ringleader himself—were there. The sorcerer was standing by a bed, weaving a spell over a third man, who lay naked on the bed. One look at the man in the bed convinced Sir James that the man was none other than the Marquis of Cherbourg himself!"

Lady Elaine touched her fingertips to her lips. "Had he been poisoned by the drug, my lord?" she asked. "Was that what had been affecting his mind?"

"The man was not your husband, my lady," Lord Darcy said gently. "He was a double, a simple-minded man in the pay of these men.

"Sir James, of course, had no way of knowing that. When he saw the Marquis in danger, he acted. Weapon in hand, he burst open the door and demanded the release of the man whom he took to be the Marquis. He told the man to get up. Seeing he was hypnotized, Sir James put his own cloak about the man's shoulders and the two of them began to back out of the room, his weapon covering the sorcerer and the ringleader.

"But there was another man in the warehouse. Sir James never saw him. This person struck him from behind as he backed out the door.

"Sir James was dazed. He dropped his weapon. The sorcerer and the ringleader jumped him. Sir James fought, but he was eventually rendered unconscious.

"In the meantime, the man whom Sir James attempted to rescue became frightened and fled. In the darkness, he tumbled down a flight of oaken stairs and fractured his skull on one of the lower steps. Hurt, dazed, and dying, he fled from the warehouse toward the only other place in Cherbourg he could call home—a bistro called the Blue Dolphin, a few blocks away. He very nearly made it. He died a block from it, in the sight of two Armsmen."

"Did they intend to use the double for some sort of impersonation of my brother?" asked the Bishop.

"In a way, my lord. I'll get to that in a moment.

"When I came here," Lord Darcy continued, "I of course knew nothing of all this. I knew only that my lord of Cherbourg was missing and that he had been working with His Majesty's Agents. Then a body was tentatively identified as his. If it *were* the Marquis, who had killed him? If it were not, what was the connection? I went to see Sir James and found that he had been missing since the same night. Again, what was the connection?

"The next clue was the identification of the drug. How could such a drug be introduced aboard ships so that almost every man would take a little each day? The taste and aroma of the brandy would be apparent in the food or water.

Obviously, then, the wine rations were drugged. And only the vintner who supplied the wine could have regularly drugged the wine of ship after ship.

"A check of the Shipping Registry showed that new vintners had bought out old wineries in shipping ports throughout the Empire in the past five years. All of them, subsidized by the Poles, could underbid their competitors. They made good wine and sold it cheaper than others could sell it. They got contracts. They didn't try to poison every ship; only a few of those on the Atlantic run—just enough to start a scare while keeping suspicion from themselves.

"There was still the problem of what had happened to My Lord Marquis. He had *not* left the castle that night. And yet he had disappeared. But how? And why?

"There were four places that the captain had not searched. I dismissed the icehouse when I discovered that people went in and out of it all day. He could not have gone to the strongroom because the door is too wide for one man to use both keys simultaneously—which must be done to open it. Sir Gwiliam had been in and out of the wine cellar. And there were indications that the tunnel had also had visitors."

"Why should he have been in any of those places, my lord?" Sir Gwiliam asked. "Mightn't he have simply left through the tunnel?"

"Hardly likely. The tunnel guard was a King's Agent. If the Marquis had gone out that night and never returned, he would have reported the fact—not to Captain Sir Androu, but to Lord

Seiger. He did not so report. Ergo, the Marquis
did not leave the castle that night."

"Then what happened to him?" Sir Gwiliam
asked.

"That brings us back to the double, Paul
Sarto," said Lord Darcy. "Would you explain,
Master Sean?"

"Well, my lady, gentle sirs," the little sorcerer
began, "My Lord Darcy deduced the use of
magic here. This Polish sorcerer—a piddling
poor one, he is, too; when I caught him in the
warehouse, he tried to cast a few spells at me and
they were nothing. He ended up docile as a lamb
when I gave him a dose of good Irish sorcery."

"Proceed, Master Sean," Lord Darcy said
dryly.

"Beggin' your pardon, my lord. Anyway, this
Polish sorcerer saw that this Paul chap was a
dead ringer for My Lord Marquis and decided
to use him to control My Lord Marquis—Law
of Similarity, d' ye see. You know the business
of sticking pins in wax dolls? Crude method of
psychic induction, but effective if the similarity
is great enough. And what could be more similar
to a man than his double?"

"You mean they used this poor unfortunate
man as a wax doll?" asked the Marquise in a
hushed voice.

"That's about it, your ladyship. In order for
the spells to work, though, the double would
have to have very low mind power. Well, he did.
So they hired him away from his old job and
went to work on him. They made him bathe and
wear fine clothes, and slowly took control of his

mind. They told him that he *was* the Marquis.
With that sort of similarity achieved, they hoped
to control the Marquis himself just as they controlled his simulacrum."

My Lady Elaine looked horrified. "*That*
caused his terrible attacks?"

"Exactly, your ladyship. When My Lord Marquis was tired or distracted, they were able to
take over for a little while. A vile business no
proper sorcerer would stoop to, but workable."

"But what did they do to my husband?" asked
the Lady of Cherbourg.

"Well, now your ladyship," said Master Sean,
"what do you suppose would happen to his
lordship when his simulacrum got his skull
crushed so bad that it killed the simulacrum?
The shock to his lordship's mind was so great
that it nearly killed him on the spot—*would* have
killed him, too, if the similarity had been better
established. He fell into a coma, my lady."

Lord Darcy took up the story again. "The
Marquis dropped where he was. He remained in
the castle until last night, when the Polish agents
came to get him. They killed the King's Agent
on guard, disposed of the body, came in through
the tunnel, got the Marquis, and took him to
their ship. When Captain Sir Androu told me
that the guard had 'deserted', I knew fully what
had happened. I knew that My Lord Marquis
was either in the vintner's warehouse or in a ship
bound for Poland. The two raids show that I was
correct."

"Do you mean," said Sir Gwiliam, "that my lord lay in that chilly tunnel all that time? How horrible!"

Lord Darcy looked at the man for long seconds. "No. Not *all* that time, Sir Gwiliam. No one—especially not the Polish agents—would have known he was there. He was taken to the tunnel after he was found the next morning—in the wine cellar."

"Ridiculous!" said Sir Gwiliam, startled. "I'd have seen him!"

"Most certainly you would have," Lord Darcy agreed. "And most certainly you *did*. It must have been quite a shock to return home after the fight in the warehouse to find the Marquis unconscious on the wine cellar floor. Once I knew you were the guilty man, I knew you had given away your employer. You told me that you had played cards with Ordwin Vayne that night; therefore I knew which vintner to raid."

White-faced, Sir Gwiliam said, "I have served my lord and lady faithfully for many years. I say you lie."

"Oh?" Lord Darcy's eyes were hard. "Someone had to tell Ordwin Vayne where the Marquis was—someone who *knew* where he was. Only the Marquis, Sir Androu, and *you* had keys to the tunnel. I saw the captain's key; it was dull and filmed when I used it. The wards of the old lock left little bright scratches on it. He hadn't used it for a long time. Only *you* had a key that would let Ordwin Vayne and his men into that tunnel."

"Pah! Your reasoning is illogical! If My Lord Marquis were unconscious, someone could have taken the key off him!"

"Not if he was in the tunnel. Why would anyone go there? The tunnel door was locked, so, even, if he *were* there, a key would have to have been used to find him. But if he had fallen in the tunnel, he would still have been there when I looked. There was no reason for you or anyone else to unlock that tunnel—*until* you were looking for a place to conceal My Lord Marquis' unconscious body!"

"Why would he have gone to the wine cellar?" Sir Gwiliam snapped. "And why lock himself in?"

"He went down to check on some bottles you had in the wine cellar. Sir James' report led him to suspect you. Warehouses and wineries are subjected to rigorous inspection. Ordwin Vayne didn't want inspectors to find that he was steeping mushrooms in brandy. So the bottles were kept *here*—the safest place in Cherbourg. Who would suspect? The Marquis never went there. But he did suspect at last, and went down to check. He locked the door because he didn't want to be interrupted. No one but you could come in, and he would be warned if you put your key in the lock. While he was there, the simulacrumized Paul fell and struck his head on an oaken step. Paul died. The Marquis went comatose.

"When I arrived yesterday, you had to get rid of the evidence. So Vayne's men came and took the bottles of drug and the Marquis. If further proof is needed, I can tell you that we found the drug on the ship, in restoppered bottles containing cheap brandy and bits of mushroom. *But the bottles were labeled Saint Couerlandt Michele '46!* Who else in Cherbourg but you would have access to such empty bottles?"

Sir Gwiliam stepped back. "Lies! All lies!"

"No!" snapped a voice from the door. "Truth! All truth!"

Lord Darcy had seen Captain Sir Androu silently open the door and let in three more men, but no one else had. Now the others turned at the sound of the voice.

Sitting in a wheelchair, looking pale but still strong, was Hugh, Marquis of Cherbourg. Behind him was Sir James le Lein. To one side stood Father Patrique.

"What Lord Darcy said is true in every particular," said my lord the Marquis in an icy voice.

Sir Gwiliam gasped and jerked his head around to look at my lady the Marquise. "You said his mind was gone!"

"A small lie—to trap a traitor." Her voice was icy.

"Sir Gwiliam de Bracy," said Sir James from behind the Marquis, "in the King's Name, I charge you with treason!"

Two things happened almost at once. Sir Gwiliam's hand started for his pocket. But by then, Lord Seiger's sword, with its curious offset hilt, was halfway from its sheath. By the time Sir Gwiliam had his pistol out, the sword had slashed through his jugular vein. Sir Gwiliam

had just time to turn and fire once before he fell
to the floor.

Lord Seiger stood there, looking down at Sir
Gwiliam, an odd smile on his face.

For a second, no one spoke or moved. Then
Father Patrique rushed over to the fallen seneschal. He was too late by far. With all his Healing power, there was nothing he could do now.

And then the Marquise walked over to Lord
Seiger and took his free hand. "My lord, others
may censure you for that act. I do not. That
monster helped send hundreds of innocent men
to insanity and death. He almost did the same
for my beloved Hugh. If anything, he died too
clean a death. I do not censure you, my lord. I
thank you."

"I thank you, my lady. But I only did my
duty." There was an odd thickness in his voice.
"I had my orders, my lady."

And then, slowly, like a deflating balloon,
Lord Seiger slumped to the floor.

Lord Darcy and Father Patrique realized at
the same moment that Sir Gwiliam's bullet must
have hit Lord Seiger, though he had shown no
sign of it till then.

Lord Seiger had had no conscience, but he
could not kill or even defend himself of his own
accord. Sir James had been his decision-maker.
Lord Seiger had been a King's Agent who would
kill without qualm on order from Sir James—
and was otherwise utterly harmless. The decision
was never left up to him, only to Sir James.

Sir James, still staring at the fallen Lord

Seiger, said: "But . . . how could he? I didn't tell him to."

"Yes, you did," Lord Darcy said wearily. "On the ship. You told him to destroy the traitors. When you called Sir Gwiliam a traitor, he acted. He had his sword halfway out before Sir Gwiliam drew that pistol. He would have killed Sir Gwiliam in cold blood if the seneschal had never moved at all. He was like a gas lamp, Sir James. You turned him on—and forgot to shut him off."

Richard, Duke of Normandy, looked down at the fallen man. Lord Seiger's face was oddly unchanged. It had rarely had any expression in life. It had none now.

"How is he, Reverend Father?" asked the Duke.

"He is dead, Your Highness."

"May the Lord have mercy on his soul," said Duke Richard.

Eight men and a woman made the Sign of the Cross in silence.

THE MUDDLE OF THE WOAD

Both pain and pride were sending their coun-
terbalancing energies through the nervous system of Walter Gotobed, Master Cabinetmaker
for His Grace, the Duke of Kent, as he opened
the door of his workshop. The pain, like the
pride, was mental in origin; in spite of his
ninety-odd years, Master Walter was still
blessed with strength in his wiry body and
steadiness in his careful hands. With his spec-
tacles perched properly on his large, thin, bony
nose, he could still draw an accurate plan for
anything from a closet to a cigar box. Come next
Trinity Sunday, the twenty-fourth of May, the
Year of Our Lord 1964, Master Walter would be
celebrating his fiftieth anniversary of his appointment as Master Cabinetmaker to the Duke.
He was now on his second Duke, the Old Duke
having died in 1927, and would serve a third
before long. The Dukes of Kent were long-lived,
but a man who works with fine woods, absorb-
ing the strength and the agelessness of the great
trees from which they come, lives longer still.

The workshop was full of woody smells—the
spiciness of cedar, the richness of oak, the warm
tang of plain pine, the fruity sweetness of apple

—and the early morning sunlight coming in through the windows cast gleaming highlights on the cabinets and desks and chairs and tables that filled the shop in various stages of progress. This was Master Walter's world, the atmosphere in which he worked and lived.

Behind Master Walter came three more men: Journeyman Henry Lavender and the two apprentices, Tom Wilderspin and Harry Venable. They followed the Master in, and the four of them walked purposefully towards a magnificent creation in polished walnut that reposed on a bench in one corner. Two paces from it, Master Walter stopped.

"How does it look, Henry?" Master Walter asked without turning his head.

Journeyman Henry, not yet forty, but already having about him the tone of a woodcraftsman, nodded with satisfaction and said: "Very beautiful, Master Walter, very beautiful." It was honest appreciation, not flattery, that spoke.

"I think Her Grace the Duchess will be pleased, eh?" the old man said.

"More than pleased, Master. Mm-m-m. There's a bit of dust on it, even since last night. You, Tom! Get a clean rag with a little lemon oil on it and give it another polish." As Tom the 'prentice scampered off in obedience, Henry Lavender continued: "His Grace the Duke will appreciate your work, Master; it's one of the finest things you've turned out for him."

"Aye. And that's something you must remember, Henry—and something you two lads must get through your heads. It's not fancy carving that makes the beauty of wood; it's the wood itself. Carving's all right in its place, mind you; I've nothing against carving if it's properly done. But the beauty's in the wood. Something plain like this, without fanciness, without ornament, shows that wood, *as wood,* is a creation of God that can't be improved upon. All you can ever hope to do is bring out the beauty that God Himself put there. Here, give me that rag, young Tom; I'll put the final polish on this myself." As he moved the oily rag, with its faint lemon scent, over the broad, flat surface, Master Walter went on: "Careful craftsmanship is what does it, lads. Careful craftsmanship. Each piece joined solidly to the next, glued tightly, screws in firmly, with no gaps or spaces—that's what makes *good* work. Matching the grain, carefully choosing your pieces, planing and sanding to a perfect surface, applying your finish, wax or varnish or shellac, to a fine smoothness—that's what makes it *fine* work. And design—ah, *design—that* makes it *art!*

"All right, now, you, Tom, take the front end. Harry, you take the other. We've a stairway to climb, but you're both strong lads and it's not too heavy. Besides, a joiner and cabinetmaker must have strong muscles to do his work and the exercise will be good for the both of you."

Obediently, the 'prentices grasped the ends they had been assigned and lifted. They had carried it before and knew to a pound how much it weighed. They heaved upwards.

And the beautifully polished walnut scarcely moved.

"Here! What's the matter?" said Master Walter. "You almost dropped it!"

"It's *heavy*, Master," said Tom. "There's somethin' in it."

"Something in it?" How could there be?" Master Walter reached out, lifted the lid. And almost dropped it again. "Good God!"

Then there was a stunned silence as the four men looked at the thing that lay within.

"A dead man," said Journeyman Henry after a moment.

That was obvious. The corpse was certainly a corpse. The eyelids were sunken and the skin waxy. The man was thoroughly, completely dead.

To make the horror even worse, the nude body—from crown of head to tip of toe—was a deep, almost indigo, blue.

Master Walter found his breath again. His feelings of surprise and horror had vanished beneath a wave of indignation. "But he don't belong here! He's got no right! No right at all!"

"Daresay it ain't his fault, Master Walter," Journeyman Henry ventured. "He didn't get there by himself."

"No," said Master Walter, gaining control of himself. "No, of course not. But what a *peculiar* place to find a corpse!"

In spite of his own feelings, it was all Apprentice Tom could do to suppress a snigger.

What better place to find a corpse than in a coffin?

Even the most dedicated of men enjoys a holiday now and then, and Lord Darcy, Chief Criminal Investigator for His Royal Highness, Prince Richard, Duke of Normandy, was no exception. He not only enjoyed his work, but preferred it above all others. His keen mind found satisfaction in solving the kind of problems that, by the very nature of the work, were continually being brought to his attention. But he also knew that a one-track brain became stale very shortly—and besides he enjoyed letting his mind drift for a while.

Then, too, there was the pleasure of coming home to England. France was fine. It was an important part of the Empire, and working for His Highness was pleasurable. But England was his home, and getting back to England once a year was . . . well, a relief. In spite of the fact that England and France had been one country for eight hundred years, the differences were still enough to make an Englishman feel faintly foreign in France. And, he supposed, vice-versa.

Lord Darcy stood at one side of the ballroom and surveyed the crowd. The orchestra was pausing between numbers, and the floor was full of people talking, waiting for the next dance. He took a drink from the whisky-and-water that he had been nursing along. This sort of thing, he congratulated himself, palled within two weeks, while his real work took fifty weeks to become irritating. Still, each was a relief from the other.

Baron Dartmoor was a decent sort, an excellent chess player, and a good man with a story now and then. Lady Dartmoor had a knack of picking the right people to come to a dinner or a ball. But one couldn't stay forever at Dartmoor House, and London society wasn't everything it was assumed to be by those who didn't live there.

Lord Darcy found himself thinking that it would be good to get back to Rouen on the twenty-second of May.

"Lord Darcy, do pardon me, but something has come up."

Darcy turned at the sound of the woman's voice and smiled. "Oh?"

"Will you come with me?"

"Certainly, my lady."

He followed her, but there was a nervousness in her manner, a tautness in her behavior, that told him there was something out of the ordinary here.

At the door to the library, she paused. "My lord, there is a . . . a gentleman who wishes to speak to you. In the library."

"A gentleman? Who is he, my lady?"

"I—" Lady Dartmoor drew herself up and took a breath. "I am not at liberty to say, my lord. He will introduce himself."

"I see." Lord Darcy unobtrusively put his hands behind his back and with his right hand drew a small pistol from the holster concealed by the tails of his green dress coat. This didn't exactly have the smell of a trap, but there was no reason to be careless.

Lady Dartmoor opened the door. "Lord Darcy, S . . . sir."

"Show him in, my lady," said a voice from within.

Lord Darcy went in, his pistol still concealed behind his back and beneath his coattails. Behind him, he heard the door close.

The man was standing with his back to the door, looking out the window at the lighted streets of London. "Lord Darcy," he said without turning. "if you are the man I have been brought to believe you are, you are dangerously close to committing the capital crime of High Treason."

But Lord Darcy, after one look at that back, had reholstered his pistol and dropped to one knee. "As Your Majesty knows, I would rather die than commit treason against Your Majesty."

The man turned, and for the first time in his life Lord Darcy found himself face to face with His Imperial Majesty, John IV, King and Emperor of England, France, Scotland, Ireland, New England, New France, Defender of the Faith, et cetera.

He looked a great deal like his younger brother, Richard of Normandy—tall, blond, and handsome, like all the Plantagenets. But he was ten years older than Duke Richard, and the difference showed. The King was only a few years younger than Lord Darcy, but the lines in his face made him look older.

"Rise, my lord," said His Majesty. He smiled. "You *did* have a gun in your hand, didn't you?"

"I did, Your Majesty," Lord Darcy said, rising smoothly. "My apologies, Sire."

"Not at all. Only what I should have expected of a man of your capabilities. Please be seated.

We will not be interrupted; my lady of Dartmoor will see to that. Thank you. We have a problem, Lord Darcy."

Darcy seated himself and the King took a chair facing him. "For the time being, my lord," said the King, "we shall forget rank. Don't interrupt me until I have given you all the data I have. Then you may ask questions as you will."

"Yes, Sire."

"Very well. I have a job for you, my lord. I know you are on holiday, and it pains me to interrupt your leisure—but this needs looking into. You are aware of the activities of the so-called Holy Society of Ancient Albion."

It was a statement, not a question. Lord Darcy and every other Officer of the King's Justice knew of the Society of Albion. They were more than just a secret society; they were a pagan sect which repudiated the Christian Church. They were reputed to dabble in Black Magic, they practiced a form of nature-worship, and they claimed direct organizational descent from the pre-Roman Druids. The Society, after a period of toleration during the last century, had been outlawed. Some said that it had remained in hiding during all the centuries since the triumph of Christianity and had only revealed itself during the easy-going Nineteenth Century, others said that its claim of antiquity was false, that it had been organized during the 1820s by the eccentric, perhaps slightly mad, Sir Edward Finnely. Probably both versions were partly true.

They had been outlawed because of their out-

spoken advocation of human sacrifice. Rejecting
the Church's teaching that the Sacrifice of the
Cross obviated for all time any further sacrifice
of human life, the Society insisted that in times
of trouble the King himself should die for the
sake of his people. The evidence that William II,
son of the Conqueror, had been killed "by an
arrow offshot" by one of his own men for just
that purpose added weight to the story of the antiquity of the Society. William Rufus, it was believed, had been a pagan himself, and had gone
willingly to his death—but it was not likely that
any modern Anglo-French monarch would do
so.

Originally, it had been one of the tenets of
their belief that the sacrificial victim must die
willingly, even gladly; mere assassination would
be pointless and utterly lacking in efficacy. But
the increasing tension between the Empire and
the Kingdom of Poland had wrought a change.
This was a time of troubles, said the Society, and
the King must die, will he or no. Evidence
showed that such sentiments had been carefully
instilled in the membership of the Society by
agents of King Casimir IX himself.

"I doubt," said King John, "that the Society
poses any real threat to the Imperial Government. There simply aren't that many fanatics in
England. But a King is as vulnerable to a lone
assassin—especially a fanatic—as any one else. I
do not consider myself indispensable to the Empire; if my death would benefit the people, I
would go to the block today. As it is, however, I

rather feel that I should like to go on living for a time.

"My own agents, I must tell you, have infiltrated the Society successfully. Thus far, they have reported that there is no hint of any really organized attempt to do away with me. But now something new has come up.

"This morning, shortly before seven o'clock, His Grace the Duke of Kent passed away. It was not unexpected. He was only sixty-two, but his health had been failing for some time and he has been failing rapidly for the past three weeks. The best Healers were called in, but the Reverend Fathers said that when a man has resigned himself to dying there is nothing the Church can do.

"At exactly seven o'clock, the Duke's Master Cabinetmaker went into his shop to get the coffin that had been prepared for His Grace. He found it already occupied—by the body of Lord Camberton, Chief Investigator for the Duchy of Kent.

"He had been stabbed—*and his body was dyed blue!*"

Lord Darcy's eyes narrowed.

"It is not known," the King continued, "how long Lord Camberton has been dead. It is possible that a preservative spell was cast over the body. He was last seen in Kent three weeks ago, when he left for a holiday in Scotland. We don't know yet if he ever arrived, though I should get a report by teleson very shortly. Those are the facts as I know them. Are there any questions, Lord Darcy?"

"None, Sire." There was no point in asking the King questions which could be better answered in Canterbury.

"My brother Richard," said the King, "has a high regard for your abilities and has communicated to me in detail regarding you. I have full respect for his judgment, which was fully borne out by your handling of the 'Atlantic Curse' case last January. My personal agents, working for months, had got nowhere; you penetrated to the heart of the matter in two days. Therefore, I am appointing you as Special Investigator for the High Court of Chivalry." He handed Lord Darcy a document which he had produced from an inside coat pocket. "I came here incognito," he went on, "because I do not want it known that I am taking a personal interest in this case. As far as the public is to know, this was a decision by the Lord Chancellor—quite routine. I want you to go to Canterbury and find out *who* killed Lord Camberton and *why*. I have no data. I want you to get me the data I need."

"I am honored, Sire," said Lord Darcy, pocketing the commission. "Your wish is my command."

"Excellent. A train leaves for Canterbury in an hour and"—His Majesty glanced at his wrist watch—"seven minutes. Can you make it?"

"Certainly, Sire."

"Fine. I have made arrangements for you to stay at the Archbishop's Palace—that will be easier, I think, and more politic than putting you in with the Ducal family. His Grace the Archbishop knows that I am interested in this case; so does Sir Thomas Leseaux. No one else does."

Lord Darcy raised an eyebrow. "Sir Thomas Leseaux, Sire? The theoretical thaumaturgist?"

The King's smile was that of a man who has perpetrated a successful surprise. "The same, my lord. A member of the Society of Albion—and my agent."

"Perfect, Sire," said Lord Darcy with a smile of appreciation. "One would hardly suspect a scientist of his standing of being either."

"I agree. Are there any further questions, my lord?"

"No. But I have a request, Sire. Sir Thomas, I understand, is not a practicing sorcerer—"

"Correct," said the King. "A theoretician only. He is perfecting something he calls the Theory of Subjective Congruency—whatever that may mean. He works entirely with the symbology of subjective algebra and leaves others to test his theories in practice."

Lord Darcy nodded. "Exactly, Sire. He could hardly be called an expert in forensic sorcery. I should like the aid of Master Sean O Lochlainn; we work well together, he and I. He is in Rouen at the moment. May I send word for him to come to Canterbury?"

His Majesty's smile grew broader. "I am happy to say that I have anticipated your request. I have already sent a teleson message to Dover. A trusted agent has already left on a special boat to Calais. He will teleson to Rouen and the boat

will be held for Master Sean at Calais to return
to Dover. From Dover, he can take the train to
Canterbury. The weather is good; he should ar-
rive some time tomorrow.''

"Sire," said Lord Darcy, "as long as the Imperial Crown decorates a head like yours, the
Empire cannot fail.''

"Neatly worded, my lord. We thank you.''
His Majesty rose from his chair and Lord Darcy
did likewise. His reversion to the royal first person plural indicated that they were no longer
speaking as man to man, but as Sovereign to
subject. "We give you carte blanche, my lord,
but there must be no further contact with Us unless absolutely necessary. When you are finished,
We want a complete and detailed report—for
Our eyes only. Arrangements for anything you
need will be made through His Grace the
Archbishop.''

"Very well, Your Majesty.''

"You have Our leave to go, Lord Darcy.''

"By Your Majesty's leave.'' Lord Darcy
dropped to one knee. By the time he had risen,
the King had turned his back and was once more
staring out the window—making it unnecessary
for Lord Darcy to back out of the room.

Lord Darcy turned and walked to the door.
As his hand touched the door handle, the King's
voice came again.

"One thing, Darcy.''

Lord Darcy turned to look, but the King still
had his back to him.

"Sire?''

"Watch yourself. I don't want you killed. I need men like you."

"Yes, Sire."

"Good luck, Darcy."

"Thank you, Sire."

Lord Darcy opened the door and went out, leaving the King alone with his thoughts.

Lord Darcy vaguely heard a bell. *Bon-n-n-ng. Bon-n-n-ng. Bon-n-n-ng.* Then a pause. During the pause, he drifted off again into sleep, but it was only a matter of seconds before the bell rang three more times. Lord Darcy came slightly more awake this time, but the second pause was almost enough to allow him to return to comfortable oblivion. At the third repetition of the three strokes, he recognized that the Angelus was ringing. It was six in the morning, and that meant that he had had exactly five hours sleep. During the final ringing of the nine strokes, he muttered the prayers rapidly, crossed himself, and closed his eyes again, resolving to go back to sleep until nine.

And, of course, couldn't sleep.

One eventually gets used to anything, he thought, feeling sleepily grumpy, *even great, clangy bells.* But the huge bronze monster in the bell tower of the cathedral church of Canterbury was not more than a hundred yards away in a direct line, and its sound made the very walls vibrate.

He pulled his head out of the pillows again, propped himself up to a sitting position, and looked around at the unfamiliar but pleasant bedroom which had been assigned him by His Grace the Archbishop. Then he looked out the window. At least the weather looked as if it would be fine.

He threw back the bedclothes, swung his legs over the edge of the bed, put his feet into his slippers, and then pulled the bell cord. He was just tying the cord of his crimson silk dressing gown—the one with the gold dragons embroidered on it—when the young monk opened the door. "Yes, my lord?"

"Just a pot of caffe and a little cream to match, Brother."

"Yes, my lord," the novice said.

By the time Lord Darcy had showered and shaved, the caffe was already waiting for him, and the young man in the Benedictine habit was standing by. "Anything else, my lord?"

"No, Brother; that will be all. Thank you."

"A pleasure, my lord." The novice went promptly.

That was one thing about the Benedictine novitiate, Lord Darcy reflected; it taught a young man from the lower classes how to behave like a gentleman and it taught humility to those who were gently born. There was no way of knowing whether the young man who had just come in was the son of a small farmer or a cadet of a noble family. If he hadn't been able to learn, he wouldn't have come even this far.

Lord Darcy sat down, sipped at the caffe, and thought. He had little enough information as yet. His Grace the Archbishop, a tall, widely-built,

elderly man with an impressive mane of white
hair and a kindly expression on his rather florid
face, had had no more information than Lord
Darcy had already received from the King. Via
teleson, Lord Darcy had contacted Sir Angus
MacReady, Chief Investigator for His Lordship
the Marquis of Edinburgh. Lord Camberton
had come to Scotland, all right; but it had not
been for a holiday. He had not told Sir Angus
what he was doing, but he had been engaged in
investigative work of some kind. Sir Angus had
promised to determine what that work had been.
"Aye, m' laird," he'd said, "I'll do the job
masel'. I'll no say a word tae anybody, and I'll
report tae ye direct."

Whether Lord Camberton's investigations in
Scotland had anything to do with the reason for
his being killed was an open question. The Holy
Society of Ancient Albion had very little following in Scotland, and the murder had almost certainly not taken place there. Taking a human
body from Edinburgh to Canterbury would be
so difficult that there would have to be a tremendous advantage to having the body found in
Canterbury that would outweigh the dangers of
transportation. He would not ignore the possibility, Lord Darcy decided, but until evidence
appeared that made it more probable, he would
look for the death spot closer to Canterbury.

The local Armsmen had definitely established
that Lord Camberton had not been killed in the
place where he was found. The deep stab wound
had, according to the chirurgeon, bled copiously
when it had been inflicted, but there was no

blood in the Duke's casket. Still, he would have
to investigate the cabinetmaker's shop himself;
the report of the Armsmen, relayed to him
through My Lord Archbishop, was not enough.

There would be no point in viewing the body
itself until Master Sean arrived; that blue dye job
had a definitely thaumaturgical feel about it,
Lord Darcy thought.

Meantime, he would stroll over to the ducal
castle and ask a few questions. But first, breakfast was definitely in order.

Master Walter Gotobed bowed and touched
his forehead as the gentleman entered the door
of his shop. "Yes, sir. What may I do for you,
sir?"

"You are Walter Gotobed, Master Cabinetmaker?" asked Lord Darcy.

"At your service, sir." said the old man politely.

"I am Lord Darcy, Special Investigator for
His Majesty's Court of Chivalry. I should like a
few moments of your time, Master Walter."

"Ah, yes. Certainly, your lordship." The old
man's eyes took on a pained expression. "About
Lord Camberton, I've no doubt. Will you come
this way, your lordship? Yes. Poor Lord Camberton, murdered like that; an awful thing, your
lordship. This is my office; we won't be disturbed here, your lordship. Would you care to
take this chair, your lordship? Here, just a moment, your lordship, let me dust the sawdust off
it. Sawdust *do* get everywhere, your lordship.
Now, what was it your lordship wanted to
know?"

"Lord Camberton's body was found here in your shop, I believe?" Lord Darcy asked.

"Ah, yes, your lordship, and a terrible thing it was, too, if I may say so. A terrible thing to have happen. Found him, so we did, in His Grace's coffin. The Healers had told me there wasn't much hope for His Grace, and Her Grace, the Duchess, asked me to make a specially nice one for His Grace, which of course I did, and yesterday morning when we came in, there he was, Lord Camberton, I mean, in the coffin where he didn't ought to be. All over blue he was, your lordship, all over blue. We didn't even recognize him because of that, not at first."

"Not an edifying sight, I dare say," Lord Darcy murmured. "Tell me what happened."

Master Walter did so, with exhausting particulars.

"You have no idea how he came here?" Lord Darcy asked when the recital was finished.

"None at all, your lordship; none at all. Chief Bertram asked us the same thing, your lordship, 'How did he get in here?' But none of us knew. The windows and the doors was all locked up tight and the back door barred. The only ones as has keys is me and my journeyman, Henry Lavender, and neither of us was here at all the night before. Chief Bertram thought maybe the 'prentices had put him in there as a practical joke —that was before Chief Bertram recognized who he was and thought they'd stole it from the Chirurgeon's College or something—but the boys swear they don't know nothing about it and I believe 'em, your lordship. They're good boys and they wouldn't pull anything like that on me. I said as much to Chief Bertram."

"I see," said Lord Darcy. "Just for the record, where were you and Journeyman Henry and the apprentices Sunday night?"

Master Walter jerked a thumb toward the ceiling. "Me and the boys were upstairs, your lordship. That's my home, and I have a room for my 'prentices. Goodwife Bailey comes in of a day to do the cleaning and fix the meals—my wife has been dead now these eighteen years, God rest her soul." He crossed himself unobtrusively.

"Then you can come in the shop from upstairs?"

Master Walter pointed toward the wall of his office. "That ladder goes up to my bedroom, your lordship; you can see the trapdoor. But it hasn't been used for nigh on ten years now. My legs aren't what they used to be, and I don't fancy a ladder any more. We all use the stairway on the outside of the building."

"Could someone have used the ladder without your knowing it, Master Walter?"

The old man shook his head firmly. "Not without my knowing of it, your lordship. If I was down here, I'd see 'em. If I was upstairs, I'd hear 'em; they'd have to move my bed from off the trapdoor. Besides, I'm a very light sleeper. A man don't sleep as well when he's past fourscore and ten as he did when he were a young man, your lordship."

"And the bolts and bars were all in place when you came down yesterday morning?"

"Indeed they were, your lordship. All locked up tight."

"Journeyman Henry had the other key, you say. Where was he?"

"He were at home, your lordship. Henry's married, has a lovely wife—a Tolliver she were afore she married, one of Ben Tolliver's daughters. That's Master Ben, the baker. Henry and his wife live outside the gates, your lordship, and the guard would have seen him if he'd come in, which he and his wife say he didn't and I believe 'em. And Henry would have no cause to do such a thing no more than the boys would."

"Have you had protective spells put on your locks and bars?" Lord Darcy asked.

"Oh, yes, your lordship; indeed I have. Wouldn't be without 'em, your lordship. The usual kind, your lordship; cost me a five-sovereign a year to have 'em kept up, but it's worth every bit."

"A licensed sorcerer, I trust? None of these hedge-magicians or witch-women?"

The old man looked shocked. "Oh, no, your lordship! Not I! I abides by the law, I do! Master Timothy has a license all right and proper, he do. Besides, the magic of them you mentioned is poor stuff at best. I don't believe none of the heresy about black magic being stronger nor white. That would be saying that the Devil were stronger nor God, and" —he crossed himself again—"I for one would never think such a thing."

"Of course not, Master Walter," Lord Darcy said soothingly. "You must understand that it is my duty to ask such questions. The place was all locked up tight, then?"

"Indeed, your lordship, indeed it was. Why, if it hadn't been that His Grace died in the night, Lord Camberton might have stayed there until this morning. But for that, we wouldn't have opened up the shop at all, it being a holiday and all."

"Holiday?" Lord Darcy looked at him questioningly. "What made the eighteenth of May a holiday?"

"Only in Canterbury, your lordship. Special day of thanksgiving it is. On that day in 1589—or '98, I misremember which—a band of assassins were smuggled into the castle by a traitor. Five of them there were. A plot to kill the Duke and his family, it were. But the plot were betrayed and the castle searched and all of 'em were found and taken before they could do anything. Hanged, they were, right out there in the courtyard." Master Walter pointed out the front of his shop. "Since then, on the anniversary, there's a day of thanksgiving for the saving of the Duke's life—though he died some years later, you understand. There's a special Mass said at the chapel and another at the cathedral, and the guard is turned out and there's a ceremonial searching of the castle, with all the Duke's Own Guard in full dress and a parade and a trooping of the colors and five effigies hanged in the courtyard and fireworks in the evening. Very colorful it is, your lordship."

"I'm sure it is," said Lord Darcy. Master Walter's recitation had recalled the facts of history to mind. "Was it carried out as usual yesterday?"

"Well, no, your lordship, it wasn't. The captain of the Duke's Own didn't think it would be right, what with the family in mourning and all. And My Lord Archbishop agreed. 'Twouldn't be proper to give thanks for the saving of the life of a Duke that's four centuries, nearly, in his grave with His late Grace not even *in* his grave yet. The Guard was turned out for five minutes of silence and a salute to His Grace instead.''

"Of course. That would be the proper thing," Lord Darcy agreed. "You would not have come into the shop until this morning, then, if His Grace had not passed away. When did you lock the shop last before you unlocked it yesterday morning?"

"Saturday evening, your lordship. That is, *I* didn't lock it. Henry did. I was a little tired and I went upstairs early. Henry usually locks up at night."

"Was the coffin empty at that time?" Lord Darcy asked.

"Positively, your lordship. I took special pride in that coffin, if I may say so, your lordship. Special pride. I wanted to make sure there weren't no sawdust or such on the satin lining."

"I understand. And at what o'clock did you lock up Saturday evening?"

"You'd best ask Henry, your lordship. *Hennnry!''*

The journeyman appeared promptly. After the introduction, Lord Darcy repeated his question.

"I locked up at half past eight, your lordship. It were still light out. I sent the 'prentices upstairs and locked up tight."

"And no one came in here at all on Sunday?"

Lord Darcy looked in turn at both men.

"No, your lordship," said Master Walter.

"Not a soul, your lordship," said Henry Lavender.

"Not a soul, perhaps," Lord Darcy said dryly. "But a body did."

Lord Darcy was waiting on the station platform when the 11:22 pulled in from Dover, and when a tubby little Irishman wearing the livery of the Duke of Normandy and carrying a large, symbol-decorated carpetbag stepped out of one of the coaches and looked around, Lord Darcy hailed him:

"Master Sean! Over here!"

"Ah! There you are, my lord! Good to see you again, my lord. Had a good holiday, I trust? What there was of it, I mean."

"To be honest, I was beginning to become a bit bored, my good Sean. I think this little problem is just what we both need to shake the cobwebs out of our brains. Come along; I have a cab waiting for us."

Once inside the cab, Lord Darcy began speaking in a low voice calculated to just barely carry above the clatter of the horses' hoofs and the rattle of the wheels. Master Sean O Lochlainn listened carefully while Lord Darcy brought him up to date on the death of the Duke and the murder of Lord Camberton, omitting nothing except the fact that the assignment had come personally from the King himself.

"I checked the locks in the shop," he concluded. "The rear door has a simple slip bar that

couldn't be opened from the outside except mag-
ically. The same with the windows. Only the
front door has a key. I'll want you to check the
spells; I have a feeling that those men are telling
the truth about locking up, that none of them
had anything to do with the murder."

"Did you get the name of the sorcerer who
serviced the locks, my lord?"

"A Master Timothy Videau."

"Aye. I'll look him up in the directory." Master Sean looked thoughtful. "I don't suppose
there's anything suspicious about the death of
His Grace the Duke, eh, my lord?"

"I am chronically suspicious of all deaths in-
timately connected with a muder case, Master
Sean. But first we will have a look at Lord
Camberton's body. It's being held in the
mortuary at the Armsmen's Headquarters."

"Would it be possible, my lord, to instruct the
cab driver to stop at an apothecary's shop before
we get to the mortuary? I should like to get something."

"Certainly." Lord Darcy gave instructions,
and the cab pulled up before a small shop. Master Sean went in and came out a few moments
later with a small jar. It appeared to be filled
with dried leaves. The whole ones were shaped
rather like an arrowhead.

"Druidic magic, eh, Master Sean?" Lord
Darcy asked.

Master Sean looked startled for a moment,
then grinned. "I ought to be used to you by now,
my lord. How did you know?"

"A blue-dyed corpse brings to mind the an-

cient Briton's habit of dying himself blue when
he went into battle. When you go into an
apothecary's shop and purchase a jar full of the
typically sagittate leaves of the woad plant, I can
see that your mind is running along the same
lines that mine had. You intend to use the leaves
for a similarity analysis."

"Correct, my lord."

A few minutes later, the cab drew up to the
front door of the Armsmen's Headquarters, and
shortly afterwards Lord Darcy and Master Sean
were in the morgue. An attendant stood by while
the two men inspected the late Lord
Camberton's earthly husk.

"He was found this way, my lord? Naked?"
Master Sean asked.

"So I am told," Lord Darcy said.

Master Sean opened his symbol-covered
carpetbag and began taking things out of it. He
was absorbed in his task of selecting the proper
material for his work when Bertram Lightly,
Chief Master-at-Arms of the City of Canterbury, entered. He did not bother Master
Sean; one does not trouble a sorcerer when he is
working.

Chief Bertram was a round-faced, pink-
skinned man with an expression that reminded
one of an amiable frog. "I was told you were
here, your lordship," he said softly. "I had to
finish up some business in the office. Can I be of
any assistance?"

"Not just at the moment, Chief Bertram, but
I have no doubt that I shall need your assistance
before this affair is over."

"Excuse me," said Master Sean without looking up from his work, "but did you have a chirurgeon look at the body, Chief Bertram?"

"Indeed we did, Master Sorcerer. Would you want to speak to him?"

"No. Not necessary at the moment. Just give me the gist of his findings."

"Well, Dr. Dell is of the opinion that his late lordship had been dead forty-eight to seventy-two hours—plus whatever time he was under a preservative spell, of course. Can't tell anything about that time lapse, naturally. Died of a stab wound in the back. A longish knife or a short thrust with a sword. Went in just below the left shoulder blade, between the ribs, and pierced the heart. Died within seconds."

"Did he say anything about bleeding?"

"Yes. He said there must have been quite a bit of blood from that stab. Quite a bit."

"Aye. So I should say. Look here, my lord."

Lord Darcy stepped closer.

"There was a preservative spell on the body, all right. It's gone now—worn off—but there's only traces of microorganisms on the surface. Nothing alive within. But the body was washed after the blood had coagulated, and it was dyed after it was washed. The wound is clean, and the dye is *in* the wound, as you see. Now, we'll see if that blue stuff is actually woad."

"Woad?" said Chief Bertram.

"Aye, woad," said Master Sean. "The Law of Similarity allows one to determine such things. The dye on the man may be exactly similar to the dye in the leaf, d'ye see. If it is, we get a reaction.

Actually, all these come under the broad Law of
Metonymy—an effect is similar to its cause, a
symbol is similar to the thing symbolized. And
vice versa, of course." Then he muttered something unintelligible under his breath and rubbed
his thumb along the leaf of woad. "We'll see,"
he said softly. "We'll see." He put the leaf on the
blue skin of the dead man's abdomen, then lifted
it off again almost immediately. The side of the
leaf that had touched the skin was blue. On the abdomen of the corpse was a white area, totally devoid
of blueness, exactly the size and shape of the leaf.

"Woad," said Master Sean with complacency.
"Definitely woad."

Master Sean was packing his materials away
in his carpetbag. Half an hour had been suffi-
cient to get all the data he needed. He dusted off
his hands. "Ready to go, my lord?"

Lord Darcy nodded, and the two of them
headed toward the door of the mortuary. Standing near the door was a smallish man in his
middle fifties. He had graying hair, a lean face,
mild blue eyes and a curiously hawklike nose.
On the floor at his feet was a symbol-decorated
carpetbag similar to Master Sean's own.

"Good day, colleague," he said in a high
voice. "I am Master Timothy Videau." Then he
gave a little bow. "Good day, your lordship. I
hope you don't mind, but I was interested in
watching your procedure. Forensic sorcery has
always interested me, although it isn't my field."

"I am Sean O Lochlainn," said the tubby little
Irishman. "This is my superior, Lord Darcy."

"Yes, yes. So Chief Bertram informed me. Isn't it terrible? Lord Camberton being murdered that way, I mean."

As he talked, he fell into step with the other two men and walked with them toward the street. "I suppose you do a lot of similarity analysis in your work, Master Sean? It is a technique with which I am not at all familiar. Protective spells, avoidance spells, repairs—that's my work. Household work. Not as exciting as your work, but I like it. Gives a man a sense of satisfaction and all that. But I like to know what my colleagues are doing."

"You came down here to watch Master Sean at work, then, Master Timothy?" Lord Darcy asked in a bland voice, betraying no trace of the thoughts in his mind.

"Oh, no, your lordship. I was asked down by Chief Bertram." He looked at Master Sean and chuckled. "You'll get a laugh out of this, Master Sean. He wanted to know what it would cost to buy a preservator big enough to serve the kitchen in the Armsmen's barracks!"

Master Sean laughed softly, then said: "I dare say that when you told him he decided to stick with a good, old-fashioned icehouse. You're the local agent, then?"

"Yes. But there's not much profit in it yet, I fear. I've only sold one, and I'm not likely to sell any more. Much too expensive. I get a small commission, but the real money for me would be in the servicing. The spell has to be reinforced every six months or so."

Master Sean smiled ingratiatingly. "Sounds

interesting. The spell must have an interesting structure."

Master Timothy returned the smile. "Yes, quite interesting. I'd like to discuss it with you. . ."

Master Sean's expression became more attentive.

". . . But unfortunately Master Simon has put the whole process under a seal of secrecy."

"I was afraid of that," Master Sean said with a sigh.

"Would I be intruding if I asked what you two are talking about?" Lord Darcy asked.

"Oh, I'm sorry, my lord," Master Sean said hurriedly. "Just shop talk. Master Simon of London has invented a new principle for protecting food from spoilage. Instead of casting a spell on each individual item—such as the big vintners do with wine casks and the like—he discovered a way to cast a spell on a specially-constructed chest, so that anything put in it is safe from spoilage. The idea being that, instead of enchanting an *object,* a *space* is given the property necessary to do the same thing. But the process is still pretty expensive."

"I see," said Lord Darcy.

Master Sean caught the tone of his voice and said: "Well, we mustn't talk shop, Master Timothy. Er . . . did your lordship want me to have a look at those locks? Might be a good idea, if Master Timothy is free for an hour."

"Locks?" said Master Timothy.

Master Sean explained about the locks on the cabinetmaker's shop.

"Why, certainly, Master Sean," said Master Timothy. "I'd be glad to be of any assistance I can."

"Excellent," said Lord Darcy. "Come to My Lord Archbishop's Palace as soon as you have the data. And thank you for your assistance, Master Timothy."

"It's a pleasure to be of service, your lordship," said the hawk-nosed little sorcerer.

In a quiet sitting room in the palace, His Grace the Archbishop introduced Lord Darcy to a tall, lean man with pale features and light brown hair brushed straight back from a broad, high forehead. He had gray-blue eyes and an engaging smile.

"Lord Darcy," said the Archbishop, "may I present Sir Thomas Leseaux."

"It is a pleasure to meet your lordship," said Sir Thomas with a smile.

"The pleasure is mine," said Lord Darcy. "I have read with great interest your popularization, 'Symbolism, Mathematics, and Magic.' I am afraid your more technical work is beyond me."

"You are most kind, my lord."

"Unless you need me," said the Archbishop, "I shall leave you two gentlemen alone. I have some pressing matters at hand."

"Certainly, Your Grace," said Lord Darcy.

When the door had closed behind His Grace, Lord Darcy waved Sir Thomas to a chair. "No one knows you're meeting me here, I trust?" he said.

"Not if I can help it, my lord," said Sir Thomas. There was a wry smile on his lips and one eyebrow lifted slightly. "Aside from the fact that I might get my throat cut, I would lose my effectiveness as a double agent if the Brotherhood found that I was having an appointment with a King's Officer. I used the tunnel that goes from the crypt in the Cathedral to the Palace cellars to get here."

"You might have been seen going into the church."

"That wouldn't bother them, my lord," Sir Thomas said with a negligent flip of one hand. "Since the Society was outlawed, we're expected to dissemble. No use calling attention to oneself by staying away from church, even if we don't believe in Christianity." His smile twisted again. "After all, why not? If a man can be expected to pretend to belief in pagan Druidism, to verbally denounce the Christian faith in grubby little meetings of fanatics, then why shouldn't those pagans pretend to the Christian faith for the same reason—to cover up their real activities. The only difference is in whether one is on one side of the law or the other."

"I should think," said Lord Darcy, "that the difference would be in whether one was for or against King and Country."

"No, no." Sir Thomas shook his head briskly. "That's where you err, my lord. The Holy Society of Ancient Albion is as strongly for King and Country as you or I."

Lord Darcy reached into his belt pouch, took out a porcelain pipe and a package of tobacco, and began to fill the bowl. "Elucidate, Sir

Thomas. I am eager to hear details of the Society
—both operational data and theory."

"Theory, then, my lord. The Society is com-
prised of those who believe that these islands
have a Destiny—with an upper-case D—to bring
peace and contentment to all mankind. In order
to do this, we must return to the practices and
beliefs of the original inhabitants of the islands
—the Keltic peoples who had them by right at
the time of the Caesarian invasion of 55 B.C."

"*Were* the Kelts the aborigines of these islands?" Lord Darcy asked.

"My lord, bear with me," Sir Thomas said
carefully. "I am trying to give you what the Society officially believes. In judging human behavior, one must go by what an individual *believes* is
true—not by what is *actually* true."

Lord Darcy fired up his pipe and nodded. "I
apologize. Continue."

"Thank you, my lord. These practices to
which I refer are based upon a pantheistic theol-
ogy. God is not just a Trinity, but an Infinity.
The Christian outlook, they hold, is true but limited. God is One—true. He is more than Three in
One, however; He is Infinity in One. They hold
that the Christian belief in the Three Persons of
God is as false—and as true—as the statement:
'There are three grains of sand on the beaches of
England.'" He spread his hands. "The world is
full of spirits—trees, rocks, animals, objects of
all kinds—all full of . . . well, call it spirit for
want of a better word. Further, each spirit is intelligent—often in ways that we can't fathom,
but intelligent, nonetheless. Each is an individ-

ual, and may be anywhere on the spectrum from 'good' to 'evil.' Some are more powerful than others. Some, like dryads, are firmly linked to a specific piece of material, just as a man is linked to his body. Others are 'free spirits'—what we might call 'ghosts', 'demons,' and 'angels.' Some—most, in fact—can be controlled; some directly, some indirectly, through other spirits. They can be appeased, bribed, and threatened.

"Now the ancient Britons knew all the secrets for appeasing these spirits—or bribing or controlling them—whatever you want. So, it appears, do the Brotherhood of Druids—the inner circle of the Society. At least, so they tell the lesser members. Most of them are of The Blood, as they call it—people from Scotland, Ireland, Wales, Brittainy, the Orkneys, the Isle of Man, and so on. Pure Keltic—or so they claim. But those of Anglo-Saxon, Norman, or Frankish descent are allowed in occasionally. No others need apply.

"Don't get the idea they're not for Country, my lord. They are. We're meant to rule the world eventually. The King of the British Isles is destined to be ruler of an empire that will cover the globe. And the King himself? He's the protection, the hex shield, the counter-charm that keeps the hordes of 'bad spirits' from taking over and making life miserable for everybody. The King keeps the storms in place, prevents earthquakes, keeps pestilence and plague away, and, in general, protects his subjects from harm.

"For King and for Country, my lord—but not in exactly the way you or I think of it."

"Interesting," Lord Darcy said thoughtfully. "How do they explain away such things as the storms and frosts that *do* hit Britain?"

"Well, that's His Majesty's fault, you see," said Sir Thomas. "If the Sovereign does not comport himself properly, in other words, if he doesn't follow the Old Faith and do things by the Druidic rules, then the Evil Ones can get through the defenses."

"I see. And one of those rules is that His Majesty must allow his life to be taken any time the Brotherhood feels like it?"

"That's not quite fair, my lord," Sir Thomas said. "Not 'anytime they feel like it'—only when danger threatens. Or every seventh year, whichever comes first."

"What about other sacrifices?"

Sir Thomas frowned. "So far as I know, there have been no human deaths. But every one of their meetings involves the ritual killing of an animal of some kind. It depends upon the time of year and the purpose of the meeting, whether one animal or another is sacrificed."

"All of which is quite illegal," Lord Darcy said.

"Quite," Sir Thomas said. "My dossiers and reports are all on file with His Grace the Archbishop. As soon as we have all the evidence we need, we will be able to make a clean sweep and round up the whole lot of them. Their pernicious doctrines have gone far enough."

"You speak with some heat, Sir Thomas."

"I do. Superstition, my lord, is the cause of much of the mental confusion among the lower

classes. They see what is done every day by
sorcerers using scientific processes and are led to
believe in every sort of foolishness because they
confuse superstition with science. That's why we
have hedge magicians, black wizards, witches'
and warlocks' covens, and all the rest of that
criminal fraternity. A person becomes ill, and instead of going to a proper Healer, he goes to a
witch, who may cover a wound with moldy
bread and make meaningless incantations or
give a patient with heart trouble a tea brewed of
foxglove or some such herb which has no symbolic relationship to his trouble at all. Oh, I tell
you, my lord, this sort of thing must be stamped
out!"

The theoretician had dropped his attitude of
bored irony. He evidently felt quite strongly
about the matter, Lord Darcy decided. Licensed
Healers, of course, used various herbs and drugs
on occasion, but always with scientific precision
according to the Laws of Magic; for the most
part, however, they relied on the Laying on of
Hands, the symbol of their Healing Art. A man
took his life in his hands whenever he trusted his
health to anyone but a priestly Healer or took
his pains and ills to anyone who operated outside the Church.

"I have no doubt of the necessity of clearing
up the whole Society, Sir Thomas," said Lord
Darcy, "but unless you intend to notify His Majesty the King that the time to strike is near, I fear
I cannot wait for the gathering in of the net. I am
looking specifically for the murderer of Lord
Camberton."

Sir Thomas stood up and thrust his hands into his coat pockets while he stared moodily at a tapestry on the wall. "I've been wondering about that ever since I heard of Lord Camberton's death."

"About what?"

"About the woad dye—I presume it *was* woad, my lord?"

"It was."

"It points clearly toward the Society, then. Some of the Inner Circle have the Talent—poorly trained and misused, but a definite Talent. There is nothing more pitiful in this world, my lord, than to see the Talent misused. It is criminal!"

Lord Darcy nodded in agreement. He knew the reason for Sir Thomas' anger. The theoretician did not, himself, possess the Talent to any marked degree. He theorized; others did his laboratory work. He proposed experiments; others, trained sorcerers, carried them out. And yet Sir Thomas wished passionately that he could do his own experimenting. To see another misuse what he himself did not have, Lord Darcy thought, must be painful indeed to Sir Thomas Leseaux.

"The trouble is," Sir Thomas went on, "that I can give you no clue. I know of no plot to kill Lord Camberton. I know of no reason why the Society should want him dead. That does not mean, of course, that no such reason exists."

"He was not, then, investigating any of the activities of the Society?"

"Not that I know of. Of course, he may have

been investigating the private activities of someone connected with the Society."

Lord Darcy looked thoughtfully at the
smoldering tobacco in the bowl of his pipe.
"And that hypothetical someone used the re-
sources of the Society to rid himself of whatever
exposure Lord Camberton might have threatened?" he suggested.

"It's possible," Sir Thomas said. "But in that
case the person would have to be rather high up
in the Inner Circle. And even then I doubt
that they would do murder for a private reason."

"It needn't have been a private reason. Suppose Camberton had found that someone in this
city was a Polish agent, but did not know he was
connected with the Society. Then what?"

"It's possible," Sir Thomas repeated. He
turned away from his inspection of the tapestry
and faced Lord Darcy. "If that were the case,
then he and other Polish agents might do away
with Lord Camberton. But that gets us no
further along, my lord. After months of work, I
still have no evidence that any one of the Inner
Circle is, in fact, a Polish agent. Further, out of
the seven members of the Inner Circle, there are
still at least three I cannot identify at all."

"They remain hidden?"

"In a way. At the meetings, the members wear
a white gown and hood, similar to a monastic
habit, while the Inner Circle wear green gowns
and hoods that completely cover the head, with
a pair of eyeholes cut in them. No one knows

who they are, presumably. I have positively identified four of them and am fairly certain of a fifth."

"Then why did you say there were at least three you could not identify? Why the qualification?"

Sir Thomas smiled. "They are shrewd men, my lord. Seven of them always appear for the functions. But there are more than seven. Possibly as many as a dozen. At any given meeting, seven wear green and the remainder wear white. They switch around, so that those not of the Inner Circle are led to believe that Master So-and-So is not a member of the Circle because they have seen him at meetings wearing common white."

"I take it, then, that the complete membership never attends any given meeting," said Lord Darcy. "Otherwise the process of elimination would eventually give the whole trick away."

"Exactly, my lord. One is notified as to date, time, and place."

"Where do they usually take place?"

"In the woods, my lord. There are several groves nearby. Perfectly safe. There are guards posted round the meeting, ready to sound the alarm if Men-at-Arms should come. And no ordinary person would come anywhere near or say a word about it to the King's Officers; they're frightened to death of the Society."

"You say there are always seven. Why seven, I wonder?"

Sir Thomas gave a sardonic chuckle. "Superstition again, my lord. It is supposed to be a mystic number. Any apprentice sorcerer could tell them that only the number five has any universal symbolic significance."

"So I understand," said Lord Darcy. "Inanimate nature tends to avoid fiveness."

"Precisely, my lord. There are no five-sided crystals. Even the duodecahedron, a regular solid with twelve pentagonal faces, does not occur naturally. I will not bore you with abstruse mathematics, but if my latest theorems hold true, the hypothetical 'basic building blocks' of the material universe—whatever they may be—cannot occur in aggregates of five. A universe made of such aggregates would go to pieces in a minute fraction of a second." He smiled. "Of course such 'building blocks', if they exist, must remain forever hypothetical, since they would have to be so small that no one could see them under the most powerful microscope. As well try to see a mathematical point on a mathematical line. These are symbolic abstractions which are all very well to work with, but their material existence is highly doubtful."

"I understand. But then living things—?"

"Living things show fiveness. The starfish. Many flowers. The fingers and toes of the human extremities. Five is a very potent number to work with, my lord, as witness the use of the pentacle or pentagram in many branches of thaumaturgy. Six also has its uses; the word 'hex' comes from 'hexagon', as in the Seal of Solomon. But that is because of the prevalence of the hexagon in nature, both animate and inanimate.

Snowflakes, honeycombs, and so on. It hasn't the power of five, but it is useful. Seven, however, is almost worthless; its usefulness is so limited as to be nearly nil. Its use in the Book of the Apocalypse of St. John the Divine is a verbal symbology which—" He stopped abruptly with a wry smile. "Pardon me, my lord. I find that I tend to fall into a pedagogical pattern if I don't watch myself."

"Not at all. I am interested," Lord Darcy said. "The question I have in mind, however, is this: Is it possible that Lord Camberton was the victim of some bizarre sacrificial rite?"

"I ... don't ... know." Sir Thomas spoke slowly, thoughtfully. He frowned for a moment in thought, then said: "It's possible, I suppose. But it would indicate that Lord Camberton himself was a member of the Inner Circle."

"How so?"

"He would have had to go *willingly* to his death. Otherwise the sacrifice would be worthless. Granted, there has been an attempt of late—fomented by Polish agents—to make an exception in the case of the King. But it hasn't taken hold very strongly. Most of these people, my lord, are misguided fanatics—but they are quite sincere. To change a tenet like that is not as easy as King Casimir IX seems to think. If His Slavonic Majesty were to be told that a marriage, in which the bride was forced to make her responses against her will at gunpoint, was a true sacrament, he would be shocked that anyone could believe such a thing. And yet he seems to think that believers in Druidism can be manipu-

lated into believing something non-Druidic very
easily. His Slavonic Majesty is not a fool, but he
has his blind spots."

"Is it possible, then," Lord Darcy asked,
"that Camberton *was* one of the Inner Circle?"

"I really don't think he was, my lord, but it's
certainly possible. Perhaps it would be of benefit
to look over my written reports. My Lord
Archbishop has copies of all of them."

"An excellent idea, Sir Thomas," said Lord
Darcy, rising from his chair. "I want a list of
known members and a list of those you suspect."
He glanced at his watch. He had two and a half
hours yet before his appointment with the family
of the late Duke of Kent. That should be time
enough.

"This way, your lordship. Their Graces and
Sir Andrew will see you now," said the liveried
footman. Lord Darcy was escorted down a long
hallway toward the room where the family of the
late Duke awaited him.

Lord Darcy had met the Duke, his wife, and
his son socially. He had not met either the
daughter, Lady Anne, or the Duchess' brother,
Sir Andrew Campbell-MacDonald.

DeKent himself had been a kindly but austere,
rather humorless man, strict in morals but
neither harsh nor unforgiving. He had been respected and honored throughout the Empire and
especially in his own duchy.

Margaret, Duchess of Kent, was some twenty
years younger than her husband, having married
the Duke in 1944, when she was twenty-one. She

was the second child and only daughter of the late Sir Austin Campbell-MacDonald. Vivacious, witty, clever, intelligent, and still a very handsome woman, she had, for two decades, been a spark of action and life playing before the quieter, more subdued background of her husband. She liked gay parties, good wines, and good food. She enjoyed dancing and riding. She was a member of The Wardens, one of the few women members of that famous London gambling club.

Nonetheless, no breath of scandal had ever touched her. She had carefully avoided any situation that might cast any suspicion of immoral behavior or wrongdoing upon either herself or her family.

There had been two children born of the union: Lord Quentin, nineteen, was the son and heir. Lady Anne, sixteen, was still a schoolgirl, but, according to what Lord Darcy had heard, she was already a beautiful young lady. Both children showed the vivaciousness of their mother, but were quite well-behaved.

The Duchess of Kent's brother, Sir Andrew, was, by repute, an easy-going, charming, witty man who had spent nearly twenty-five years in New England, the northern continent of the New World, and now, nearing sixty, he had been back in England for some five years.

The Dowager Duchess was seated in a brocaded chair. She was a handsome woman with a figure that maturity had ripened but not overpadded and rich auburn hair that showed no touch of gray. The expression on her face showed that she had been under a strain, but her eyes were clear.

Her son, Lord Quentin, stood tall, straight and somber by her side. Heir Apparent to the Ducal Throne of Kent, he was already allowed to assume the courtesy titles of "Your Grace" and "My Lord Duke", although he could not assume control of the government unless and until his position was confirmed by the King.

Standing a short, respectful distance away was Sir Andrew Campbell-MacDonald.

Lord Darcy bowed. "Your Grace, Sir Andrew, I am grieved that we should have to meet again under these circumstances. I was, as you know, long an admirer of His late Grace."

"You are most kind, my lord," said the Dowager Duchess.

"I am further grieved," Lord Darcy continued, "that I must come here in an official capacity as well as in a personal capacity to pay my respects to His Late Grace."

Young Lord Quentin cleared his throat a little. "No apologies are necessary, my lord. We understand your duty."

"Thank you, Your Grace. I will begin, then, by asking when was the last time any of you saw Lord Camberton alive."

"About three weeks ago," said Lord Quentin. "The latter part of April. He went to Scotland for a holiday."

The Dowager Duchess nodded. "It was a Saturday. That would have been the twenty-fifth."

"That's right," the young Duke agreed. "The twenty-fifth of April. None of us has seen him since. Not alive, I mean. I identified the body positively for the Chief Master-at-Arms."

"I see. Does any of you know of any reason why anyone would want to do away with Lord Camberton?"

Lord Quentin blinked. Before he could say anything, his mother said: "Certainly not. Lord Camberton was a fine and wonderful man."

Lord Quentin's face cleared. "Of course he was. I know of no reason why anyone should want to take his life."

"If I may say so, my lords," said Sir Andrew, "Lord Camberton had, I believe, turned many a malefactor over to the mercies of the King's Justice. I have heard that he was threatened with violence on more than one such occasion, threatened by men who were sentenced to prison after their crimes were uncovered through his efforts. Is it not possible that such a person may have carried out his threat?"

"Eminently possible," Lord Darcy agreed. He had already spoken to Chief Bertram about investigations along those lines. It was routine in the investigation of the death of an Officer of the King's Justice. "That may very likely be the explanation. But I am, naturally, bound to explore every avenue of investigation."

"You are not suggesting, my lord," the Dowager Duchess said coldly, "that anyone of the House of Kent was involved in this dreadful crime?"

"I suggest nothing, Your Grace," Lord Darcy replied. "It is not my place to suggest; it is my duty to discover facts. When all the facts have been brought to light, there will be no need to make suggestions or innuendoes. The truth, whatever it may be, always points in the right direction."

"Of course," said the Duchess softly. "You must forgive me, my lord; I am overwrought."

"You must forgive my sister, my lord," Sir Andrew said smoothly, "her nerves are not of the best."

"I can speak for myself, Andrew," the Dowager Duchess said, closing her eyes for a moment. "But my brother is right, Lord Darcy," she added. "I have not been well of late."

"Pray forgive me, Your Grace," Lord Darcy said gently. "I have no desire to upset you at so trying a time. I think I have no further questions at the moment. Consider my official duties to be at an end for the time being. Is there any way in which I can serve you personally?"

She closed her eyes again. "Not at the moment, my lord, though it is most kind of you to offer. Quentin?"

"Nothing at the moment," Lord Quentin repeated. "If there is any way in which you can help, my lord, rest assured that I will inform you."

"Then, with Your Graces' permission, I shall take my leave. Again, my apologies."

As he walked down the corridor that led toward the great doorway, escorted by the seneschal, Lord Darcy was suddenly confronted by a young girl who stepped out of a nearby doorway. He recognized her immediately; the resemblance to her mother was strong.

"Lord Darcy?" she said in a clear young voice. "I am Lady Anne." She offered her hand.

Lord Darcy smiled just a little and bowed. The kissing of young ladies' hands was now considered a bit old-fashioned, but Lady Anne, at sixteen, evidently felt quite grown up and wanted to show it.

But when he took her hand, he knew that was not the reason. He touched his lips to the back of her hand. "I am honored, my lady," he said as he dexterously palmed the folded paper she had held.

"I am sorry I could not welcome you, my lord," she said calmly, "but I have not been well. I have a terrible headache."

"Perfectly all right, my lady. I trust you will soon be feeling better."

"Thank you, my lord. Until then—" And she walked on past him. Lord Darcy went on without turning, but he knew that one of the three he had left in the room behind him had opened the door and observed the exchange between himself and Lady Anne.

Not until he had left the main gates of the Ducal Palace did he look at the slip of paper.

It said:

"My lord, I must speak with you. Meet me at the Cathedral, near the Shrine of St. Thomas, at six. *Please!*"

It was signed "Anne of Kent."

At five thirty, Lord Darcy was sitting in his rooms in the archiepiscopal palace listening to Master Sean make his report.

"Master Timothy and I checked the locks and bars on the cabinetmaker's shop doors and windows, just as you instructed, my lord. Good spells they are, my lord: solid, competent work. Of course, I could have opened any one of 'em myself, but it would take a sorcerer who knew his stuff. No ordinary thief could have done it, nor an amateur sorcerer."

"What condition are they in, then?" Lord Darcy asked.

"As far as Master Timothy and myself could tell, not a one of 'em had been broken. O' course, that doesn't mean that they hadn't been tampered with. Just as a good locksmith can open a lock and relock it again without leaving any trace, so a good sorcerer could have opened those spells and re-set 'em without leaving a trace. But it would take a top-flight man, my lord."

"Indeed." Lord Darcy looked thoughtful. "Have you checked the Guild Register, Sean?"

Master Sean smiled. "First thing I did, my lord. According to the Register of the Sorcerer's Guild, there is only one man in Canterbury who has the necessary skill to do the job—aside from meself, that is."

"That exception is always granted, my good Sean," said Lord Darcy with a smile. "Only one? Then obviously—"

"Exactly, my lord. Master Timothy himself."

Lord Darcy nodded with satisfaction and tapped the dottle from his pipe. "Very good. I will see you later, Master Sean. I must do a little more investigating. We need more facts."

"Where are you going to look for them, my lord?"

"In church, Master Sean; in church."

As his lordship walked out, Master Sean gazed after him in perplexity. What had he meant by that?

"Maybe," Master Sean murmured to himself, half in jest, "he's going to pray that the Almighty will tell him who did it."

The cathedral was almost empty. Two women were praying at the magnificently jeweled Shrine of St. Thomas Becket, and there were a few more people at other shrines. In spite of the late evening sun, the ancient church was dim within; the sun's rays came through the stained glass windows almost horizontally, illuminating the walls but leaving the floor in comparative darkness.

St. Thomas was still a popular saint. The issues for which he had fought and died eight centuries before were very dead issues indeed. Even the question of whether Henry II, the first Plantagenet King, had been intentionally involved in the death of Archbishop Thomas was now of interest only to historians and would probably never be settled. After his near-death from a crossbow bolt at the Siege of Chaluz, Richard the Lion Hearted had taken pains to exonerate his father, even though he had fought with old Henry till the day of his death. Young Arthur— the "Good King Arthur" who was so often confused in popular legend with Arthur of Camelot —had, as grandson of Henry II, probably done a bit of white-washing, too. It matters little now.

Arthur's decendants, including the present John IV, held on to the Empire that Henry had founded.

Henry II had his place in history as Thomas had his in Heaven.

As he neared the shrine, Lord Darcy saw that one of the two kneeling women was Lady Anne. He stopped a few yards away and waited. When the girl rose from prayer, she looked around, saw Lord Darcy, and came directly toward him.

"Thank you for coming, my lord," she said in a low voice. "I'm sorry I had to meet you this way. The family thought it would be better for me not to talk to you because they think I'm being a silly hero-worshiping girl. But that's not so, really—though I *do* think you're just wonderful." She was looking up at him with wide gray eyes. "You see, my lord, I know all about you. Lady Yvonne is a schoolmate of mine. She says you're the best Investigator in the Empire."

"I try to be, my lady," Lord Darcy said. He had not spoken more than a score of words to Yvonne, daughter of the Marquis of Rouen, but evidently she had been smitten by a schoolgirl crush—and from the look in Lady Anne's eyes, the disease was contagious.

"I think the sooner you solve the murder of Lord Camberton, the better for everyone, don't you?" Lady Anne asked. "I prayed to St. Thomas to help you. He ought to know something about murders, oughtn't he?"

"I should think so, yes, my lady," Lord Darcy admitted. "Do you feel that I will need special intercession by St. Thomas to solve this problem?"

Lady Anne blinked, startled—then she saw the gleam of humor in the tall man's steel-gray eyes. She smiled back. "I don't think so, my lord, but one should never take things for granted. Besides, St. Thomas won't help you unless you really need it."

"I blush, my lady," Lord Darcy said without doing so. "I assure you there is no professional jealousy between St. Thomas and myself. Since I work in the interests of justice, Heavenly intervention often comes to my assistance, whether I ask for it or not."

Looking suddenly serious, she said: "Does Heaven never interfere with your work? In the interest of Divine Mercy, I mean?"

"Perhaps, sometimes," Lord Darcy admitted somberly. "But I should not call it 'interference'; I should call it, rather, an 'illumination of compassion'—if you follow me, my lady."

She nodded. "I think I do. Yes, I think I do. I'm glad to hear you say so, my lord."

The thought flashed through Lord Darcy's mind that Lady Anne suspected someone—someone she hoped would not be punished. But was that necessarily true? Might it not simply be compassion on her own part?

Wait and see. Lord Darcy cautioned himself. *Wait and see.*

"The reason I wanted to talk to you, my lord," Lady Anne said in a low voice, "is that I think I found a Clue."

Lord Darcy could almost hear the capital letter. "Indeed, my lady? Tell me about it."

"Well, *two* Clues, really," she said, dropping her voice still further to a conspiratorial whisper. "The first one is something I saw. I saw Lord Camberton on the night of the eleventh, last Monday, when he came back from Scotland."

"Come, this is most gratifying!" Lord Darcy's voice was a brisk whisper. "When and where, my lady?"

"At the castle, at home. It was very late—nearly midnight, for the bells struck shortly afterward. I couldn't sleep. Father was so ill, and I—" She stopped and swallowed, forcing back tears. "I was worried and couldn't sleep. I was looking out the window—my rooms are on the second floor—and I saw him come in the side entrance. There's a gas lamp there that burns all night. I saw his face clearly."

"Do you know what he did after he came in?"

"I don't know, my lord. I thought nothing of it. I stayed in my rooms and finally went to sleep."

"Did you ever see Lord Camberton alive again?"

"No, my lord. Nor dead either, if it comes to that. Was he *really* stained blue, my lord?"

"Yes, my lady, he was." He paused then: "What was the other clue, my lady?"

"Well, I don't know if it means anything. I'll leave that for you to judge. Last Monday night, when Lord Camberton came home, he was carrying a green cloak folded across his arm. I noticed it particularly because he was wearing a dark blue cloak and I wondered why he needed two cloaks."

Lord Darcy's eyes narrowed just a trifle. "And—?"

"And yesterday . . . well, I wasn't feeling very well, you understand, my lord. My Father and I were very close, my lord, and—" Again she stopped for a moment to fight back tears. "At any rate, I was just walking through the halls. I wanted to be alone for a while. I was in the West Wing. It's unused, except for guests, and there's no one there at the present time. I smelled smoke —a funny odor, not like wood or coal burning. I tracked the smell to one of the guest rooms. Someone had built a fire in the fireplace, and I thought that was odd, for yesterday was quite mild and sunny, like today. There was still smoke coming from the ashes, though they had been all stirred up. The smoke smelled like cloth burning, and I thought *that* was very odd, too, so I poked about a bit—and I found *this!*" With a flourish, she took something from the purse at her belt, holding it out to Lord Darcy between thumb and forefinger.

"I think, my lord, that one of the servants at the castle knows something about Lord Camberton's murder!"

She was holding a small piece of green cloth, burnt at the edges.

Master Sean O Lochlainn came into Lord Darcy's room bearing a large box under one arm and a beaming smile on his round Irish face. "I found some, my lord!" he said triumphantly.

"One of the draper's shops had a barrel of it. Almost the same color, too."

"Will it work, then?" Lord Darcy asked.

"Aye, my lord." He set the box on the nearby table. "It'll take a bit o' doing, but we'll get the results you want. By the by, my lord, I stopped by the hospital at the abbey and spoke to the Healer who performed the autopsy on His late Grace, the Duke. The good Father and the chirurgeon who assisted both agree: His Grace died of natural causes. No traces of poison."

"Excellent! A natural death fits my hypothesis much better than a subtle murder would have." He pointed at the box that Master Sean had put on the table. "Let's have a look at this floc."

Master Sean obediently opened the box. It was filled to the brim with several pounds of fine green fuzz. "That's floc, my lord. It's finely-chopped linen, such as that bit of cloth was made of. It's just lint, is all it is. But it's the only thing that'll serve our purpose." He looked around and spotted the piece of equipment he was looking for. "Ah! I see you got the tumbling barrel."

"Yes. My Lord Archbishop was good enough to have one of his coopers make it for us."

The device was a small barrel, with a volume of perhaps a dozen gallons, with a crank at one end, and mounted in a frame so that turning the crank would cause the barrel to rotate. The other end of the barrel was fitted with a tight lid.

Master Sean went over to the closet and took out his large, symbol-decorated carpet bag. He put it on the table and began taking various objects out of it. "Now, this is quite a long process, my lord. Not the simplest thing in the world by any means. Master Timothy Videau prides himself on being able to join a rip in a piece of cloth so that the seam can't be found, but that's a simple bit of magic compared to a job like this. There, all he has to do is make use of the Law of Relevance, and the two edges of a rip in cloth have such high relevance to each other that the job's a snap.

"But this floc, d'ye see, has no direct relevance to the bit o' cloth at all. For this, we have to use the Law of Synecdoche, which says that the part is equivalent to the whole—and contrariwise. Now, let's see. Is everything dry?"

As he spoke, he worked, getting out the instruments and materials he needed for the spells he was about to cast.

It was always a pleasure for Lord Darcy to watch Master Sean at work and listen to his detailed explanations of each step. He had heard much of it countless times before, but there was always something new to be learned each time, something to be stored away in the memory for future reference. Not, of course, that Lord Darcy could make direct use of it himself; he had neither the Talent nor the inclination. But in his line of work, every bit of pertinent knowledge was useful.

"Now, you've seen, my lord," Master Sean went on, "how a bit of amber will pick up little pieces of lint or paper if you rub it with a piece of wool first, or a glass rod will do the same if you rub it with silk. Well, this is much the same process, basically, but it requires patterning and concentration of the power, d'ye see. That's the difficult part. Now, I must have absolute silence for a bit, my lord."

It took the better part of an hour for Master Sean to get the entire experiment prepared to his satisfaction. He dusted the floc and the bit of scorched cloth with powders, muttered incantations, and made symbolic designs in the air with his wand. During it all, Lord Darcy sat in utter silence. It is dangerous to disturb a magician at work.

Finally, Master Sean dumped the box of floc into the barrel and put the bit of green cloth in with the fluffy lint. He clamped the cover on and made more symbolic tracings with his wand while he spoke in a low tone.

Then he said: "Now comes the tedious part, my lord. This is pretty fine floc, but that barrel will still have to be turned for an hour and a half at least. It's a matter of probability, my lord. The damaged edges of the cloth will try to find a bit of floc that is most nearly identical to the one that was there previously. Then that bit of floc finds another that was most like the next one and so on. Now, it's a rule that the finer things are divided, the more nearly identical they become. It is theorized that if a pure substance, such as salt, were to be reduced to its ultimate particles, they'd all be identical. In a gas—but that's neither here nor there. The point is that if I had used, say, pieces of half-inch green thread, I'd have to use tons of the stuff and the tumbling would take days. I won't bore you with the mathematics of the thing. Anyhow, this will take time, so—"

Lord Darcy smiled and raised a hand. "Patience, my dear Sean. I have anticipated you." He thought of how the King had done the same to him only the day before. He pulled a bell rope.

A knock came at the door and when Lord Darcy said "Come in" a young monk clad in novice's robes entered timidly.

"Brother Daniel, I think?" said his lordship.

"Y-yes, my lord."

"Brother Daniel, this is Master Sean. Master Sean, the Novice Master informs me that Brother Daniel is guilty of a minor infraction of the rules of his Order. His punishment is to be a couple of hours of monotonous work. Since you are a licensed sorcerer, and therefore privileged, it is lawful for a lay brother to accept punishment from you if he so wills it. What say you, Brother Daniel?"

"Whatever my lord says," the youth said humbly.

"Excellent. I leave Brother Daniel to your care, Master Sean. I shall return in two hours. Will that be plenty of time?"

"Plenty, my lord. Sit down on this stool, Brother. All you have to do is turn this crank— slowly, gently, but steadily. Like this. That's it. Fine. Now, no talking. I'll see you later, my lord."

When Lord Darcy returned, he was accompanied by Sir Thomas Leseaux. Brother Daniel was thanked and dismissed from his labors.

"Are we ready, Master Sean?" Lord Darcy asked.

"Ready, indeed, my lord. Let's have a look at it, shall we?"

Lord Darcy and Sir Thomas watched with interest as Master Sean opened the end of the barrel.

The tubby little sorcerer drew on a pair of thin leather gloves. "Can't get it damp, you see," he said as he put his hands into the end of the wooden cylinder, "nor let it touch metal. Falls apart if you do. Come out, now . . . easy . . . easy . . . ahhhhh!"

Even as he drew it out, tiny bits of floc floated away from the delicate web of cloth he held. For what he held was no longer a mass of undifferentiated floc; it had acquired texture and form. It was a long robe of rather fuzzy green linen, with an attached hood. There were eyeholes in the front of the hood so that if it were brought down over the head the wearer could still see out.

Carefully, the round little Irish sorcerer put the reconstituted robe on the table. Lord Darcy and Sir Thomas looked at it without touching it.

"No question of it," Sir Thomas said after a moment. "The original piece came from one of the costumes worn by the Seven of the Society of Albion." Then he looked at the sorcerer. "A beautiful bit of work, Master Sorcerer. I don't believe I've ever seen a finer reconstruction. Most of them fall apart if one tries to lift them. How strong is it?"

"About that of a soft tissue paper, sir. Fortunately, the weather has been dry lately. In damp weather"— he smiled—"well, it's more like damp tissue paper."

"Elegantly put, Master Sean," said Sir Thomas with a smile.

"Thank you, Sir Thomas." Master Sean whipped out a tape measure and proceeded to go over the reconstituted garment carefully, jotting down the numbers in his notebook. When he was through, he looked at Lord Darcy. "That's about it, my lord. Will we be needing it any further?"

"I think not. In itself it does not constitute evidence; besides, it would dissolve long before we could take it to court."

"That's so, my lord." He picked up the flimsy garment by the left shoulder, where the original scrap of material was located, and lowered most of the hooded cloak into the box which had held the floc. Then, still holding to the original bit of cloth with gloved thumb and forefinger, he touched the main body of the cloak with a silver wand. With startling suddenness, the material slumped into a pile of formless lint again, leaving the original cloth scrap in Master Sean's fingers.

"I'll file this away, my lord," he said.

Three days later, on Friday the twenty-second, Lord Darcy found himself becoming impatient. He wrote more on the first draft of the report which would eventually be sent to His Majesty and reviewed what he had already written. He didn't like it. Nothing new had come up. No

new clues, no new information of any kind. He
was still waiting for a report from Sir Angus
MacReady in Edinburgh, hoping that would
clear matters up. So far, nothing.

His late Grace, the Duke of Kent had been
buried on Thursday, with My Lord Archbishop
officiating at the Requiem Mass. Half the nobility of the Empire had been there, as had His Majesty. And Lord Darcy had induced My Lord
Archbishop to allow him to sit in choir in the
sanctuary so that he could watch the faces of
those who came. Those faces had told him
almost nothing.

Sir Thomas Leseaux had information that
showed that either Lord Camberton himself or
Sir Andrew Campbell-MacDonald or both were
very likely members of the Society of Albion.
But that proved nothing; it was extremely possible that one or both might have been agents
sent in by the Duke himself.

"The question, good Sean," he had said to the
tubby little Irish sorcerer on Thursday afternoon, "remains as it was on Monday. Who
killed Lord Camberton and why? We have a
great deal of data, but they are, thus far, unexplained data. Why was Lord Camberton placed
in the Duke's coffin? When was he killed? Where
was he between the time he was killed and the
time he was found?

"Why was Lord Camberton carrying a green
costume? Was it the same one that was burnt on
Monday? If so, why did whoever burnt it wait
until Monday afternoon to destroy it? The green
habit would have fit either Lord Camberton or

Sir Andrew, both of whom are tall men. It certainly did not belong to any of the de Kents; the tallest is Lord Quentin, and he is a good six inches too short to have worn that outfit without tripping all over the hem.

"I am deeply suspicious, Sean; I don't like the way the evidence is pointing."

"I don't quite follow you, my lord," Master Sean had said.

"Attend. You have been out in the city; you have heard what people are saying. You have seen the editorials in the *Canterbury Herald*. The people are convinced that Lord Camberton was murdered by the Society of Albion. The clue of the woad was not wasted upon Goodman Jack, the proverbial average man.

"And what is the result? The members of the Society are half scared to death. Most of them are pretty harmless people, in the long run; belonging to an illegal organization gives them the naughty feeling a little boy gets when he's stealing apples. But now the Christian community is up in arms against the pagans, demanding that something be done. Not just here, but all over England, Scotland, and Wales.

"Lord Camberton wasn't killed as a sacrifice, willing or otherwise. He'd have been disposed of elsewhere—buried in the woods, most likely.

"He was killed somewhere inside the curtain wall of Castle Canterbury, and it was murder—not sacrifice. Then why the woad?"

"As a preservative spell, my Lord," Master Sean had said. "The ancient Britons knew enough about symbolism to realize that the arrowhead leaves of the woad plant could be used protectively. They wore woad into battle. What they didn't know, of course, was that the protective spells don't work that way. They—"

"Would you use woad for a protective spell, as a preservative to prevent decomposition of a body?" interrupted Lord Darcy.

"Why . . . no, my lord. There are much better spells, as you know. Any woad spell would take quite a long time, and the body has to be thoroughly covered. Besides, such spells aren't very efficient."

"Then why was it used?"

"Ah! I see your point, my lord!" Master Sean's broad Irish face had suddenly come all over smiles. "Of course! The body was *meant* to be found! The woad was used to throw the blame on the Holy Society of Ancient Albion and divert suspicion from somewhere else. Or, possibly, the entire purpose of the murder was to give the Society a bad time, eh?"

"Both hypotheses have their good points, Master Sean, but we still do not have enough data. We need *facts,* my good Sean. *Facts!*"

And now, nearly twenty-four hours had passed and no new facts had come to light. Lord Darcy dipped his pen in the ink bottle and wrote down that disheartening fact.

The door opened and Master Sean came in, followed almost immediately by a young novice bearing a tray which contained the light luncheon his lordship had asked for. Lord Darcy pushed his papers to one side to indicate where

the tray should be placed. Master Sean held out
an envelope in one hand. "Special delivery, my
lord. From Sir Angus MacReady in Edinburgh."

Lord Darcy reached eagerly for the envelope.
What happened was no one's fault, really.
Three people were crowded around the table,
each trying to do something, and the young novice, in trying to maneuver the tray, had to move
it aside when Master Sean handed over the envelope to Lord Darcy. The corner of the tray
caught the neck of the ink bottle, and that there-
tofore upright little container promptly toppled
over on its side and disgorged its contents all
over the manuscript Lord Darcy had been working on.

There was a moment of stunned silence, broken by the profuse apologies of the novice. Lord
Darcy inhaled slowly, then calmly told the lad
that there was no damage done, that he was certainly not at fault, and that Lord Darcy was not
the least bit angry. He was thanked for bringing
up the tray and dismissed.

"And don't worry about the mess, Brother,"
Master Sean said. "I shall clean it up myself."

When the novice had left, Lord Darcy looked
ruefully at the inkstained sheets and then at the
envelope he had taken from Master Sean's fingers. "My good Sean," he said quietly, "I am
not, as you know, a nervous or excitable man. If,
however, this envelope does not contain good
news and useful information, I shall undoubtedly throw myself on the floor in a raving convulsion of pure fury and chew holes in the rug."

"I shouldn't blame you in the least, my lord,"
said Master Sean, who knew perfectly well that
his lordship would do no such thing. "Go sit
down in the easy-chair, my lord, while I do
something about this minor catastrophe."

Lord Darcy sat in the big chair near the window. Master Sean brought over the tray and put
it on the small table at his lordship's elbow. Lord
Darcy munched a sandwich and drank a cup of
caffe while he read the report from Edinburgh.

Lord Camberton's movements in Scotland,
while not exactly done in a blaze of publicity,
had not been gone about furtively by any means.
He had gone to certain places and asked certain
questions and looked at certain records. Sir
Angus had followed that trail and learned what
Lord Camberton had learned, although he confessed that he had no notion of what his late
lordship had intended to do with that information or what hypothesis he may have been working on or whether the information he had obtained meant anything, even to Lord Camberton.

His lordship had visited, among other places,
the Public Records Office and the Church Marriage Register. He had been checking on
Margaret Campbell-MacDonald, the present
Dowager Duchess of Kent.

In 1941, when she was only nineteen, she had
married a man named Chester Lowell, a man of
most unsavory antecedents. His father had been
imprisoned for a time for embezzlement and had
finally drowned under mysterious circum-

stances. Chester's younger brother, Ian, had been arrested and tried twice on charges of practicing magic without a license, but had been released both times after a verdict of "Not Proven", and had finally gone up for six years for a confidence game which had involved illegal magic and had been released in 1959. Chester Lowell himself was a gambler of the worst sort, a man who cheated at cards and dice to keep his pockets lined.

After only three weeks of marriage, Margaret had left Chester Lowell and returned home. Evidently the loss had meant little to Lowell; he did not bother to try to get her back. Six months later, he had fled to Spain under a cloud of suspicion; the authorities in Scotland believed that he had been connected with the disappearance of six thousand sovereigns from a banking house in Glasgow. The evidence against him, however, was not strong enough to extradite him from the protection of the King of Aragon. In 1942, the Aragonese authorities reported that the "Inglés", Chester Lowell, had been shot to death in Zaragoza after an argument over a card game. The Scottish authorities sent an investigator who knew Lowell to identify the body, and the case against him was marked "Closed".

So! thought Lord Darcy, *Margaret de Kent is twice a widow.*

There had been no children born of her brief union with Lowell. In 1944, after an eight months courtship, Margaret had become the Duchess of Kent. Sir Angus MacReady did not

know whether the Duke had been aware then of
the previous marriage, or, indeed, whether he
had ever known.

Sir Andrew Campbell-MacDonald had also
had his history investigated by Lord Camberton.
There was certainly nothing shady in his past; he
had had a good reputation in Scotland. In 1939,
he had gone to New England and had served for
a time in the Imperial Legion. He had com-
ported himself with honor in three battles
against the red aborigines and had left the service with a captain's commission and an excellent record. In 1957, the small village in which
he had been living was raided by the red
barbarians and burnt to the ground after great
carnage, and it had been believed for a time that
Sir Andrew had been killed in the raid. He had
returned to England in 1959, nearly penniless,
his small fortune having vanished as a result of
the destruction during the raid. He had been giv-
en a minor position and a pension by the Duke
of Kent and had lived with his sister and
brother-in-law for the past five years.

Lord Darcy put the letter aside and thoughtfully finished his caffe. He did not look at all as
though he were about to have a rug-chewing fit
of fury.

"The only thing missing is the magician," he
said to himself. "Where is the magician in this?
Or, rather, *who* is he? The only sorcerer in plain
sight is Master Timothy Videau, and he does not
apparently have any close connection with Lord
Camberton or the Ducal Palace. Sir Thomas

suspects that Sir Andrew might be a member of the Society of Albion, but that does not necessarily mean he knows anything about sorcery."

Furthermore, Lord Darcy was quite certain that Sir Andrew, if he was a member of the Inner Circle, would not draw attention to the Society in such a blatant manner.

"Here is your report, my lord," said Master Sean.

Lord Darcy came out of his reverie to see Master Sean standing by his side with a sheaf of papers in his hand. His lordship had been vaguely aware that the tubby little Irish sorcerer had been at work at the other end of the room, and now it was obvious what he had been doing. Except for a very slight dampness, there was no trace of the ink that had been spilled across the pages, although the clear, neat curves of Lord Darcy's handwriting remained without change. It was, Lord Darcy knew, simply a matter of differentiation by intention. The handwriting had been put there with intention, with purpose, while the spilled ink had got here by accident; thus it was possible for a removal spell to differentiate between them.

"Thank you, my good Sean. As usual, your work is both quick and accurate."

"It would've taken longer if you'd been using these new indelible inks," Master Sean said deprecatively.

"Indeed?" Lord Darcy said absently as he looked over the papers in his hand.

"Aye, my lord. There's a spell cast on the ink itself to make it indelible. That makes it fine for

documents and bank drafts and such things as
you don't want changed, but it makes it hard as
the very Devil to get off after it's been spilled.
Master Timothy was telling me that it took him
a good two hours to get the stain out of the
carpet in the Ducal study a couple of weeks
ago."

"No doubt," said Lord Darcy, still looking at
his report. Then, suddenly, he seemed to freeze
for a second. After a moment, he turned his head
slowly and looked up at Master Sean. "Did Master Timothy mention exactly what day that
was?"

"Why . . . no, my lord, he didn't."

Lord Darcy put his report aside and rose from
his chair. "Come along, Master Sean. We have
some important questions to ask Master
Timothy Videau—very important."

"About ink, my lord?" Master Sean asked,
puzzled.

"About ink, yes. And about something so expensive that he has sold only one of them in
Canterbury." He took his blue cloak from the
closet and draped it around his shoulders.
"Come along, Master Sean."

"So," said Lord Darcy some three-quarters of
an hour later, as he and Master Sean strolled
through the great gate in the outer curtain wall
of Castle Canterbury, "we find that the work
was done on the afternoon of May 11th. Now we
need one or two more tiny bits of evidence, and
the lacunae in my hypothesis will be filled."

They headed straight for Master Walter
Gotobed's shop.

Master Walter, Journeyman Henry Lavender informed them, was not in at the moment. He and young Tom Wilderspin had taken the cart and mule to deliver a table to a gentleman in the city.

"That is perfectly all right, Goodman Henry," Lord Darcy said. "Perhaps you can help us. Do you have any zebrawood?"

"Zebrawood, my Lord? Why, I think we have a little. Don't get much call for it, my lord. It's very dear, my lord."

"Perhaps you would be so good as to find out how much you have on hand, Goodman Henry? I am particularly eager to know."

"O' course, my lord. Certainly." The journeyman joiner went back to the huge room at the rear of the shop.

As soon as he had disappeared from sight, Lord Darcy sprang to the rear door of the shop. It had a simple drop bar as a lock; there was no way to open it from the outside. Lord Darcy looked at the sawdust, shavings, and wood chips at his feet. His eye spied the one he wanted. He picked up the wood chip and then lifted the bar of the door and wedged the chip in so that it held the bar up above the two brackets that it fitted in when the door was locked. Then he took a long piece of string from his pocket and looped it over the wood chip. He opened the door and went outside, trailing the two ends of the string under the door. Then he closed the door.

Inside, Master Sean watched closely. The string, pulled by Lord Darcy from outside, tightened. Suddenly the bit of wood was jerked out from between the bar and the door. Now unsupported, the bar fell with a dull thump. The door was locked.

Quickly, Master Sean lifted the bar again, and Lord Darcy re-entered. Neither man said a word, but there was a smile of satisfaction on both their faces.

Journeyman Henry came in a few minutes later; evidently he had not heard the muffled sound of the door bar falling. "We ain't got very much zebrawood, my lord," he said dolefully. "Just scrap. Two three-foot lengths of six-by-three-eights. Leftovers from a job Master Walter done some years ago. We'd have to order it from London or Liverpool, my lord." He put the two boards on a nearby workbench. Even in their unfinished state, the alternate dark and light bands of the wood gave it distinction.

"Oh, there's quite enough there." Lord Darcy said. "What I had in mind was a tobacco humidor. Something functional—plain but elegant. No carving; I want the beauty of the wood to show."

Henry Lavender's eyes lit up. "Quite so, my lord! To be sure, my lord! What particular design did my lord have in mind?"

"I shall leave that up to you and Master Walter. It should be of about two pounds capacity."

After a few minutes, they agreed upon a price and a delivery date. Then: "Oh, by the by, Goodman Henry . . . I believe you had a slip of the memory when I questioned you last Tuesday."

"My lord?" Journeyman Henry looked startled, puzzled, and just a little frightened.

"You told me that you locked up tight on Saturday night at half past eight. You neglected to tell me that you were not alone. I put it to you that a gentleman came in just before you locked up. That he asked you for something which you fetched for him. That he went out the front door with you and stood nearby while you locked that door. Is that not so, my good Henry?"

"It's true as Gospel, my lord," said the joiner in awe. "How on Earth did you know that, my lord?"

"Because that is the only way it could have happened."

"That's just how it did happen, my lord. It were Lord Quentin, my lord. That is, the new Duke; he were Lord Quentin then. He asked me for a bit of teak to use as a paperweight. He knew we had a polished piece and he offered to buy it, so I sold it to him. But I never thought nothing wrong of it, my lord!"

"You did nothing wrong, my good Henry—except to forget to tell me that the incident had happened. It is of no consequence, but you should have mentioned it earlier."

"I humbly beg your pardon, my lord. But I didn't think nothing of it."

"Of course not. But in future, if you should be asked questions by a King's Officer, be sure to remember details. Next time, it might be more important."

"I'll remember, my lord."

"Very good. Good day to you, Goodman Henry. I shall look forward to seeing that humidor."

Outside the shop, the two men walked across the busy courtyard toward the great gate. Master Sean said: "What if he hadn't had any zebrawood, my lord? How would you have got him out of the shop?"

"I'd have asked for teak," Lord Darcy said dryly. "Now we must make a teleson call to Scotland. I think that within twenty-four hours I shall be able to make my final report."

There were six people in the room. Margaret, Dowager Duchess of Kent, looked pale and drawn but still regal, still mistress of her own drawing room. Quentin, heir to the Duchy of Kent, stood with somber face near the fireplace, his eyes hooded and watchful. Sir Andrew Campbell-MacDonald stood solemnly by the window, his hands in the pockets of his dress jacket, his legs braced a little apart. Lady Anne sat in a small, straightbacked chair near Sir Andrew. Lord Darcy and Master Sean faced them.

"Again I apologize to Your Graces for intruding upon your bereavement in this manner," Lord Darcy said, "but there is a little matter of the King's Business to be cleared up. A little matter of willful murder. On the 11th of May last, Lord Camberton returned secretly from Scotland after finding some very interesting information—information that, viewed in the proper light, could lend itself very easily to blackmail. Lord Camberton was murdered because of what he had discovered. His body was then hidden away until last Saturday night or early Sunday morning, at which time it was put in the coffin designed for His late Grace, the Duke.

"The information was more than scandalous; if used in the right way, it could be disastrous to the Ducal Family. If someone had offered proof that the first husband of Her Grace the Duchess was still living, she would no longer have any claim to her title, but would still be Margaret Lowell of Edinburgh—and her children would be illegitimate and therefore unable to claim any share in the estates or government of the Duchy of Kent."

As he spoke, the Dowager Duchess walked over to a nearby chair and quietly sat down. Her face remained impassive.

Lord Quentin did not move.

Lady Anne looked as though someone had slapped her in the face.

Sir Andrew merely shifted a little on his feet.

"Before we go any further, I should like you to meet a colleague of mine. Show him in, Master Sean."

The tubby little Irish sorcerer opened the door, and a sharp-faced, sandy-haired man stepped in.

"Ladies and gentlemen," said Lord Darcy. "I should like you to meet Plainsclothes Master-at-Arms Alexander Glencannon."

Master Alexander bowed to the silent four. "Your Graces. Lady Anne. An honor, I assure ye." Then he lifted his eyes and looked straight at Sir Andrew. "Good morrow to ye, Lowell."

The man who had called himself Sir Andrew merely smiled. "Good morrow, Glencannon. So I'm trapped, am I?"

"If ye wish to put it that way, Lowell."

"Oh, I think not." With a sudden move, Lowell, the erstwhile "Sir Andrew" was behind Lady Anne's chair. One hand, still in his jacket pocket, was thrust against the girl's side. "I would hesitate to attempt to shoot it out with two of His Majesty's Officers, but if there is any trouble about this, the girl dies. You can only hang me once, you know." His voice had the coolness of a man who was used to handling desperate situations.

"Lady Anne," said Lord Darcy in a quiet voice, "do exactly as he says. *Exactly,* do you understand? So must the rest of us." Irritated as he was with himself for not anticipating what Lowell would do, he still had to think and think fast. He was not even certain that Lowell had a gun in that pocket, but he had to assume that a gun was there. He dared not do otherwise.

"Thank you, my lord," Lowell said with a twisted smile. "I trust no one will be so foolish as not to take his lordship's advice."

"What next, then?" Lord Darcy asked.

"Lady Anne and I are leaving. We are walking out the door, across the courtyard, and out the gate. Don't any of you leave here for twenty-four hours. I should be safe by then. If I am, Lady Anne will be allowed to return—unharmed. If there is any hue and cry . . . well, well, there won't be, will there?" His twisted smile widened. "Now clear away from that door.

Come, Anne—let's go on a nice trip with your dear uncle."

Lady Anne rose from her chair and went out the door of the room with Lowell, who never took his eyes off the others. He closed the door. "I shouldn't like to hear that door opened before I leave," his voice said from the other side. Then footsteps echoed away down the corridor.

There was another door to the room. Lord Darcy headed for it.

"No! Let him go!"

"He'll kill Anne, you fool!"

Lord Quentin and the Duchess both spoke at once.

Lord Darcy ignored them. "Master Sean! Master Alexander! See that these people are kept quiet and that they do not leave the room until I return!" And then he was out the door.

Lord Darcy knew all the ins and outs of Castle Canterbury. He had made a practice of studying the plans to every one of the great castles of the Empire. He ran down a corridor and then went up a stone stairway, taking the steps two at a time. Up and up he went, flight after flight of stairs, heading for the battlements atop the great stone edifice.

On the roof, he paused for breath. He looked out over the battlement wall. Sixty feet below, he saw Lowell and Lady Anne, walking across the courtyard—slowly, so as to attract no attention from the crowds of people. They were scarcely a quarter of the way across.

Lord Darcy raced for the curtain wall.

Here, the wall was only six feet wide. He was
protected from being seen from below by the
crenelated walls on either side of the path atop
the greater curtain wall. At a crouch, he ran for
the tower that topped the great front gate. There
was no one to stop him; no soldiers walked these
battlements; the castle had not been attacked for
centuries.

Inside the gate tower was the great portcullis,
a vast mass of crossed iron bars that could be
lowered rapidly in case of attack. It was locked
into place now, besides being held up by the
heavy counterwieght in the deep well below the
gate entrance.

Lord Darcy did not look over the wall to see
where his quarry was now. He should be in front
of them, and if he was, Lowell might—just might
—glance up and see him. He couldn't take that
chance.

He did not take the stairs. He went down the
shaft that held the great chain that connected the
portcullis to its counterweight, climbing down
the chain hand over hand to the flagstones sixty
feet beneath him.

There was no Guardsman in the chamber
below during the day, for which Lord Darcy was
profoundly grateful. He had no time to answer
questions or to try to keep an inquisitive soldier
quiet.

There were several times when he feared that
his life, not Lady Anne's, would be forfeit this
day. The chain was kept well oiled and in read-
iness, even after centuries of peace, for such was
the ancient law and custom. Even with his legs
wrapped around the chain and his hands grip-

ping tightly, he slipped several times, burning his palms and thighs and calves. The chain, with its huge, eight-inch links, was as rigid as an iron bar, held taut by the great pull of the massive counterweight below.

The chain disappeared through a foot-wide hole that led to the well beneath, where the counterweight hung. Lord Darcy swung his feet wide and dropped lightly to the flagstoned floor.

Then, cautiously, he opened the heavy oak door just a crack.

Had Lowell and the girl already passed?

Of the two chains that held up the great portcullis, Lord Darcy had taken the one that would put him on the side of the gate to Lowell's left. The gun had been in Lowell's right hand, and—

They walked by the door, Lady Anne first, Lowell following slightly behind. Lord Darcy flung open the door and hurled himself across the intervening space.

His body slammed into Lowell's, hurling the man aside, pushing his gun off the girl's body, just before the gun went off with a roar.

The two men tumbled to the pavement and people scattered as they rolled over and over, fighting for possession of the firearm.

Guardsmen rushed out of their places, converging on the struggling figures.

They were too late. The gun went off a second time.

For a moment, both men lay still.

Then, slowly, Lord Darcy got to his feet, the gun in his hand.

Lowell was still conscious, but there was a

widening stain of red on his left side. "I'll get you Darcy," he said in a hoarse whisper. "I'll get you if it's the last thing I do."

Lord Darcy ignored him and faced the Guardsmen who had surrounded them. "I am Lord Darcy, Investigator on a Special Commission from His Majesty's Court of Chivalry," he told them. "This man is under arrest for willful murder. Take charge of him and get a Healer quickly."

The Dowager Duchess and Lord Quentin were still waiting when Lord Darcy brought Lady Anne back to the palace.

The girl rushed into the Duchess' arms. "Oh, Mama! Mama! Lord Darcy saved my life! He's wonderful! You should have seen him!"

The Duchess looked at Lord Darcy. "I am grateful to you, my lord. You have saved my daughter's life. But you have ruined it. Ruined us all.

"No, let me speak," she said as Lord Darcy started to say something. "It has come out, now. I may as well explain.

"Yes, I thought my first husband was dead. You can imagine how I felt when he showed up again five years ago. What could I do? I had no choice. He assumed the identity of my dead brother, Andrew. No one here had ever seen either of them, so that was easy. Not even my husband the Duke knew. I could not tell him.

"Chester did not ask much. He did not try to bleed me white as most blackmailers would have. He was content with the modest position and pension my husband granted him, and he behaved himself with decorum. He—" She stopped suddenly, looking at her son, who had become pale.

"I ... I'm sorry, Quentin," she said softly. "Truly I am. I know how you feel, but—"

Lord Quentin cut his mother short. "Do you mean, Mother, that it was Uncle An ... *that man* who was blackmailing you?"

"Why, yes."

"And Father didn't know? No one was blackmailing Father?"

"Of course not! How could they? Who—?"

"Perhaps," said Lord Darcy quietly, "you had best tell your mother what you thought had happened on the night of May 11th."

"I heard a quarrel," Lord Quentin said, apparently in a daze. "In Father's study. There was a scuffle, a fight. It was hard to hear through the door. I knocked, but everything had become quiet. I opened the door and went in. Father was lying on the floor, unconscious. Lord Camberton was on the floor nearby—dead—a letter opener from Father's desk in his heart."

"And you found a sheaf of papers disclosing the family skeleton in Lord Camberton's hand."

"Yes."

"Further, during the struggle, a bottle of indelible ink had fallen over, and Lord Camberton's body was splashed with it."

"Yes, yes. It was all over his face. But how did you know?"

"It is my business to know these things," Lord Darcy said. "Let me tell the rest of it. You asssumed immediately that Lord Camberton had been attempting to blackmail your father on the strength of the evidence he had found."

"Yes. I heard the word 'blackmail' through the door."

"So you assumed that your father had attacked Lord Camberton with the letter opener and then, because of his frail health, fallen in a swoon to the floor. You knew that you had to do something to save the family honor and save your father from the silken noose.

"You had to get rid of the body. But where? Then you remembered the preservator you had bought."

Lord Quentin nodded. "Yes. Father gave me the money. It was to have been a present for Mother. She sometimes likes a snack during the day, and we thought it would be convenient if she could have a preservator full of food in her rooms instead of having to call to the kitchen every time."

"Quite so," said Lord Darcy. "So you put Lord Camberton's body in it. Master Timothy Videau has explained to me that the spell cast upon the wooden chest keeps a preservative spell on whatever is kept within, so long as the door is closed. Lord Camberton was supposed to be in Scotland, so no one would miss him. Your father never completely recovered his senses after that night, so he said nothing.

"Actually, he probably never knew. I feel he probably collapsed when Lord Camberton, who had been sent to Scotland by your father for that purpose, confirmed the terrible blackmail secret.

Lowell was there in the room, having been taken in to confront the Duke. When His Grace collapsed, Lord Camberton's attention was diverted for a moment. Lowell grabbed the letter opener and stabbed him. He knew the Duke would say nothing, but Lord Camberton's oath as a King's Officer would force him to arrest Lowell.

"Lowell, by the by, was a member of the Holy Society of Ancient Albion. Camberton had found that out, too. Lowell probably had lodgings somewhere in the city under another name, where he kept his paraphernalia. Camberton discovered it and brought along the green costume Lowell owned for proof. When Lowell talks, we will be able to find out where that secret lodging is.

"He left the room with the Duke and Lord Camberton still on the floor, taking the green robe with him. He may or may not have heard you knock, Lord Quentin. I doubt it, but it doesn't matter. How long did it take you to clean up the room, Your Grace?"

"I . . . I put Father to bed first. Then I cleaned the blood off the floor. I couldn't clean up the spilled ink, though. Then I took Lord Camberton to the cellar and put him in the preservator. We'd put it there to wait for Mother's birthday—which is next week. It was to be a surprise. It—" He stopped.

"How long were you actually in the room?" Lord Darcy repeated.

"Twenty minutes, perhaps."

"We don't know what Lowell was doing during those twenty minutes. He must have been surprised on returning to find the body gone and the room looking tidy."

"He was," said Lord Quentin. "I called Sir Bertram, our seneschal, and Father Joseph, the Healer, and we were all in Father's room when ... *he* ... came back. He looked surprised, all right. But I thought it was just shock at finding Father ill."

"Understandable," said Lord Darcy. "Meanwhile, you had to decide what to do with Lord Camberton's body. You couldn't leave it in that preservator forever."

"No. I thought I would get it outside, away from the castle. Let it be found a long ways away, so there would be no connection."

"But there was the matter of the blue ink-stain," Lord Darcy said. "You couldn't remove it. You knew that you would have to get Master Timothy, the sorcerer, to remove the stain from the rug, but if the corpse were found later with a similar stain, Master Timothy might be suspicious. So you covered up. Literally. You stained the body with woad."

"Yes. I thought perhaps the blame would fall on the Society of Albion and divert attention from us."

"Indeed. And it very nearly succeeded. Between the use of the preservator and the use of woad, it looked very much like the work of a sorcerer.

"But then came last Monday. It is a holiday in Canterbury, to celebrate the saving of a Duke's life in the Sixteenth Century. A part of the celebration includes a ritual searching of the castle. Lord Camberton's body would be found."

"I hadn't been able to find a way of getting it out," Lord Quentin said. "I'm not used to that sort of thing. I was becoming nervous about it, but I couldn't get it out of the courtyard without being seen."

"But you had to hide it that day. So you made sure the shop of Master Walter was unlocked on Saturday night and you put the body in the coffin, thinking it would stay there until after the ceremony, after which you could put it back in the preservator.

"Unfortunately—in several senses of the word—your father passed away early Monday morning. The body of Lord Camberton was found."

"Exactly, my lord."

"Lowell must have nearly gone into panic himself when he heard that the body had been found covered with woad. He knew it connected him—especially if anyone knew he was a member of the Society. So, that afternoon, he burnt his green robe in a fireplace, thinking to destroy any evidence that he was linked with the Society. He was not thorough enough."

The Duchess spoke again. "Well, you have found your murderer, my lord. And you have found what my son has done to try to save the honor of our family. But it was all unsuccessful in the end. Chester Lowell, my first husband, still lives. My children are illegitimate and we are penniless."

Master-at-Arms Alexander Glencannon coughed slightly. "Beggin' your pardon, Your Grace, but I'm happy to say you're wrong. I've known those thievin' Lowells for years. 'Twas I who went to Zaragoza back in '42 to identify Chester Lowell. I saw him masael', and 'twas him, richt enow. The resemblance is close, but this one happen tae be his younger brother, Ian Lowell, released from prison in 1959. He was nae a card-sharp, like his brother Chester, but he's a bad 'un, a' the same."

The Dowager Duchess could only gape.

"It was not difficult to do, Your Grace," said Lord Darcy. "Chester had undoubtedly told Ian all about his marriage to you—perhaps even the more intimate details. You had only known Chester a matter of two months. The younger brother looked much like him. How could you have been expected to tell the difference after nearly a quarter of a century? Especially since you did not even know of the existence of the younger Ian."

"Is it true? Really true? Oh, thank God!"

"It is true, Your Grace, in every particular," Lord Darcy said. "You have reason to be thankful to Him. There was no need for Ian Lowell to bleed you white, as you put it. To have done so might have made you desperate—for all he knew, desperate enough to kill him. He might have avoided that by taking money and staying out of your reach, but that was not what he wanted.

"He didn't want money, Your Grace. He wanted protection, a hiding place in such plain sight that no one would think of looking for him there. He wanted a front. He wanted camouflage.

"Actually, he is in a rather high position in the Holy Society of Ancient Albion—a rather lucrative position, since the leaders of the Society are not accountable to the membership for the way they spend the monies paid them by the members. In addition, I have reason to believe that he is in the pay of His Slavonic Majesty, Casimir of Poland—although, I suspect, under false pretenses, since he must know that it is not so easy to corrupt the beliefs of a religion as King Casimir seems to think it is. Nonetheless, Ian Lowell was not above taking Polish gold and sending highly colored reports back to His Slavonic Majesty.

"And who would suspect that Sir Andrew Campbell-MacDonald, a man whose record was that of an honorable soldier and an upright gentleman, of being a Polish spy and a leader of the subversive Holy Society of Albion?

"Someone finally did, of course. We may never know what led His late Grace and Lord Camberton to suspect him, although perhaps we can get Ian Lowell to tell us. But their suspicion has at last brought about Lowell's downfall, though it cost both of them their lives."

There was a knock at the door. Lord Darcy opened it. Standing there was a priest in Benedictine habit. "Yes, Reverend Father?" Lord Darcy said.

"I am Father Joseph. You are Lord Darcy?"

"Yes, I am, Reverend Father."

"I am the Healer the guardsmen called in to take care of your prisoner. I regret to say I could do nothing, my lord. He passed away a few minutes ago from a gunshot wound."

Lord Darcy turned and looked at the Ducal Family. It was all over. The scandal need never come out, now. Why should it, since it had never really existed?

Sir Thomas Leseaux would soon finish his work. The Society of Albion would be rendered impotent as soon as its leaders were rounded up and confronted with the King's High Justice. All would be well.

"I should like to speak to the bereaved family," said Father Joseph.

"Not just now, Reverend Father," said the Dowager Duchess in a clear voice. "I would like to make my confession to you in a few minutes. Would you wait outside, please?"

The priest sensed that there was something odd in the air. "Certainly, my daughter. I will be waiting." He closed the door.

The Duchess, Lord Darcy knew, would tell all, but it would be safe under the seal of the confessional.

It was Lord Quentin who summed up their feelings.

"This," he said coldly, "will be a funeral I will really enjoy. We thank you, my lord."

"The pleasure was mine, Your Grace. Come, Master Sean; we have a Channel crossing awaiting us."

A STRETCH OF THE IMAGINATION

Late afternoon is not a usual time for suicide, but in Lord Arlen's case, it appeared that his death could hardly be attributable to any other cause.

Lord Arlen was the owner and head of one of the most important publishing houses in Normandy, Mayard House. Its editorial offices occupied the whole of a rather large building located in the heart of the Old City, not too far from the Cathedral of St. Ouen. On the day of the Vigil of the Feast of St. Edward the Confessor, Thursday, October 12, 1972, Lord Arlen was in his private office, sound asleep. He was accustomed to taking a nap at that time, and staff were well aware of it, so they moved quietly and spoke in low tones and only when necessary. No one had gone in or out of his office for nearly an hour.

At five minutes past four, three members of staff—Damoselle Barbara, and Goodmen Wober and Andray—heard an odd thump and further strange noises through the thick door of the private office. They all hesitated and looked at each other. They felt that something was wrong, but not one of them quite dared to open that door, fearing Lord Arlen's temper.

Within thirty seconds, Sir Stefan Imbry came charging into the room. "What's happened?" he barked. "I was in the library. Heard a noise. Chair falling, I think. Now it sounds as though my lord is being sick at his stomach." He didn't pause as he spoke, but went straight to the door of the inner office. The staff members felt a momentary sense of relief; only Chief Editor Sir Stefan would dare break in on Lord Arlen.

He flung open the door and stopped suddenly. "Good God!" he said in a strangled voice. Then, to staff, "Quickly! Help me!"

Lord Arlen was hanging by his neck from a rope that had been thrown over a massive wooden beam. He was still twitching. Below his feet was an overturned chair.

He was still just barely alive when they took him down, but his larynx had been crushed, and he died before medical aid or a Healer could be summoned.

Lord Darcy, Chief Criminal Investigator for His Royal Highness, Richard, Duke of Normandy, looked down at the small and rather pitiful body that lay on the office couch. Lord Arlen had been a short man—five-four—and weighed nine stone. In death, he no longer showed the driving, fanatical, and—at times— almost hysterical energy that had made him one of the most feared and respected men in his field. Now he looked like a boy in his teens.

Dr. Pateley, the Chirugeon, had finished his examination of the body and looked up at Lord

Darcy. "Master Sean and I can give you more accurate information after the autopsy, my lord, but I'd say he's been dead between half an hour and forty-five minutes." He smoothed his gray hair and adjusted his pince-nez glasses. "That fits in with the time your office was notified, my lord."

"Indeed it does," murmured Lord Darcy. Tall, lean, and handsome, he spoke Anglo-French with a definite English accent. "Master Sean? How goes it?"

Master Sean O Lochlainn, Chief Forensic Sorcerer to His Highness, was busy with a small golden wand which had a curious spiral pattern inscribed upon its gleaming surface. It is not wise to interrupt a magician while he is working, but Lord Darcy sensed that the tubby little Irish sorcerer had finished his work and was merely musing.

He was right. Master Sean turned, a half smile on his round face. "Well, me lord, I haven't had time for a complete analysis, but the facts stand out very clearly." He twirled the wand in his fingers. "There was no one else in the room at the time he died, me lord, and hadn't been for an hour. Time of death was fourteen minutes after four, give or take a minute. The time of the psychic shock of the hanging itself was five after. No evil influence in the room; no sign of Black Magic."

"Thank you, my good Sean," Lord Darcy said, his eyes focused upon the overhead beam. "As always, your evidence is invaluable."

His lordship turned to the fourth man in the

room, Master-at-Arms Gwiliam de Lisles, a large, beefy, tough-looking man with huge black mustaches and the mind of a keen investigator.

"Master Gwiliam," Lord Darcy said, "would you have one of your men fetch me a ladder that can reach that beam?" He gestured upward.

"Immediately, my lord."

Two uniformed Men-at-Arms were given instructions, and the ladder was brought. Lord Darcy, with a powerful magnifying lens in his hand, climbed up the ladder to the heavy beam, ten feet above the floor, two and a half feet below the ceiling.

The rope which had hanged Lord Arlen was still in place, and Lord Darcy examined the beam and the rope itself very carefully.

Master Sean, staring upward with his blue Irish eyes, said: "May I ask what it is you might be looking for, me lord?"

"As you see," Lord Darcy said, still scrutinizing the wood, "the rope goes up over the beam, here, and is held firmly at the far end, tied to the pipe that runs just below the window behind the desk. It might be possible that Lord Arlen was strangled, the rope put about his neck, and hauled up to the position in which he was found. In that case, the friction of the rope against the wood would displace the fibers of both in an upward and backward direction. But—" He sighed and began climbing back down the ladder. "But no. The evidence is that he actually did drop from the end of that rope and was hanged."

"Would there have been time, my lord," Master Gwiliam asked, "to have hauled him up like that?"

"Possibly not, my dear Master Gwiliam, but every bit of evidence must be checked. If the fibers had showed friction the other direction, we might have been forced to recheck the timing."

"Thank you, my lord," said the plainclothes Master-at-Arms.

Lord Darcy went over to check the other end of the rope.

There was only one window in the office. Lord Arlen had liked dimness and quiet in his office, and one window was enough for him. It was directly behind his desk, and opened into a three-foot-wide air shaft that let in hardly any light, even at high noon. For illumination, his lordship had depended upon the usual gaslights, even in the daytime. They were all alight, but Lord Darcy, being his usual suspicious self, had sniffed the air for any signs of raw gas. There was none. Gas had nothing to do with the problem.

The window itself was of the usual double-hung type. To provide air flow, the upper lite was open about three inches. It was a high, narrow window, and the top of the casing was nine feet above the floor. The bottom pane was open about eight inches, and the end of the rope ran through it to tie to an exterior pipe about six inches from the bottom of the sill. It slanted up to the beam near the ceiling, and dropped to its fatal end.

A careful examination showed that the window had not been opened any farther than it was now; the whole apparatus had been varnished at least twice, and the varnish in the joints and cracks had almost sealed the window lites in place. That window hadn't been opened fully for years.

"Eight inches at the bottom and three inches at the top," Lord Darcy said thoughtfully. "Hardly enough room for a man to crawl through. And, aside from the door, there are no other ways in or out of this room." He looked at Master Sean. "None?"

"None, me lord," said the round little Irish sorcerer. "Master Gwiliam and meself have checked that over thoroughly. There's no hidden passages, no secret panels. Nothing of the like." He paused a moment, then said: "But there's no gloom."

Lord Darcy's gray eyes narrowed. "No gloom, Master Sean? Pray elucidate."

"Well, me lord, in a suicide's room, there is always a sense of gloom, of deep depression, permeating the walls. The kind of mental state a man has to be in to do away with himself nearly always leaves that kind of psychic impression. But there's no trace of that here."

"Indeed?" His lordship made a mental note. His gray eyes surveyed the room once more. "Very well. Cast a preservative spell over the body, Master Sean; I shall go out and get information from the witnesses."

"As you say, me lord," said Master Sean.

Lord Darcy headed for the library. "Come with me, Master Gwiliam," he said as he opened the door. The big Master-at-Arms followed.

In the library, five people were waiting, guarded by two husky Men-at-Arms wearing the black-and-silver uniforms of Keepers of the King's Peace. Three of the five were staff: the brown-haired, dark-eyed Damoselle Barbara; the round-faced, balding Goodman Wober; the lanky, nearsighted Goodman Andray. The fourth was Chief Editor Sir Stefan Imbry, a powerful, six-foot-four giant of a man. The fifth —a bull-like brute with a hard, handsome face— was one that Lord Darcy did not know.

Sir Stefan came to his feet. "My lord, may I ask why we are being held here? I have a dinner engagement, and these others wish to go home. Why should His Royal Highness the Duke send your lordship to investigate such a routine business, anyway?"

"It's the law," said Lord Darcy, "as you, Sir Stefan, should well know. When a member of the aristocracy dies by violence—whether intentional, accidental, or self-inflicted—it is mandatory that I enter the case. As for why you are being held here: I am an Officer of the King's Justice."

Sir Stefan paled a trifle.

Not out of fear, but out of profound respect. His Majesty, John IV, by the Grace of God, King and Emperor of England, France, Scotland, Ireland, New England and New France, King of the Romans and Emperor of the Holy Roman Empire, Defender of the Faith, was the latest of the long line of Plantagenet kings who had ruled the Anglo-French Empire since the time of Henry II. King John had all the strength, ability, and wisdom that was typical of the oldest ruling family in Europe. He was descended from King Arthur the Great, grandson of Henry II and nephew to Richard the Lion-Hearted, who, after surviving a wound from a crossbow bolt in 1199, had been a great solidifying force for the Empire until his death in 1219. John IV was a direct descendant of Richard the Great, who had reformed and strengthened the Empire in the latter half of the fifteenth century.

The reminder that Lord Darcy was a Royal Officer cooled even Sir Stefan Imbry's ire.

"Of course, my lord," he said in a controlled voice. "I was merely asking for information."

"And that is all I am doing, Sir Stefan," Lord Darcy said gently. "I am collecting information." He gestured. "My duty."

"Certainly, certainly," Imbry said hurriedly, and rather abashedly. "No offense intended." Imbry was used to giving orders around Mayard House, but he knew when to defer to a superior.

"And none taken," Lord Darcy said. "Now, as to information, who is this gentleman?" He indicated the fifth member of the waiting group, the heavily muscled, hard-faced, handsome man with the dark, curly hair.

Sir Stefan Imbry made the formal introduction as the man in question stood up. "My Lord Darcy, may I present Goodman Ernesto Norman, one of our finest authors. Goodman Ernesto, Lord Darcy, Chief Investigator for His Royal Highness."

Ernesto looked at Lord Darcy with smoldering brown eyes and gave a medium bow. "An honor, your lordship."

"The honor is mine," said Lord Darcy. "I have read several of your books. One day, if you are of a mind, I should like to discuss them with you."

"A pleasure, your lordship," Goodman Ernesto said as he sat down. But there was an undertone of surliness in his voice.

Lord Darcy looked about the huge room. It was richly appointed and spacious; the walls beneath an eighteen-foot ceiling were lined with well-filled bookcases ten feet high. Above the bookcases, the walls were decorated with swords, battleaxes, maces, and shields of various designs. Several helms sat upright on the top of the bookcases. Flanking the door were two suits of sixteenth-century armor, each holding in one gauntlet a fifteen-foot cavalry lance. The window draperies were heavy dark green velvet; the gas lamps were intricately shaped and gold plated.

The pause to survey the room was filled with silence. Lord Darcy had firmly established his authority.

He looked at Sir Stefan. "I know that you have gone through this several times already, but I must ask you to repeat it again—" He glanced briefly at the other four. "—all of you."

Master-at-Arms Gwiliam, standing near the door, unobtrusively took out his notebook to record the entire conversation in shorthand.

Sir Stefan Imbry looked grim and said: "I don't see the reason for such fuss over a suicide, my lord, but it seems—"

"*It was* not *suicide!*" Damoselle Barbara's

voice seemed to snap through the air.

Sir Stefan jerked his head around and looked at her angrily, but before he could speak, Lord Darcy said: "Let her speak, Sir Stefan!" Then, more softly: "Upon what do you base that statement, Damoselle?"

There were tears in her eyes, and she looked extraordinarily beautiful as she said, in a soft voice: "No material evidence. Nothing concrete that I could prove. But—as is well known—I have been My Lord Arlen's mistress for over a year. I know him. He would never have killed himself."

"I see," Lord Darcy said. "Do you have the Talent, Damoselle?"

"To a slight degree," she said calmly. "I have been tested for it. My Talent is above normal, but not markedly so."

"I understand," Lord Darcy said. "Then you have no evidence to give except your knowledge of his late lordship and your intuition?"

"None, my lord," she said in a subdued voice.

"Very well. I thank you, Damoselle Barbara. And now, Sir Stefan, if you will continue with your recitation."

Sir Stefan had calmed down, but Lord Darcy noticed that Ernesto Norman had given the Damoselle Barbara a suppressed glare of hatred.

Jealousy, Lord Darcy thought. *Hard jealousy. A stupid reaction. The man needs a Healer.*

Sir Stefan, looming tall and strong, began his story for the third time.

"At approximately half-past two . . ."

*   *   *

At approximately half-past two, Lord Arlen had come in from having luncheon at the Mayson du Shah and ignored a spiteful look from the Damoselle Barbara. She had been brought up in the north of England by rather straitlaced parents and did not understand that it was perfectly permissible for a gentleman to go to the Mayson du Shah for nothing but luncheon. She was used to the more staid English gentlemen's clubs of York or Carlisle.

"Where's Sir Stefan?" he snapped at Goodman Andray.

"Not come back from lunch yet, my lord," Andray said.

"Any other business waiting?"

"Goodman Ernesto is waiting for you, my lord. In the library."

"Ernesto Norman? He can wait. I'll let you know. Send Sir Stefan in as soon as he comes back."

Lord Arlen had stalked into his office.

At half-past two, he had bellowed sharply: "Barbara!"

She had, according to her testimony, said "Yes, my lord," and rushed into the inner office. He had, she said, been seated behind his desk. It was an impressive desk, some seven feet long by three feet wide. Behind it, Lord Arlen seemed impressively tall as he sat in his chair—for the very simple reason that his chair was elevated an extra six inches, and he had a six-inch high footstool hidden beneath the desk. Anyone who sat in the guest chair, unless he was exceedingly tall, had to look up at Lord Arlen.

The Damoselle Barbara had, she said, gone into the office and stood at attention, as was proper, and said: "You called, my lord?"

Without looking up from the manuscript he was reading, he said, "Yes, my love, I did. Send in Ernesto."

"Yes, my lord." And she had gone to fetch the waiting author.

Goodman Ernesto Norman had been waiting in the library. Notified by the Damoselle Barbara that Lord Arlen would see him, he had strode angrily out, down the hall, and around to his lordship's office, and had walked in without knocking, slamming the door behind him.

Norman's testimony was: "I was ready to strangle the little jerk, my lord. Or slap him silly. Whichever was the handiest. I'd just read the galley proofs of my latest novel, *A Knight of the Armies*. The beak-faced little name-of-a-dog had *butchered* it! I told him I wouldn't have it published that way. He told me that he'd bought the rights and I had nothing to say about it. We exchanged words, I lost the argument, and I walked out."

The staff admitted that they had heard sharp voices, but none of them had heard any of the words.

Goodman Ernesto had slammed out of the inner office at fifteen minutes of three.

Sir Stefan Imbry had walked into the outer office as Norman had stormed out of the inner. The two ignored each other as Norman went on out.

"What the devil's eating him?" Sir Stefan had asked.

"Don't know, Sir Stefan," Goodman Wober had said. "His lordship asked you to report immediately you came in, sir."

Sir Stefan's testimony was that he had gone immediately into the office, where Lord Arlen was drinking caffe—which had been brought to him by Goodman Andray a few minutes before.

"It was just a short business conference, my lord," Sir Stefan said. "I was given instructions to the format of three books we will be publishing. Entirely routine stuff, but if you want the details, my lord . . ."

"Later, perhaps. Pray continue."

"I left his office at a minute or two after three. He always naps from three to four. I went to the Art Department to check on some book illustrations, then came in here to the library to do some research, checking some of the points in a book on magic we're publishing in the spring."

"A scholarly work?" Lord Darcy asked.

"It is. *Psychologistics* by Sir Thomas Leseaux, Th.D."

"Ah! An excellent man. Master Sean will be eager to obtain a copy."

Sir Stefan nodded. "The firm will be happy to supply him with two copies. Perhaps—" His eyes brightened. "Perhaps Master Sean would consent to review it for the Rouen *Times?*"

"He might, if you approached him properly," Lord Darcy murmured. Then, more briskly: "You were here in the library, then, sir, when Lord Arlen was hanged?"

"I was, my lord."

"May I ask, then, how it was that you were apprised of the fact?" Lord Darcy was fairly certain that he knew the answer to the question, but he wanted to hear Sir Stefan's answer. "You were in the outer office, apparently, within seconds after the—ah—unfortunate incident. How did you know of it?"

"I heard the noise, my lord," said Sir Stefan. He pointed toward a window on the north, shrouded with green velvet. As he pointed, he rose to his feet. "That window, my lord, opens directly to the air shaft."

He went over and moved the curtains aside. "As you see."

The air shaft outside the window was three feet wide. A yard away was the window of Lord Arlen's office. The window itself was partially open at top and bottom, as his lordship had noted previously. So was the library window. Lord Darcy tested it. Unlike the window in Lord Arlen's office, the lites slid up and down easily; they had not been varnished over.

"Master Sean?" Lord Darcy called in a normal conversational tone.

The Irish sorcerer's round face appeared from between the closed curtains on the other side. "Aye, me lord?"

"All going well?"

"Quite well, me lord."

"Very good. Carry on."

Lord Darcy drew the curtains to, turned, and faced the others in the flickering gaslight. "Very well, Sir Stefan; that explains that. One more question."

"Yes, my lord?"

"Why was it that when you rushed in to Lord

Arlen's office and found him hanging—you did not cut him down? A simple flick of a pocketknife would have released the strangling tension of the rope around his throat, would it not? Instead, you *untied the knot. Why?*"

It was the Damoselle Barbara who answered. "You didn't know, my lord?"

Lord Darcy had expected that all eyes would have gone to Sir Stefan; instead, they had come to him. He recovered quickly.

"Elucidate, Damoselle," he said calmly.

"Lord Arlen was deathly afraid of sharp instruments," the girl said. "It was an obsession with him. He never went to the Art Department, for instance, because of the razor-sharp instruments they use for making paste-ups, and that sort of thing."

Lord Darcy's eyes narrowed. "He was, I believe, smooth-shaven?"

"Smooth, yes," she answered calmly. "Shaven, no. His barber used a depilatory wax which pulled the hairs out by the roots. It was painful, but he preferred it to being approached by a razor. He would not permit anyone near him to even carry a knife. We all obeyed."

"Not even a letter opener?" Lord Darcy asked.

"Not even a letter opener," she said. She gestured toward the walls above the bookcases that lined the room. "Look at those ancient weapons. Not one of them has an edge or a sharp point. Does that answer your question about Sir Stefan's cutting down My Lord Arlen?"

"Quite adequately, Damoselle," said Lord Darcy with a slight bow.

Great God! he thought. *They all seem a little mad, and their late employer was the maddest of them all.*

Seven o'clock. Nearly three hours had passed since Lord Arlen had died. Outside, the sky was dark and clouded, and the air held an autumn chill. Inside, in Lord Arlen's office, the gas lamps and the fireplace gave the room a summery warmth. The body of Lord Arlen, covered by a blanket and a preservative spell, rested silently.

Sean O Lochlainn, Master Sorcerer, stood in the soft gaslight and eyed the end of the fatal rope. Behind him, respectfully silent, stood Lord Darcy, Dr. Pateley, and Master-at-Arms Gwiliam. It is not wise to disturb a magician at work.

After a moment, Master Sean bent over, opened his large, symbol-decorated carpetbag, and took out several items, including a silver-tipped ebon wand.

"There's no difficulty here, my lord," Master Sean said. "The psychic shock of sudden death has charged the hemp quite strongly." Master Sean liked to lecture, and when he assumed his pedagogical manner, his brogue faded to paleness. "The Law of Relevance is involved here; scientifically speaking, we have here a psychic force field which, given the proper impetus, will tend to return to its former state."

Then his wand moved in intricate curves, and his lips formed certain ritual syllables.

Gently, gracefully, the rope began to move. As if an unseen hand were guiding it, the hempen twist made itself into a loop. Quickly, smoothly, it tied itself. For half a second, it hung in the air, an almost perfect circle. Then, suddenly, it drooped limply.

"There you are, my lord," said Master Sean with a gesture.

Lord Darcy walked over and looked at the looped and knotted rope without touching it. "Interesting. A simple slip knot, not a hangman's knot." Without looking up, he added: "Master Gwiliam, may I borrow your measuring tape?"

The burly Master-at-Arms unclipped his tape measure from his belt and handed it to his lordship.

Lord Darcy measured the distance from the floor to the noose. Then he measured the overturned chair from the leg to the seat. Then, with all due reverence, he measured the corpse from heel to neck.

Finally, he said: "Dr. Pateley, you are the lightest of us, I think. What is your weight?"

"Ten stone, my lord," said the chirurgeon. "Perhaps a pound or two under."

"You'll do, Doctor. Grab hold of that rope and put your weight on it."

Dr. Pateley blinked. "My lord?"

"Take hold of the rope above the noose and lift your feet off the floor. That's it." He mea-

sured again. "Less than a quarter of an inch of
stretch. That's negligible. You may let go now,
Doctor. Thank you."

Lord Darcy handed Master-at-Arms Gwiliam
his tape measure back.

Lord Darcy tilted his head back and looked
up at the overhead beam which held the rope.
"A singularly foolish thing to do," he said,
almost to himself.

"That's true, my lord," said Master Gwiliam.
"I've always considered suicide to be a very
foolish act. Besides, as someone once said, 'It's
so *per*manent.' "

"I am not speaking of suicide, but of murder,
my good Master-at-Arms. And it is equally permanent."

"Murder, me lord?" Master Sean O
Lochlainn raised his eyebrows. "Well, if you say
so. It's glad I am that I am not in the detective
business."

"But you are, my dear Sean," Lord Darcy
said with some surprise.

Master Sean grinned and shook his round
Irish head. "No, me lord. I am a sorcerer. I'm a
technician who digs up facts that ordinary observation wouldn't discover. But all the clues in
the world don't help a man if he can't put them
together to form a coherent whole. And that is
your touch of the Talent, my lord."

"*I?*" Lord Darcy looked even more surprised.
"I have no Talent, Sean. I'm no thaumaturge."

"Now, come, me lord. You have that touch of
the Talent that all the really great detectives of
history have had—the ability to leap from an un-

warranted assumption to a foregone conclusion without covering the distance between the two. You then know where to look for the clues that will justify your conclusion. You knew it was murder two hours ago, and you knew who did it."

"Well, of course! Those two points were obvious from the start. The question was not 'Who did it?' but 'How was it done?' " His lordship smiled broadly. "And now, naturally, the answer to that last question is plain as a pikestaff!"

"How are you so certain it was murder, my lord?" asked Master Gwiliam.

"For one thing, the measurements we have just made show that the late Lord Arlen's feet were seventeen inches off the ground when he was hanged. The seat of the chair is but eighteen inches from the floor. If—I say if—he had put up that noose and then kicked the chair away, he would have dropped one inch. He would have been strangled, surely, no question of that. But you have seen the cruel marks of that deeply imbedded rope in the throat of his late lordship, and you have heard Dr. Pateley testify that the larynx was crushed. By the bye, Doctor, was the neck broken?"

"No, my lord," said the chirurgeon. "Badly dislocated—stretched, as it were—but not broken."

"He was a light man," Lord Darcy continued. "Nine stone. A drop of one inch could not have done all that damage." He looked at Master Sean. "Therefore, you see, it didn't happen that way. All that was necessary was to use one's imagination to see how it *might* have happened, and then check the evidence to see if it *did* happen that way. The final step is to check the evidence to make sure it could not have happened any other way. Having done that, we shall be ready to make our arrest."

Fifteen minutes later, Lord Darcy, Master Sean, and Master Gwiliam entered the library, where four Men-at-Arms held the five suspects under guard. Master Sean, his symbol-decorated carpetbag in hand, stopped at the door, flanked by the pair of standing suits of armor with their fifteen-foot spears.

Sir Stefan Imbry, who had been reading a book, let it drop to the floor and stood up. "How much longer has this got to go on, Lord Darcy?" he asked angrily.

"Only a few minutes, Sir Stefan. We have nearly completed our investigation." All the eyes in the room, except for Master Sean's, were on his lordship.

Sir Stefan sighed. "Good. I'm glad it's over with, my lord. There will have to be a Coroner's Inquest, of course. I do hope the jury will be kind enough to bring in a verdict of 'Suicide while of unsound mind.' "

"I do not," said Lord Darcy. "It is my fond belief that they will decide that it was an act of premeditated murder and that they pray the Court of the King's High Justice to try Sir Stefan Imbry for the crime."

Sir Stefan paled. "Are you mad?"

"Only at times. And this is not one of them."

The Damoselle Barbara gasped and said: "But Sir Stefan was nowhere near the office at the time!"

"Oh, but he was, Damoselle. He was here, in this room, alone, scarcely a dozen feet from where Lord Arlen was hanged. The whole procedure was quite simple. He went into Lord Arlen's office and slipped a drug into Lord Arlen's caffe. It is one of the more powerful, quick acting drugs. Within a few minutes, his lordship was unconscious. He affixed the rope to the pipe outside the window, threw the other end over the beam, and tied that end around Lord Arlen's neck in a slip knot."

"But the little snot wasn't hanged till an hour later," Goodman Ernesto Norman interrupted.

"True. Let me finish. Sir Stefan then put the unfortunate Lord Arlen's unconscious body *up on that beam.*"

"Just a minute, your lordship," Goodman Ernesto interrupted again. "I have no love for Sir Stefan particularly, but, tall as he is, he couldn't have lifted Lord Arlen ten feet in the air, even if he stood on the chair. And there was no ladder in the office."

"An acute observation, Goodman Ernesto. But you failed to take into account the fact that there was another chair in the room. Lord Arlen's desk chair is a full twenty-four inches high, as opposed to the normal eighteen."

"An extra six inches?" Ernesto Norman shook his head. "Still wouldn't have done it. He'd need at least another six—" He stopped suddenly. His eyes widened. "The footstool!"

"Exactly," Lord Darcy said. "Put that on top of the chair, and you have your needed six inches. I could almost do it myself, and Sir Stefan is taller than I. And nine stone is no great load for a strong man to lift."

"Even supposing I had done all that," said Sir Stefan through ashen lips, but with a controlled voice, "what am I supposed to have done next?"

"Why, my dear fellow, you left the office—after replacing the desk chair and footstool behind the desk. And after quietly putting the guest chair on its side. Then you went out and did what you told us you did, knowing that no one would disturb Lord Arlen after three o'clock."

"But we heard the chair fall at four!" the Damoselle Barbara said in a hushed voice.

"No. By your own testimony, you heard a thump. But it was Sir Stefan's statement that he heard the chair fall that influenced your thinking. The thump you heard was the sound of the beam when the shock of Lord Arlen's body, dropping nearly four feet, slammed that rope against the wood."

The Damoselle Barbara closed her eyes and shuddered. The other two members of staff just sat silently and stared.

"You waited for an hour, Sir Stefan. Then, at four o'clock, you—" Lord Darcy stopped as he got a signal from Master Sean. "Yes, Master Sean?"

"This one, me lord. Definite." He jerked a thumb toward the suit of armor standing to the left of the door.

"That completes the investigation," Lord Darcy said with a hard smile. "You, Sir Stefan, took that fifteen-foot spear, which—like every other weapon in here—has no edge or point, and used it to push Lord Arlen's body off the beam. Then you put the spear back in the gauntlet of the empty armor and went running to the office. You knew it would take some time to untie the knot, and you knew that by that time Arlen would be dead.

"But the whole thing was incredibly stupid. You were up against a dilemma. The problem was the length of the rope. If he dropped too far, his neck would break, and that would be inconsistent with an eighteen-inch chair. But if he only dropped far enough to strangle himself, his feet would have been higher off the floor than the seat of the chair. So you tried a middle road. But the stupid thing was that you did not see that the physical evidence could not, in any case, be reconciled."

Lord Darcy turned to Master Gwiliam. "Master-at-Arms Gwiliam de Lisle, I, as an Officer of the King's Justice, request that you, as an Officer of the King's Peace, arrest this man upon suspicion of murder."

As the Men-at-Arms took the broken Sir Stefan off, the shocked Damoselle Barbara said: "But *why*, my lord? Why did he do it?"

"I checked at the Records Office on Lord Arlen's will before I came here," Lord Darcy told her. "He left half his interest in the firm to you, and half to Sir Stefan. He wanted control. Now you will get it all."

The Damoselle Barbara began to cry.

But Lord Darcy noticed that Goodman Ernesto Norman had a half smile on his face, as though he were thinking, *Now I can get my novel published the way I wrote it.*

Lord Darcy sighed. "Come, Master Sean. We have an appointment for dinner, and the hour grows late."